Praise for
Nine Ways to Die

"Kate Hallock has written, in *Nine Ways to Die*, an old-fashioned, who-done-it novel. A murder mystery, a sex trafficking ring, a ticking clock on saving a kidnapped girl, and an Enneagram subplot to entice and entertain would-be sleuths all combine to make for a great read and a satisfying ending with a twist. *Nine Ways to Die* is good fun and impossible to put down. A well-told story with dysfunctional family dynamics from hell. Buy this book, but don't put it on your bedside table, unless you don't mind reading all night."

—**Randy Sanders**, Author of *Mighty Peculiar Elections: New South Gubernatorial Campaigns of 1970 and the Changing Politics of Race*

"I loved reading *Nine Ways to Die*, a combo thriller/locked-door mystery—so clever! It is a fun puzzle for the readers to figure out. I loved making an Enneagram attempt and getting a response with the correct answer, causing me to analyze my understanding of each number."

—**Michelle Krueger**, SWContent

"What sets the Enneagram apart from other personality tools is that it identifies someone's core motivation. It provides insight into the 'why' behind the 'what.' In Kate Hallock's *Nine Ways to Die*, she cleverly depicts the motivations of all nine types in a way that captures the importance of motivational differences and the impact they have on one's actions. Whether you're an Enneagram enthusiast or just like a good mystery, *Nine Ways to Die* is a fun read that keeps you intrigued and allows you to explore different personalities with an interesting and fun approach!"

—**Hilarie Kay**, Enneagram Coach, Trainer, and Author of *Unlock Your Potential at Work: A Beginner's Guide to Using the Enneagram*

"Kate Hallock's murder mystery, *Nine Ways to Die*, is one of those novels that begs to be read in one sitting. The author's overlay of an Enneagram puzzle onto a traditional murder mystery is imaginative and wonderfully engaging. Who is which Enneagram personality type? Who is the killer? Through action and dialogue, characters reveal their essential natures and at one time or other each person seems to be the possible murderer. Twists in the narrative lead the reader to false conclusions up until the final reveal—a final reveal that unlocks whole new insights into most of the characters."

—**R. Barbara Gitenstein**, President Emerita, The College of New Jersey, Author of *Experience is the Angled Road: Memoir of an Academic*

"Kate Hallock's *Nine Ways to Die: An Enneagram Murder Mystery* is reminiscent of a good ole Agatha Christie novel where there is a dead body, and everyone present in a large, stately home has a motive. It is a fun whodunit that keeps you guessing as you quickly turn the pages. Hallock addresses a real problem—human trafficking—with knowledge and concern but adds twists and turns. This literary mind got lost in the story and didn't try the Enneagram puzzle. But, never mind, it was well worth the time and energy just to keep up with the fast-paced plot. I challenge you to read this book and see if you can figure out the surprise ending!"

—**Dr. Carolyn Curry**, Author of *Suffer and Grow Strong: The Life of Ella Gertrude Clanton Thomas: 1934-2007* and *Sudden Death: A Novel*, Georgia Author of the Year Award 2015

Nine Ways to Die: An Enneagram Murder Mystery

by Kate Hallock

ISBN 978-1-64663-964-9

Published by

 köehlerbooks™

3705 Shore Drive
Virginia Beach, VA 23455
800-435-4811
www.koehlerbooks.com

KATE HALLOCK

NINE WAYS TO DIE

An Enneagram
Murder Mystery

VIRGINIA BEACH
CAPE CHARLES

To Adam

AUTHOR'S NOTE

Dear Reader,

Before you dive in, I'd like to address the Enneagram in the room. That is to say, the Enneagram in the book. For those unfamiliar with the term, an Enneagram is a geometric figure with nine points, each classifying a personality type. In *Nine Ways to Die*, you will come across nine suspects, each a different number on the Enneagram. It is your job to figure out which suspect is which number on the Enneagram. The characters are listed in the back of the book with room to keep notes to help you keep track. In the back, you'll also find brief descriptions of each type to help you on your journey.

From this point forward, the Enneagram will not be mentioned. You'll go along for the ride as if you were reading any other murder mystery. But hidden within are hints and clues that will illuminate the deeper motivations, and Enneagram number of each character.

If you don't know anything about the Enneagram, no worries. You can use the descriptions in the back to make your own guesses, or you can ignore that element of the book completely.

Keep in mind that the characters are caricatures of their type, and all are on the unhealthy side of their number. Their flaws and traits are exaggerated. Please do not be offended or take these depictions too seriously. It is meant to be fun.

I apologize in advance to those of you who share a number with the murderer. But that couldn't possibly be your number, right?

Enjoy!

—Kate Hallock

SATURDAY MORNING

MICHAEL HIGGINS

I t was the first sunrise in sixty-one years in which the heart of Michael Higgins did not beat. Not that he ever paid attention to sunrises or other things of such frivolity. Michael Higgins was a businessman, the cold, hard, driven type, consumed more with the nuances of his various companies' stock price openings than of the colors in the rising sun outside his window.

On the Saturday morning after his son's twenty-fifth birthday party, Michael's cold blank eyes reflected the pink, wispy clouds of a cotton candy sunrise as his body lay lifeless on the travertine surround of his saltwater pool.

Michael Higgins had been murdered. But this is not where our story begins. Our story begins five days prior on Monday morning, a morning marked by another death.

CHAPTER 1

MONDAY

TARA

Tara scooched the faux fur tufted desk chair closer to the rose gold keyboard as she hacked into the GBI website. Nothing new since yesterday. The case was getting cold. Too much time had passed.

She'd just woken from a nightmare, the same nightmare. Most nights, she fell asleep at her desk while searching for answers, answers about Cara, until the pull of sleep became too strong to overcome.

She slipped her glasses on and walked across her apartment to the coffee pot in the kitchen. She pulled her brown hair into a knot on her head. As she made coffee, she replayed a dream still fresh in her mind.

Tara's eleven-year-old sister, Cara, was walking down the street. The sky was purple, and she was happy. Her freckled cheeks broke into a broad grin as she smiled at Tara. But behind her, a van slowly approached. Tara tried to call out, but her voice was mute. The van she had imagined was black with a logo on the side that was always changing. Sometimes it was in focus and other times not. The van slammed on the gas. Tara tried to run to Cara, but her feet were stuck. The van pulled up next to Cara and yanked her inside. Cara hadn't had time to scream or react. She was just gone.

Tara hadn't witnessed Cara's actual kidnapping; no one had. But the dream burned in her as if it were truth. She had been haunted by it since that day three months earlier when Cara disappeared.

Tara had spent every waking moment since that day hunting for her sister. Tara had always been good with computers. Better than good. She was and had been for some time a hacker. Now she used those skills to scour the internet for any clue, any hint of her sister. She had followed rabbit hole after rabbit hole and had not left her apartment for weeks. Hadn't showered for days. Hadn't brushed her teeth yesterday, or had she? It didn't matter. Only one thing mattered . . . finding Cara.

RUNNER

For nearly two weeks, the temperature in Atlanta had not dipped below ninety-five degrees. The entire city had taken on a rather oppressed temperament. People walked as if the effect of gravity had been increased, with hunched shoulders and a slow pace, every step a concerted effort. Speaking became efficient and brief. Even those most prone to exaggeration and descriptive liberties cut themselves short from weariness. Patrons in restaurants ordered smoothies and salads, too hot to add anything warm to their bellies.

One lone runner, a doctor, braved the appalling heat. He knew to take it easy. He'd seen numerous heat-exhaustion cases just this week in the ER. He stopped at the water fountain as he crossed through Piedmont Park and put his head under the water before taking a gulp of the relatively cool liquid. When he resumed his run, he saw the poor girl stumbling toward him. Her eyes fixed on some point on the horizon. He realized immediately she was not well and dialed 911 as he ran to her.

Grabbing her by the shoulders, he noticed her skin was cold to the touch, cold like death.

"911, what's your emergency?" the operator said.

"I need an ambulance, Piedmont Park, Tenth Street entrance. I've got a girl who appears to be suffering from hypothermia."

The silence on the other end made him realize the absurdity of what he had just said. With no time for explanations, he quickly changed his story.

"Sorry, I don't know what is wrong with her, maybe heatstroke. Please send help."

"An ambulance is on the way."

He clicked off the phone, and fully aware it would look wrong for a grown man to hug a young teenage girl, he wrapped his arms around her bare shoulders and held her tight anyway. His body heat was what she needed most in this moment—screw societal norms. She flinched when he touched her.

"It's okay. I'm not going to hurt you," he said.

"So cold . . . don't tell . . . O'Hara." She shivered violently. "Hide me, don't let them find me. Please. He's coming on Saturday at midnight . . . . he kills them all."

"Who's coming? O'Hara?" the runner asked.

"No . . . Mr. Green. He's going to kill us."

"Who is us?"

"Me . . . and—" She was struggling to talk. Her eyes were going out of focus. "Me and Cara." She collapsed in his arms.

"Help is on the way."

He placed her gently on the concrete. As he started CPR and heard the sirens approaching, he knew from years of experience that it was too late.

BETSY

Detective Betsy Turner walked toward the small white tent in the middle of Piedmont Park with her partner Henry Sanders. She only hoped that the young dead girl inside was not Cara Sharp, who they'd been searching for all summer. Betsy wore a white T-shirt, gray slacks, and black and white checkered Vans, her long brown wavy hair pulled up into a tight ponytail.

Betsy had been with the Atlanta Police Department for nearly five years. She'd started with them shortly after moving south from her small hometown in Connecticut. She still felt like an outsider but had lately caught herself saying *y'all* and drinking sweet tea with every meal.

She took a deep breath as she stepped inside the tent. This part never got easier.

Inside, the sight of the small lifeless body filled her with deep sadness and a dash of relief. The girl was young, maybe thirteen, with dark brown hair and tan skin. This was not Cara Sharp. Cara had brownish-red hair, fair skin, and freckles. At least she wouldn't have to make that call to Cara's sister, Tara—not yet, not today. For now, there was still hope, although Betsy knew from personal experience that any answer was better than years of not knowing.

Henry Sanders began to take notes on his iPad with a stylus. Henry had been Betsy's partner ever since her first day. When they'd first started working together, Betsy got a cold feeling from Henry. But over time, she came to realize he was just a deep thinker. He could talk about nearly any subject but never engaged in idle chitchat. He usually skipped greetings, instead getting straight to the point. He was a few years older than Betsy's twenty-eight years and had a wife and toddler daughter at home. He wore black glasses that set off his deep brown skin and often a bow tie.

The medical examiner, Aja Patel, knelt next to the body. Aja was around Betsy's age. She spoke with a deep Southern accent, which caught Betsy off guard, since Aja was Indian.

"I'm gonna have to look into it a bit more," Aja said. "But it looks to me like this girl died of hypothermia."

Henry stopped writing and looked at Betsy and then at Aja.

"Did you say hypothermia?" Betsy asked. "Or did you mean heatstroke?"

"No. She froze to death," Aja said.

"But we're in the middle of a heat wave."

"Yeah."

"And you're telling me this girl died of hypothermia?"

"That's what I'm telling you."

"But—"

"You're the detective. I guess you'll have to puzzle it out," Aja said, smiling.

Betsy kneeled next to the body, pulled on latex gloves, and touched the shoulder of the girl gently. She was ice-cold. She carefully lifted the hands. The fingers were pale blue.

"What's that under her fingernails?" Betsy said, looking closer. "It's red. It could be blood." She took the hand in her own to inspect the liquid. As she moved the hand, the substance dripped onto the pavement. Henry kneeled to inspect it.

"That's not blood," Henry said.

"I'll bag it and send it to the lab," Aja said. "There's also a tattoo on her wrist." She gently turned the wrist of the deceased upward. On the inside of her wrist was a tattoo with a single black outline of a triangle with a semicircle at the base. "That may help you in identifying her."

"I haven't seen this one before. Could be the mark of human traffickers. Can you tell how old it is?"

"It is well healed. I'd say she's had it at least a year, but that's just an educated guess."

"Thanks, Aja."

"No problem. I'll keep you posted."

"Don't jump to conclusions," Henry said as he and Betsy walked back to the squad car after speaking to the only witness.

"She said the name Cara, right before she died. It was her last word."

"You don't know she meant Cara Sharp."

"No, we don't know for sure, but if not, it's a pretty big coincidence. We need to find out who this girl was and where she came from before Saturday. Or we may never solve the Cara Sharp case."

"In the meantime, you'd better call Tara," Henry said. "If she hears a girl was found, she'll jump to conclusions."

O'HARA

Across town on a loading dock that looked like hundreds of others around the city, a truck driver discussed the events of the morning with his boss, O'Hara.

"So, she escaped and died in a public place. That's what you're saying?" O'Hara asked.

"Yes," the driver said, looking down at the ground. "I'm sorry. I—"

"Do you realize what you've done? You've compromised the entire operation!"

"I'm sorry. She got away from me."

"You were overpowered by a tween? A dying tween? Is that what you are telling me?"

"I just . . . I was caught off guard," said the driver.

"Get used to that," O'Hara said.

"What do you—?"

The gun appeared as if from nowhere. Before the driver could react, a shot hit him in the head, and he fell, lifeless, to the ground with a thud.

"This heat is affecting my imbecile tolerance," O'Hara mumbled.

MICHAEL

Michael Higgins sat in his corner office with his back to the view of the city while his secretary read off the items on his schedule for the week, as she did every Monday morning.

"Now that we've finished with the business calendar," she said, "here are the personal items for this week. Lunch today at twelve-thirty at Pricci for two. Tomorrow you have a doctor's appointment at eight-thirty. And Friday is Mike's birthday party. Nikki said to make sure you leave here by six to have enough time to change and be ready when guests arrive at seven. That's it for this week. Next week you're heading to Africa for the big game hunt."

Michael nodded and waved his hand to dismiss her.

TARA

Tara Sharp stood in the dining room of her apartment staring at the wall. In the center was an 8x11 glossy photo of Cara smiling at the camera with the standard blue background of everyone's school photos. Tara looked like her younger sister. They had the same brownish-red hair, the same freckles, the same green eyes, only Tara wore glasses. Surrounding the photo were papers and photos pinned to the wall. Red string connected some of the papers to each other. It was a tangle of clues and logic that only made sense to Tara. She moved to the floor and opened her laptop.

Tara studied computer science at Georgia Tech. She had taken the summer semester off to focus on Cara, who hadn't been seen since late May. She had not expected the search to take this long. Now, at the end of August, she only had a week until fall classes would start. If she didn't have answers by then, she'd have to defer. Finding Cara was an all-consuming endeavor.

She logged into her computer and once again studied the passenger logs for flights in and out of Atlanta. Tara had learned how to access websites and information, access that wasn't, strictly speaking, legal. She was able to get information the police couldn't. In high school, she made a ton of money by offering to change grades for other students. And although the faculty had caught on, she hadn't been caught. No one turned her in because they knew she could change their grades for the worse if they did.

She now used those skills to hunt for her sister. But even her skills had come up short. She'd found nothing but dead ends.

Her cell phone rang. She grabbed it off the floor. The screen read *Detective Betsy*. She froze. She was scared to answer it, scared to know the truth. But if it had been the worst, they wouldn't call. That was news they'd give in person. In a moment of bravery, she answered.

"Hello," she said.

"Hi, Tara, it's Detective Turner. How are you?"

"Do you know something? Did you find her?"

"No. I called because a girl died today in Piedmont Park. It is not Cara. It will be on the news, but she is unidentified, so they won't release a name. I didn't want you to worry."

Tara forced herself to breathe. *Not Cara!* Why was she so upset? It wasn't Cara, but it could have been. Someone somewhere else was going to get news that their search for a missing daughter, sister, friend . . . was over. She laid back onto the floor. Tara had to find Cara. She had to. She would not get that news. She vowed it to herself.

"Tara? Are you alright?" Betsy asked.

"How did she die? Was it . . . was she killed?"

"We don't know. The official cause of death is hypothermia," Betsy said.

Tara stood and walked over to her wall of notes. "Did you say hypothermia?"

"Yeah. We have to wrap our heads around that one, with the excessive heat we've been having."

Tara grabbed a photo of Cara that was pinned to the wall and ripped it free from its thumbtack. She stared at it.

"I've got to go," Tara said.

"Wait. Can you come by the station? There is something I'd like to talk to you about."

"Sure," Tara said, but she wasn't really listening as she ended the call. She plopped down on the floor with her laptop and started a new search.

SLOAN

Sloan Peterson sat at a bench with a telephoto camera lens, waiting for the perfect shot. Despite the heat, Sloan wore a seersucker suit. He pulled a handkerchief from his pocket and wiped his shiny bald head. He watched his business partner, Michael Higgins, in the restaurant across the street.

Michael Higgins had the dashing smile and full handsome head of gray hair you'd expect to find on a distinguished movie star. He could charm anyone into almost anything. But those who succumbed felt almost immediately that they had been used and regretted whatever they had agreed to. A philanderer, an opportunist, a misogynist, a racist, and most probably a narcissist, Michael Higgins pushed everyone around him to the absolute limit of patience. His good looks had always allowed him to get away with being a self-righteous jackass.

Michael sat across the table from a young blond. He paid the check and rose from the table. They did not see nor suspect that they were being watched. They walked outside to the corner where they stopped for a deep passionate kiss. Sloan snapped a few clicks of the camera and stowed it as the two walked away in separate directions.

For the last six months, Sloan had argued with Michael about the sale of his company, Butler's Ice Cream. Butler's was Sloan's baby. He'd started it right out of culinary school. He put a Southern spin on classic flavors: Georgia Peachy Keen, Scarlett's Red Raspberry, Muscadine Vine, Chocolate Drenched Strawberry, and Rocking Chair Chip were a few of the signature flavors. Unfortunately, in the early days of his business, he sold fifty-one percent of his company to Michael, more than he wanted to sell. But he'd needed the money. It had bought little Cindy some time and comfort in her final days, and that, he knew, was priceless. He didn't regret it.

Their partnership hadn't affected the day-to-day, but now that the company was doing so well, Michael was set on selling it. Sloan could not have that. These photos would give him leverage.

CHAPTER 2

TUESDAY

ADDISON

"Dementia." The doctor's words hung thick in the air. Addison's father, Michael Higgins, was already an unreasonable man; add dementia, and he'd become an unpredictable entity. Addison had gone with her father to the doctor, but she hadn't expected this. He didn't act like a man with dementia. She hadn't seen the signs. The impact of the doctor's words hit her like a gut punch. Her father, who would never admit to any form of weakness, sat silently, probably trying to figure out how it was possible that his own mind, his greatest asset, betrayed him.

Her father's health had started to deteriorate a few years ago. Only Addison knew about his health problems. Michael didn't have much use or respect for women. But somehow, Addison, his only daughter, had wormed her way into his heart at some point between her third and fifth year of life. He had never been much of a fan of babies and avoided spending much time with his children in the first two years of their lives. Michael found he bonded with them once they were a bit more engaging.

Addison and her brothers had been forced to work for their father. Her brothers worked at his venture capitalist firm, but she was not so lucky. Her father had coerced Addison into being his nurse. Michael didn't want to put that kind of burden on his wife, or strain on his marriage.

Addison had tried to convince him to hire a nurse. He certainly had the money, but he said he didn't want a stranger knowing so much about him. He'd told Addison that if she wanted to keep getting money for medical school and stay in his will, she would have to take care of him. So, she capitulated. He had been diagnosed with diabetes and high blood pressure.

The last year of school had nearly killed her. Michael was getting pills three times a day and insisted Addison be the one to administer them. Luckily, his house wasn't far from Georgia Tech, and she had scheduled her classes accordingly. She'd pushed herself to the limit to take care of him as well as complete her undergraduate in four years, graduating with honors in chemistry and biology. She'd been accepted to Emory Medical School and planned to start there next week, but the school was on the other side of Atlanta, making it impossible to administer all medication to her father three times a day.

Addison pushed her square glasses up as she looked at her father. What would he expect from her now? The idea of continuing to care for him as he became less and less rational terrified her. Would she be able to continue at this unforgiving pace as his needs for her help increased? Medical school wasn't exactly the kind of thing you could schedule around your father's pill times.

There were only so many hours in a day, and she was wasting them doing a job a trained monkey could do. Anyone could dole out a few pills and take blood pressure. A nurse would happily do it for what Michael could pay. *But damn him!*

"Why would you waste time studying when your duty is to me and this family?" he had said the last time it had come up. "And besides," he'd said, "sooner or later you'll meet someone and get to the business of making me grandchildren."

The doctor's words to Michael broke her thoughts, bringing her back to the present.

"It might be a good idea to get your affairs in order now before your mental capabilities deteriorate," the doctor said.

"How much time are we talking about?" Michael asked.

"There's no telling. Some cases progress very rapidly, others take longer."

Addison swept a strand of hair back into the messy bun, wrapping it around the pencil that held her brown wavy hair out of her face. She didn't know much about dementia, but she knew that her job was about to get harder, a lot harder.

Addison's life flashed before her eyes. Her only escape was her father's demise. But he could live another decade like this, maybe two.

Michael turned to his daughter.

"This stays between us. If anyone finds out about this, I will hold you responsible. Is that clear?"

"I won't tell anyone as long as you hand the company over. Prepare Mike or whoever is taking over for you."

"Don't tell me what I need to do. I know perfectly well how to handle my affairs," he said.

"And Daddy, I cannot continue to care for you. You need to hire a professional."

"If you don't continue to care for me, I will not send the check to Emory. You can forget about medical school. It's a waste of money if you ask me. A lady doctor." He shook his head.

The doctor's mouth fell open at his comment. He looked at Addison in shock. She gave him a knowing shrug.

SLOAN

Sloan sat in his small office at Michael Higgins Industries, staring at a blank wall. He preferred to work from his office at Butler's Ice Cream. He loved seeing the customers and hearing the jingle of the bell as they came and went. He found he was the most inspired to create new flavors in that setting. Maybe it was the smell of fresh waffle cones wafting upstairs. But here, where it smelled of disinfectant and printer ink, he never had much success with flavor combinations.

His office here was sparse with only one photo on his desk of his daughter, Cindy, sitting on his shoulders when she was a toddler at the zoo. That was before she'd gotten sick.

Michael walked past his office, just coming back from his doctor appointment. Sloan followed him into his large corner office with a northeastern view. Stone Mountain poked out of the trees in the distance.

"Michael, it's nearly five, how about a drink?" Sloan said, wandering over to the small bar area at the back of his office.

"I could use one," Michael said.

Sloan poured scotch into two glasses. Michael used the intercom to call his secretary. "I need an appointment Monday with my estate lawyer."

Sloan smiled to himself as he carried the drink over to Michael. "Making some changes?"

Michael looked at him, "Why do you care?"

"Just making conversation. I did want to talk to you about the new flavor. I've been over at R&D testing the samples. I'm not happy with it yet."

"I'm telling you for the last time, grits ice cream is never going to work. Even if it's delicious, the idea of it is revolting."

"You'll come around." Sloan paused and gulped his drink. Michael had turned his attention to his computer.

"Are you still considering selling Butler's? I heard you had a meeting with Nestle."

"Yeah."

"I should have been there, Michael."

"Why? I own the controlling portion of Butler's," Michael snapped.

"But I started this company, and I own forty-nine percent."

"You're too emotionally invested. You've made up your mind no matter what kind of offer they make."

"Yeah. We have a good thing here. Don't ruin it over money."

"What did you think would happen? I'm in the business of buying and selling companies. Did you think we'd make ice cream together forever? Did you think that your company meant more to me than any of the others?"

"I thought we were friends," Sloan said.

"What does that have to do with anything?"

"I thought you'd take my opinion into account!"

"I did. But my fifty-one percent opinion outweighs your forty-nine."

Sloan picked up his drink and downed it. "It's not the right time to sell. Just give me a year or two, and you'll see I can turn Butler's into a household name."

"With grits ice cream? Your best ideas are behind you, and we need to sell at the peak of this thing, which is now."

"Just give me another year."

"No can do. I've agreed to the Nestle deal."

"What?"

"Don't worry, you'll get your forty-nine percent. You'll be pleased when the check arrives."

"But I didn't sign anything! It can't be a done deal."

"It's not. Just a verbal agreement. We'll sign the papers Monday. I want to have it finalized before I leave the country. I've got the Africa hunt next week."

"Michael, you shouldn't have agreed without talking to me. You'll regret this," Sloan said.

"What is that supposed to mean?"

"Nothing," Sloan said, walking out the office door.

He turned down the hall toward the office of Michael's middle son, Harris. Harris sat at his desk in his attempt at work attire—unripped jeans, a half-button gray T-shirt, and fire-engine red Nikes. His brown hair hung in his face. He was playing a game of desk pool on a tiny table someone had given him as a joke.

"Hey, Sloan, what can I do for you?"

"Want to join your dad and me for golf Monday?"

"Sure. What time?"

"Your father just made an appointment to see his estate lawyer. Since his office is near Ansley Golf Club, he thought we'd have a round. I'll have my secretary set it up. Should be late morning."

"What's he meeting his estate lawyer about?"

"He didn't say. You don't think he's going to make any changes to his will, do you? I'm sure you have nothing to worry about."

"Of course, I'm sure you're right," Harris said, putting down the tiny pool cue and looking out the window.

Sloan left Harris's office and went to find Mike Jr., Michael's eldest son. Mike was working on his computer in his corner office. Sloan stuck his head in.

"Hey, Mike, are you up for a round of golf Monday? Your father has a meeting with the estate lawyer, so he wants to go to Ansley."

"Golf? I don't know if I feel like golf again," Mike said, looking up briefly and then returning to his work.

"What do you think he's meeting with the estate lawyer about?" Sloan asked.

"No clue," Mike said, not even looking up this time.

"You don't think he's going to change his will?"

Mike stopped working and looked at Sloan. "I'm sure he is making a change. Why else would he see the lawyer? It's probably some silly tax loophole or something. I'm sure there's nothing to worry about."

"Of course. I'll let you know about golf."

"Okay."

BETSY

The roundhouse kick hit the long punching bag a good two inches above the last one; the sweat trails made it obvious to anyone who was paying attention. No one was. Detective Betsy Turner alternated legs and pummeled the unsuspecting bag from the other side. She brought her leg down and rolled her neck while bouncing slightly on her feet.

She stood in the center of the police workout room with the windows open in the hopes of a breeze. Sweat rolled off her forehead onto the cement floor. She then began to attack the bag with a continuous barrage of jabs. Her hands moving in rhythm began to feel like they were leading her brain and not the other way around.

Her phone chimed, breaking her rhythm. She glanced at it resting on a nearby bench. There was a text from her partner, Henry Sanders.

Tara Sharp is here to see you.

Betsy sighed. She didn't want to face the disappointment that lived on Tara's face, the same disappointment that lived in her own heart, the disappointment of not knowing, of having no answers.

She saw herself in Tara, who recently felt the sting of an imperfect world interrupting her previously safe life. But this world was not a safe place. It was a horror show. Betsy had felt the same shadowing of her world, the same blackening of her youthful innocence. It was probably the reason she connected with Tara. They both had sisters taken from them.

Tara was the twenty-two-year-old sister of a missing eleven-year-old girl named Cara. Betsy wasn't sure if it was cute or weird that the sisters had rhyming names.

Betsy's twin sister, Hillary, had gone missing when they were seniors in high school. They'd gone to a movie in their small hometown in Connecticut. They walked home partway together, but Hillary had left her purse behind at the theater. Betsy did not want to walk back. It was late and she was tired. Hillary said to go on and she'd catch up to her. Only she never had. No one had ever seen Hillary again. It would be ten years in November.

The police looked into it and considered her a runaway. But Betsy knew better; Hillary didn't run away. She just didn't. Hillary was smart. If she was running away, she would have made a plan. And she would have told Betsy. They told each other everything. Besides, Hillary had a crush, or more of an obsession, with a local boy. It was all she ever talked about. She wouldn't have run away as long as the promise of sitting next to him in math class on Monday awaited.

Betsy's entire life changed after that. Something horrible had happened to Hillary, and Betsy was never the same.

She'd pursued a criminal justice degree at her local community college, eventually becoming a police officer and now a detective. She'd transferred to Atlanta because it was a hotspot for human trafficking, which she suspected had played a role in the disappearance of her sister. She vowed that she would have compassion and listen to people about who their loved ones were and not just assume that a missing teenager had run away.

That's why she empathized with Tara. That's why she wanted to help her find Cara. It was redemption for her failure with Hillary.

* * *

Henry was at his desk, opposite hers, when Betsy arrived in the office. He was talking to Tara while holding a book about serial killers.

"I like to know as much as I can about how they work. There's one on the FBI's ten most wanted list now. They've nicknamed him The Hunter's Hunter . . ." Betsy smiled to herself as Henry blathered on about serial killers. He looked for patterns in their behaviors. It was a hobby of his. One of his greatest goals was to catch one.

"Thanks for coming in," Betsy said. "I wasn't sure if you would."

Tara looked confused.

"I asked you on the phone yesterday to come in," Betsy said.

"You did?"

"Yes. The reason I asked you to come in today is to talk about the girl who died yesterday." Betsy pulled a picture of the girl out of a folder and showed it to Tara. "Do you recognize her?"

Tara studied the photo. "No," she said, shaking her head.

"It was a long shot."

"Why?" Tara asked.

"Before she died, she mentioned the name Cara."

"What? What did she say?" Tara asked.

"She mentioned three names: O'Hara, Mr. Green, and Cara. Do the other names mean anything to you?"

"No. But what did she say about Cara?"

"Nothing specific," Betsy said, avoiding Tara's eyes. "The witness just mentioned the names."

"So, there must be a connection?"

"It's possible," Henry said. "We're looking into it. You must have had another reason for coming in today. Can we help you with something?"

Tara nodded and took a deep breath. "Yes, I think I may have stumbled onto something."

Betsy and Henry looked at each other.

"I know you want to find your sister, but you have to leave the investigative work up to us," Betsy said, knowing that if it were her, she'd be doing the same thing.

"I know. I know I had the wrong idea before, but this time, this time I think I really have something."

"We took the leads you gave us seriously, and they didn't pan out. I'm sorry, but they just didn't. We can't spend any more time chasing wild theories," Betsy said. "It's time for you to move on with your life."

"How can I move on? She's still out there somewhere."

"I know it's hard. But we're handling this."

"Are you?" Tara asked and stormed out of the office.

TARA

Tara pushed the down button for the elevator. The police station was housed inside an old mill off Ponce de Leon Avenue. She knew that Betsy had not been entirely truthful. Something more, something specific, had been said about Cara by the unidentified girl. Tara suspected that Betsy was probably trying to spare her the hard truth, but if Tara was going to find her sister, she needed the truth no matter how brutal. She needed to see the file. The elevator door opened. Tara turned around and walked back toward the detectives' office. She slipped past them sitting at their desks and into the bathroom at the end of the hall.

She didn't have to wait long before Betsy and Henry left their desks. She darted in and sat at Betsy's desk. The file was still out on top. She looked around. No one was watching. She quickly opened the file, thumbing past the picture of the dead girl to the witness statement. She read what the runner had said; someone was coming on Saturday to kill her and Cara.

Tara dropped the folder onto the desk. *Kill Cara! On Saturday!* That meant Cara was alive. But only until Saturday. Tara had four days to find Cara and bring her home.

HARRIS

Harris shook the long bangs out of his eyes. Even if it was sometimes annoying, Harris liked to keep his hair longer. He didn't want to be another suit at his father's company. Not that he needed to worry. Even the way Harris moved was marked by his light and airy attitude, as if, like life's problems, even gravity had a lesser effect on him.

Harris knocked on the open door to his father's office.

"Yes," Michael said without looking up.

"Hey, Dad, listen, I had an idea. I was thinking of taking some of my inheritance and using it to start a zip-line company. There is some property on both sides of the Chattahoochee, right near downtown. With little investment, a zip line could be installed over the river and around the property. I believe it would be a big draw for tourists."

His father put his pen down and glared, taking a deep breath.

"Harris. You aren't an idea man. You are my numbers guy, remember? I need you running analysis on the companies we are considering investing in."

"I know, Dad, but you could hire someone who would do a better job at that than me. I'm just not a numbers guy."

"You underestimate yourself."

"But you invest in companies. Why not this company? I think there is a market for it."

"I invest in proven businesses. I don't risk my money on unproven ideas."

"But Dad—"

"Enough. Go back to work." He waved Harris away.

Harris stepped into the hallway and walked slowly back to his office. He thought about his father and how he was always controlling his life. He wanted his life to be his own. He wanted the money he had earned by jumping through his father's hoops for years. And there was only one way to get it.

CHAPTER 3

WEDNESDAY

YVETTE

The elevator opened on level seventy-two at Michael Higgins Industries. A large white desk stretched across the lobby in front of a red wall where the letters MHI hung in white, illuminated from behind. Yvette, a tall blonde wearing a designer suit in cream with a light-pink blouse approached the desk.

"Can I help you?" asked the woman behind the desk.

"Yes, I'm here for my nine o'clock interview," Yvette said, forcing confidence into her voice.

The receptionist looked down at her calendar. "Okay. I'll go find out. Please have a seat." The receptionist walked through glass doors and disappeared.

Yvette sat on a gray leather tufted chair. As she waited, a few workers arrived and walked past her into the office. The third guy to do so wore a tailored blue suit with a printed orange and navy button-down shirt underneath. He had brown hair, which was long enough to be pulled into a half bun on top of his head. He wore black-rimmed glasses and smiled at her as he entered.

The receptionist returned, "I'm sorry, we don't have an interview for today. What position was it you were interviewing for?"

"Oh, uh . . ."

"What's this?" Half Bun asked.

"Good morning, Mr. Higgins," the receptionist said.

Yvette's eyes darted back to the man.

"Mr. Higgins is my father; you can call me Mike or Mr. Mike."

"Yes sir. There appears to be a mix up. She is here for a nine o'clock interview, but no one seems to have a record of it."

Yvette noticed the way Mike was looking at her. She would follow the receptionist's lead and stay aloof and civil.

"Of course, I hate that I came all the way down here. I could have sworn it was today at nine. Maybe if I can just find the paper where I wrote down the name of who I spoke to. Usually I'm quite good with names, but I think in my excitement at the prospect of the interview, I just forgot. It's a tough job market out there."

"Is it?" Mike asked. "I'm sure she's here to interview for Susan's replacement. Her maternity leave can't be that far off."

"I believe she's not due until February, sir."

"Follow me. We'll go talk to Steve in HR," Mike said. "What was your name?"

"Oh . . . uh . . . Yvette."

"Nice to meet you, Yvette," Mike said, holding the door open for her.

"Hey, Steve," Mike said as he poked his head into a small windowless office. "There seems to be a mix up. This is Yvette. She's supposed to have an interview today. Would you speak with her and see if we have a suitable position?"

Steve knew that there'd been no interview and eyed her with disdain.

"Mr. Higgins," he said.

"Just Mike, please."

"I'm quite sure there was no interview scheduled for today. I think this lady may be trying to get away with something," Steve said.

Mike laughed. "Like what? Finding a job in a difficult market? Well, more power to her. That takes a lot of inner confidence to invent an interview. That's the kind of talent we need here."

"What if she's a corporate spy?" Steve asked.

Mike looked at Yvette with squinty eyes. "I think she's safe. But feel free to background check her."

Yvette began to look uncomfortable.

"We don't have positions available," Steve huffed.

"Why don't you just call me the next time you have an opening?" Yvette said meekly.

"She can be Susan's replacement, unless she's overqualified to be a secretary," Mike said.

"Oh no, not at all," Yvette said, smiling.

"Susan isn't due until February."

"Well, better to be prepared," Mike said. "I'll leave you to it." He left the room.

Yvette stood in awkward silence.

The interview did not go well. Steve had no intention of hiring her. She did her best to charm him, but it was not enough. He rolled through some basic questions. After just ten minutes or so, he was showing her out.

"Have a nice day," the receptionist said.

She entered the elevator and sighed heavily. Just as the doors were about to close, Mike entered the elevator.

"Oh, hello again," he said. "How'd it go? That was fast."

"Uh, not well. I don't think we'll be coworkers anytime soon."

"Well, I guess that's for the best."

"What?"

"As a policy, I don't date coworkers, and I've been thinking about you ever since we met. Would you like to have dinner, tonight?"

"Yes."

BETSY

Betsy's eyes were going out of focus. She could only look at a screen for so long. Nearly twenty-four hours had passed since Jane Doe died in the park. Betsy searched through all the missing person databases and was no closer to finding her identity. The only clue was a tattoo on the girl's wrist, a triangle with a semicircle on the end.

Betsy searched the police database of tattoos, but to no avail. Either the symbol was not linked to any known organization, or it was too new to be cataloged in the system.

Henry interrupted her search. "Aja asked to see us downstairs."

They took the elevator down to the medical examiner's office for an update.

"Well, my assessment in the field was correct," Aja said. "It was hypothermia. I don't envy you trying to figure that one out. It's completely illogical."

"It seems that way, but once we get to the truth, it will be a straight arrow of logic," Henry said.

Betsy couldn't wrap her head around hypothermia in this heat. She rode the elevator upstairs with Henry.

"Any ideas?" she asked him.

"A couple. But nothing solid," Henry said.

"Are there any poisons that mimic hypothermia?"

"I don't know. If there are, Aja would have caught them. I think the girl was just cold. The witness said she was cold to the touch."

TARA

The police needed proof before they would listen, and Tara was going to get it. She'd gone down the rabbit hole, and she wasn't coming back without Cara. Her research had led her to an address in downtown Atlanta. Tara's white Volvo sedan passed by the front of the small Victorian-style house with a front porch that wrapped around one side. The front door had a stained-glass window. She drove past the house, pulled a quick U-turn around a thin tree-lined median, and pulled to the curb across the street, far back enough that she could see, but without being conspicuous.

It was too bright out to be able to see in the windows. At three in the afternoon, it was the hottest part of the day. Luckily, she had stopped to get a frosted orange from the Varsity on her way over here and, of course, some onion rings. She'd chosen good stakeout food at least. The stifling heat forced her to keep the air-conditioning on as she crunched away on the rings.

A yellow Corvette approached from the opposite direction. Tara slid down and watched through the hole in her steering wheel. The Corvette turned into the driveway of the house. The license plate read ISCREAM. A shiver ran down her spine.

A balding man in his fifties exited the car. He walked around to the trunk and opened it. Tara held her breath. He pulled out two reusable grocery bags filled to overflowing. He picked up a third bag of groceries and approached the front door. He used a key to unlock it while balancing the groceries with his knee. He returned a moment later, retrieving four more grocery bags. She wondered who he shared the home with. How many groceries did this guy need? As he pulled the bags from the trunk, he dropped one on the ground. Four large boxes of tampons fell to the ground. One of the boxes opened, and the man cursed as he leaned over to pick them up and put them back in the box.

Her phone chirped. She grabbed it and read the text. It was already after four. She had better get going. She pulled the list of properties to investigate off the passenger seat and scratched through this one. It was clearly a private residence. She buckled up and headed for home. She'd have to check out the next address tomorrow.

Tara was getting closer to finding her sister. She could feel it. She could sense it. She knew what she had to do, but her mind kept running to the worst-case scenario. What she was doing was dangerous, and although she was normally risk-avoidant, she had to try. No matter the consequence, she had to try. She had time for one more stop tonight. She pulled into the parking lot, grabbed her leather tote bag, and headed into the small spy shop. If she was going to do this, she needed the right gear.

LIZA

Liza trudged over the lawn with her camping chair slung over her shoulder, headed to watch her youngest son, Harris, play a game called Spikeball, a relatively new sport, at least to her.

She heard laughter, splashing, and joyful screams from the large public pool, crowded with families looking to escape the heat that had persisted into the evening, as it had for the last two weeks. Liza thought back to the days of dragging her three kids to the same pool, carrying a large bag with towels, goggles, snacks, sunblock, and pool toys. She could almost feel Harris's tiny toddler hand in hers as they walked. Now his hand dwarfed hers. Not that she wanted to go back. She missed those sweet little babies, but she hadn't forgotten the long selfless days. And now her kids were grown. She'd raised her own best friends, and she loved watching them navigate the world and hearing their struggles and successes. Soon enough, they'd give her grandbabies to snuggle.

She wiped sweat off her eyebrows, running her hand over her bouncy pixie haircut. She'd allowed it to turn gray as she aged. Many of her friends thought she was crazy, but it didn't bother her. Why pay for brown when the gray was free and pretty in its own way? She saw Harris on the far field talking with the team before the match. Harris was captain of The Hedgehogs. Harris had always been athletically gifted and was offered college scholarships for track and swimming, but his father had insisted he go to Emory for business. He joined the swim team there, but it was not competitive nationally. Just one more thing his father had stolen from her son.

Liza did not want to be annoyed with her ex-husband. She took a deep breath, trying to suppress her anger, but sometimes it wiggled around inside her and set her teeth on edge.

The team huddle broke up. Harris saw his mother and waved as he bounded over.

"Hey, Mom," he said. He took the chair from her, smiling like a little boy, proud she had come. "These are just games for fun."

"I know, but I like watching you play. You're very good."

"Thanks, Mom."

Harris set up her chair on the sideline beside a few other girlfriends and supporters. After a few seasons of watching Spikeball, Liza had gotten friendly with some of the other spectators. She said hello and made a comment about the heat before sitting down.

"Game point," Harris said. She watched as he and his teammate hit the ball back and forth before Harris slammed it down against the small trampoline. His teammate gave him a high five and a chest bump. Harris ran over to his mom, a look of childish pride upon his brow.

"Wonderfully played," Liza said.

"Thanks for coming."

"I'll see you at dinner on Friday. Try not to be late, okay? It's important to your brother."

"Okay. Hey, Mom, before you go, I'd like to talk to you about something."

"Sure, honey, anything."

"I'll walk you to your car."

Harris picked up her camping chair and threw it over his shoulder. "I'll be right back!" he shouted at his teammates. Once out of earshot of anyone, he said, "I tried to go out on my own and start a business, but dad said he wouldn't support me. Plus, he's meeting with his estate lawyer Monday. Do you think he is cutting us out of the will?"

"No. Why would you think that?"

"I don't know. Why else would he meet with the estate lawyer?"

"He wouldn't do that. You went to business school like he wanted and worked at the company like he wanted, surely you've earned your inheritance."

"Yeah, you're probably right. I just wish he couldn't hold the money over our heads. I feel so powerless."

"You've given that man more than he deserves. You are the master of your destiny."

"Yeah, I am. Thanks, Mom. You're the best." Harris threw the chair into the trunk of her gray BMW sedan.

Liza drove home, but her mind drifted to her ex-husband and his self-centered, manipulative tactics. She'd tried to put a positive spin on it for Harris's sake, but she knew him too well to consider this move as anything other than another power play. She'd gained her freedom from him with the divorce, but her three children never would.

MIKE

The air smelled sweeter and the heat less oppressive. Mike's thoughts had been on only one thing since that morning. The lovely Yvette. He felt that fate had brought them together. Something about her, not just her stunning good looks, but something about her eyes. Her green eyes made him think of soft moss, wet after rain.

He offered to pick her up, but she'd said she would just meet him outside the office building where he worked. He hadn't even gone home but had stayed late, for the first time in ages, willing the clock to go faster. Finally, 6:30 p.m. had arrived, and he stood on the sidewalk waiting for her with butterflies in his stomach.

Although it annoyed his father, Mike kept his brown curly hair shoulder length, often pulling it back into a tight man bun when hard at work. He wore round tortoise shell glasses and had a three-day beard presently, but not always. His brown eyes were connected directly to his heart, and he often felt the emotions of others just from seeing them. His father, who disdained men showing emotions, especially in the workplace, was disappointed when his namesake son did. Mike tried to suppress them until he was alone, but with limited success.

He saw Yvette approaching from down the block. He waved when she neared, and she smiled back at him. He opened the door of his chauffeured car for Yvette, and she slipped inside. She smiled brightly, but there was something wary in her eyes.

The car pulled away from the curb and into traffic.

"I thought we could go eat at Nikolai's Roof. Have you been there?"

"Nope. I've never heard of it."

Mike smiled.

"What?" Yvette asked.

"I don't know. I just have a good feeling."

A loud pop interrupted the silence. The driver pulled over into a gas station and exited the car.

"I'll be right back," Mike said.

Yvette slipped out behind him.

"Dreadfully sorry, sir," the chauffeur said. "It appears we have a flat tire."

Even at nearly seven, the heat was stifling. Sweat appeared on the driver's forehead as he took off his coat and laid it over the trunk.

"Are you going to change the tire?" Mike asked.

"Yes, sir. I apologize again. It shouldn't take too long."

"It's too hot for you to deal with that."

"I don't mind, sir. It is my job. I will call another car to pick you up."

"No, don't bother calling another car. I have a better idea. If you insist on changing the tire, don't forget there are cold waters and cokes in the back. Make sure to drink something, then park the car and meet us over there," Mike said, pointing toward a restaurant across the street and a couple of blocks down.

"Yes, sir."

Mike turned to Yvette. "Change of plans," he said, offering her his arm.

She took it, and they walked up the street to a house that had been converted into a Mexican Restaurant with a large sun on the sign. Mike held the door open for her. He waved at the hostess and walked past her to a large corner table.

"I hope you like tacos. These are the best in the city. It was lucky, us getting the flat tire right outside."

Yvette didn't say anything. She had probably been expecting something fancier. He looked around the beloved restaurant with new eyes. It wasn't fancy, but it was clean.

The waitress arrived and placed two large waters on the table.

YVETTE

Yvette picked up the water and drank it down heartily. She felt her shoulders drop and her stress evaporate. She wasn't a fancy restaurant person, but she could definitely do tacos and guacamole.

"Are you disappointed? Did you want to go to Nikolai's?" Mike asked.

"Not at all. This is more comfortable for me."

"That's surprising. Most girls I've dated don't count a meal like this as a date. They always wanted expensive meals. If I took my ex here, she wouldn't have spoken to me for a week. Sometimes I wondered if she liked the fancy dinners more than she liked me."

"Well, I like tacos. You've set a high bar if you want me to like you more than tacos," Yvette said with an exaggerated wink. He was easy to talk to.

The waitress returned with chips and guacamole. She realized immediately that she was ravenous. The nerves, the anticipation of the evening, and thinking through every possible problem that might arise had left her empty.

"Can I get you anything besides water to drink?" the waitress asked.

"A beer for me. How about a Dos Equis?" Mike said.

"I'll just have a Coke," Yvette said. She looked at Mike. "I don't drink."

"Noted," Mike said.

They ordered their tacos. As the waitress turned to leave, Yvette dipped a chip into the guac and ate it.

"I was so nervous," Yvette said. "Is it weird to admit that?"

"No, I was nervous too."

"Why were you nervous?" Yvette asked.

"I don't know. Why were you nervous?"

"I'm not used to fancy restaurants and being driven by a chauffeur . . . not that any of that is bad, I just . . . whew, I was so nervous. I feel better now." Yvette picked up her water and took a long drink.

"To be honest, I prefer low-key myself. I like to find unique places that have something special or different to offer. I'm not really into chain restaurants."

"Where I grew up, there were only two restaurants. There was some fast food at the interstate, but that was over thirty minutes away. We'd drive over sometimes if we were bored."

"I grew up in downtown Atlanta. There were plenty of options. But I could have anything I wanted at home. We had a chef."

"Wow. I cannot relate to that. Tell me about your family."

"My dad is Michael Higgins. He owns several companies, and I work for him at his firm. He invests in various companies. That's boring, sorry. My mom is Liza, and they got divorced when I was eight. I think she only stayed around that long because she's a saint. My dad is impossible. We put up with him, but sometimes I want to throw him through a wall. I have a younger sister, Addison. She's going to be an amazing doctor someday. She is very logical and smart. She's going to start med school at Emory next week. My brother is Harris. You'll like him. He's a lot of fun. My dad remarried Nikki when I was ten. She's, well, she's loud and critical and the opposite of my mom in a lot of ways. It was hard for us to like her. But now that I don't live with her, I don't mind her. Then my youngest brother, well half-brother, is Kieran. He is Nikki's only child. He's only twelve, and we all spoil him, but he's too cool to be rotten or anything like that. What about your family?"

"Oh, uh . . ." Yvette was interrupted by the waitress delivering their tacos. "Our tacos have arrived," she said, dancing her head a little and smiling, relieved not to have to talk about herself.

"You really like tacos."

"Okay, if I'm honest, I feel this way about most food."

"So, what's your favorite food?"

"Pizza. You?"

"Sushi, probably."

Six tacos, two Cokes, and one beer later, they were back outside. The sun had sunk below the tree line, and the temperature had dropped to ninety-six.

"Want to walk a bit?"

"Sure."

They wandered down the street until they came to Centennial Park and meandered through. Children were running through the fountains, getting a bit of relief from the heat.

"Do you like working for your dad?"

"Eh, it's a job."

"If you didn't work for your dad, what would you do?"

"I'd paint. I love to paint. I wanted to go to school for it, but my dad insisted on business school."

"What do you paint?"

"Oh, anything really, people or places, landscapes, but I like to add abstract elements to otherwise standard paintings. I also really love to paint space, like outer space. I sometimes paint a night scene and dominate the subject with a huge starry sky with deep purples and nebulas."

"Wow, I'd love to see some of them."

"Really? No one ever wants to see them, except Mom. What about you? I know you are looking for work. What kind of job are you looking for?"

"Oh, just something stable that will help me pay the bills. I'm actually pretty good with computers."

They meandered around and talked for hours. Hanging out with Mike was like being with an old friend instead of a first date. Yvette let her guard down for the first time in ages. She floated home and had to remind herself that there was a job to do.

CHAPTER 4

THURSDAY

HARRIS

Harris sat in Mike's office drinking his morning coffee. It had become a habit of Harris's to waste the first hour or so of work, hanging out with his brother and mentally preparing for the next few hours to be spent behind a screen looking at spreadsheets.

"I'm worried, Mike," Harris said.

"That's not like you."

"Dad's got a meeting with his estate lawyer on Monday. Did you know?"

"Yeah, Sloan mentioned it."

"He's cutting us off. I can feel it."

"Maybe, but unlikely." Mike's phone chimed. He picked it up and smiled.

"What are you so happy about?" Harris asked.

Mike looked up from his phone. "Oh, just this girl I met. I'm going to ask her to come to my party tomorrow."

"What girl?"

"Her name's Yvette."

"Look at you, you're all flustered. She must be special."

"She is. Have you ever met someone and felt that you'd known them your whole life?"

"Nope," Harris said, shaking his head. "I hope she comes to the party. I want to meet her. Oh, I might be a bit late to the party. I've got a Spikeball tournament tomorrow afternoon."

"I hope the weather holds out for you. I'm a little concerned about it, actually. That hurricane in the gulf is supposed to move up here by tomorrow and could cause some nasty storms."

"Yeah, I heard. Hopefully it will fizzle out. Mom said she might come watch my Spikeball match. She's coming to the party too, right?"

"Yeah. I made sure she was invited," Mike said.

"Awkward. She and Nikki really don't get along."

"Mom gets along with everyone," Mike said.

"Yeah, and Nikki gets along with no one, except maybe Kieran," Harris said.

Sloan poked his head into the office.

"We're on for golf at eleven on Monday after your father meets with the estate lawyer. You guys didn't do anything to get yourselves written out of the will, I hope." Sloan chuckled. Harris and Mike exchanged a nervous look. "Struck a nerve? I was only teasing," Sloan said.

CHEF JOE

Chef Joe stood over the cutting board, chopping vegetables. He had the roundish build that inspired confidence in his culinary abilities. Short wavy hair stuck out from the chef's hat Miss Nikki insisted he wear. He pushed his black glasses up his nose as he worked.

Joe worked skillfully, biding his time. He served dinner every night in the opulent dining room dominated by the large stuffed elephant head, tusks and trunk included, its dead black eyes staring down at him. It had taken him a month to be able to walk into the room without gagging. Joe had always been passionate about two things—food and animal rights.

The world was full of monsters; Chef Joe knew that all too well.

He had spent his life fighting many of them through various wildlife organizations. But it didn't matter. Every time they made a step forward in one area, they lost ground in another.

It may have seemed like a contradiction for an animal lover to be a chef; he was by no means a vegetarian chef. He felt that the death of an animal should never be wasted. He often cooked with parts that others discarded. He used animal giblets and skin in creative and delicious ways, trying to honor by avoiding waste. But to kill an animal for fun? That sickened him.

Nikki entered his kitchen. "Let's discuss the menu for Mike's birthday party tomorrow night."

"Yes, ma'am. I have printed a menu for your approval." He handed it to her. "Additionally, I'll be doing my signature chocolate cake for your son's party."

"He's not my son," Nikki said sharply. "Now, this menu might work if we make a few changes."

MIKE

Mike's feet hadn't touched the ground since he'd met Yvette. She brought him out of the funk he'd been in since he'd started working for his father. He'd numbed to his dreams and aspirations. After their first date, he'd pulled out his paints for the first time in ages and gotten right to work. He painted for hours, finally heading to bed around three. He was late to work, not that anyone would dare to tell on the boss's son. Heck, Harris was late every day and there was no consequence. Mike thought about his job here and how he loathed it. He felt like a cog in a machine, a hamster on a wheel. It was a business that neither invented nor created anything. They just bet on other companies by investing in them and then riding their coattails to success.

Mike wanted to create, a passion that had stirred and now called for all his attention. He did not think he could make it through one more day. But he'd have to. His father would never let him go. He was his father's namesake, his legacy, and as such, Michael had tried to control every detail of Mike Jr.'s life. It was stifling.

Michael was worth somewhere in the range of $200 million, the kind of money that would be hard for even the most disgruntled son to walk away from. He had often let his mind wander to the freedom he'd gain if his father was dead. He'd get his share of the inheritance and he could go wherever he wanted and live his life painting. Now that vision included Yvette.

He'd dwelled on his father's death since he was about twelve. The idea came to him when his father had taken him to South Georgia to partake in a tradition called the Rattlesnake Roundup. A large pit had been dug in the middle of a field. Over the course of the weekend, the men would gather up rattlesnakes and throw them in the pit. By the time Mike and his father had arrived, the pit was already four feet deep with the creatures writhing over each other in a moving sea of snakes. Mike didn't particularly like snakes, but he felt sad for them. Their death imminent, in a mass grave. Even if they were of an inferior mental capacity, surely, they saw the writing on the wall. The atmosphere in the crowd was jubilant and mostly drunk. Every now and then, you'd hear the crack of a shotgun go off as someone got too close to one and it had to be shot before even making it to the pit. At the end of the last day, they poured gasoline into the pit and burned the snakes alive. Mike had cried seeing the snakes erratic with pain and melting together into nothingness. His father had pulled him aside and slapped him.

"We don't cry for those beneath us, and everything and everyone is beneath us."

Young Mike managed to hold his tears in until he was alone, but he'd cried half the night for those snakes. They said it was important to keep the rattlesnake population under control, to keep their numbers from steadily climbing, to keep people safe. But Mike wondered if there wasn't a more humane way to do that.

His father had bought one of the snakes before they'd been burned alive. At the time, Mike thought he'd done it to rescue it from a terrible fate, but he realized later that his father enjoyed having control over something so powerful.

He milked the snake for its venom. He'd forced his young son to partake in the ritual, showing him how to grasp the snake and hold it firm as it bit into the cloth-covered beaker, the venom dripping down and collecting in the bottom. Mike hated it. His father knew this.

"I think we need to visit Zeus," he'd say. And Michael would follow him to his office where Zeus was kept in a large terrarium. Mike would hang his head and stare at the snake in the terrarium until he got up the nerve to reach in, pull it out, and force it to bite the beaker. He would cry the whole time, feeling the snake's fear.

As this ritual of fear continued, Mike began to imagine his father was the beaker. How easy it would be to grab the snake and turn on his father, forcing the snake's teeth to puncture his skin and release its venom into the cruel man. *I could make it look like an accident,* Mike had concluded.

The daydream surfaced once more as he thought of Zeus III, the latest iteration of the beast, biting into his father.

YVETTE

Yvette's phone rang. It was Mike. She was glad to hear from him so soon after their date.

"Hello," she said.

"Good morning," Mike said. "I hope it's not too soon to call."

"Not at all. I'm actually impressed. All I usually get after a date is a text three days later, saying, 'What's up.'"

"So . . . what's up?" Mike said. "Just kidding. I was up most of the night painting. You really inspired me."

Yvette's heart fluttered, even though she didn't want it to. "That's great. What did you paint?"

"Lots of things . . . you."

Yvette smiled. "That I'd like to see."

"Maybe one day. Actually, I was calling to see if you were busy Friday. It's my birthday, and I'm having dinner at my family's. Is it too soon for you to come with me?"

"Great. I'd love to come," Yvette said.

"Are you sure? It will be my whole family. I almost didn't ask, but I want you to be there."

"I wouldn't miss it," Yvette said, smiling.

"Great."

TARA

Tara stepped out of her apartment complex into the parking garage. She pulled her sunglasses on immediately. It wasn't even eleven and the sun was in full force. The heat hit her like a wave as soon as she'd left the comfortable air-conditioning. She walked down the stairs toward the parking lot, her mind on the best route through the city to investigate the remaining properties on her list, those owned by her top suspect in Cara's disappearance. She had two days left to find her.

She walked across the lot to her white Volvo and stopped in shock. The driver's side window was broken. She looked around the parking garage. No one was there. She slowly approached the window and saw a rock about the size of a grapefruit sitting on the passenger seat. Tara darted back inside the house and called Detective Betsy.

Ten minutes later, Detectives Turner and Sanders arrived with a backup car. Betsy pulled on a pair of gloves as she approached the Volvo sedan's broken window. She could see the rock that had smashed in the window and come to rest on the passenger seat. She opened the side door to retrieve the rock. A rubber band held a note to the rock. It said, *Stop Snooping*.

Betsy handed the rock over to an officer who put it in an evidence bag.

"Send that to the lab for analysis," Betsy told the patrolman. She walked over to Tara. "You changed your hair."

Tara reached up and touched her hair. "Yeah. Do you think I look like a hussy?"

Betsy choked on her coffee. "A hussy?" She laughed. "I've never heard anyone use that word. But no. It looks nice."

Tara grinned.

"I thought I told you to stop investigating," Betsy said. "I can't lose you too."

"I've hit a nerve. I must be on the right track."

"Okay, come by the station this afternoon and we'll go over everything you have. I will continue to work from where you left off, but maybe it's time for you to leave the police work up to me. Promise me you will drop this."

"I promise," Tara said, her fingers crossed behind her back.

Tara watched as they drove away. The police were finally ready to listen, but she knew they'd want proof and Tara was going to get it.

Back inside, she pulled the bag of purchases from her visit to the spy shop out onto the table. She opened the large leather tote next to it as she began to pack. First, she pulled out the bulletproof vest she'd bought. It had been expensive but was thinner and less noticeable than traditional vests. Next, she tested a taser. It cracked and sparked in the air. She tossed it in the bag. She added a roll of duct tape, a handful of zip ties, a first aid kit, and a length of rope. Satisfied with her supplies, she turned to the kitchen and threw a couple of granola bars and a bottle of water into the bag and then headed back out to check out her list of properties.

BETSY

Betsy dripped with sweat. The police station had spotty air-conditioning. She hoped they would get something from the rock that was thrown at Tara's car, but she doubted it. Tara must be on the right track. She had spooked someone. Hopefully she'd head this way shortly to go over her latest theory. Maybe she should have listened to her earlier this week. It was Thursday and she had made zero progress on either case.

She turned her attention back to the Jane Doe. She'd had no luck connecting the symbol on Jane's arm to anything. Her gut told her it had to do with human trafficking, but there was no intel on it.

Betsy walked over to the kitchenette for a coffee. Another detective led a teenage girl with her arms cuffed in front of her past Betsy toward the interview room. As she walked past, Betsy noticed a small symbol on her wrist, a black outline of a triangle with a semicircle attached to it.

SLOAN

Sloan reached down deep into the three-gallon tub of Washington Carver's Delight, a Dutch chocolate base with peanut bits as well as a ribbon of peanut butter, and scooped out the remainder of the ice cream, the frozen ribbon of peanut butter snapped as he rolled the ice cream into a ball. He pulled his arm keeping his wrist straight rather than spinning it, which would lead to carpel tunnel and an uneven scoop, the same way he taught all his employees. He used the scoop to round out and form the chocolate mass into a ball, which he slipped into the freshly made waffle cone. Even though he was the CEO of Butler's Ice Cream, he still loved to serve his loyal customers.

He handed the cone off to one of his employees to ring it up and wiped his arms off on the black apron he'd put over his Brooks Brothers slacks and pink button-down shirt. The flagship store, an old house he'd converted into a quaint ice cream haven in downtown Atlanta, was busy. The heat was good for business. Each of the rooms of the rambling old house was filled with overstuffed chairs and cozy tables with mismatched dining chairs. It felt more like a comfy coffeehouse than the sterile franchises of his competitors. Sloan's office was upstairs, an area off limits to customers and roped off. He pulled the rope open, let himself through, and climbed the steps to his office.

Sloan talked to both customers and employees easily, each feeling a bit of inexplicable camaraderie from him. Able to talk to anyone about anything with an air of actual interest, Sloan was well liked and cordial.

What had started as a dream was now five stores around the greater Atlanta area. He wouldn't have had this much success without the partnership to Michael Higgins, but he'd grown more and more wary of his majority partner the longer they were in business together. Michael was gruff and often irrational. He had a mind for business, that much was clear, but he didn't bend once he had decided on something. And it seemed his mind was set on selling Butlers' to Nestle.

Sloan felt that he had made a deal with the devil when he'd taken his money all those years ago. He had done all the hard work of inventing the flavors that everyone loved, yet he felt he was always answering to Michael. One of the reasons he started his own business was to not have to answer to anyone but himself. But he had no way out.

He looked at the two pictures pinned to the wall of his precious daughter, Cindy. One was of a little girl about five with long red hair smiling on a swing. The other was a bald girl in a hospital bed, hugging her beloved bear. But the smile was the same in both, big and carefree. When she'd gotten sick, Sloan had no health insurance. He was quickly overwhelmed with medical debt. He'd never had debt in his life and took pride in that fact, but he soon faced hundreds of thousands of dollars he owed for hospital visits and medications. His ex-wife had to quit her job to take care of Cindy. It was up to him to find the money. He had to mortgage the store and was on the brink of losing it when he reached out to investors. In the end, all the money in the world couldn't have saved her. He'd left nothing on the table.

Despite his growing dislike of his business partner, Sloan would go to Michael's home to celebrate the birthday of young Mike. He'd been to the Higgins's estate for dinner many times, but this time, he felt a deep foreboding at the impending event. He sighed deeply.

KIERAN

Kieran stood at the edge of the driveway watching cars pass as he waited for an Uber. Most of his friends weren't allowed to take Ubers, but most of his friends had moms or nannies to chauffer them. Kieran's mom was a busy woman. She wanted her son to be worldly, and not a sheltered rich boy with no idea of how the world works. So, she gave him a phone and a credit card and let him go. He was on his own most days. The long summer days did drag. Luckily, school would start back in a couple of weeks.

The combination of Nikki's Colombian genes and Michael's good looks had blended perfectly in Kieran. He was tan, with his father's green eyes and his mother's dark brown hair. At twelve, he could've passed for fifteen, standing five-foot-eight with no indication of slowing down. Only a whisper of babyness in his face hinted at his youth. He already found the eyes of girls and young women. But still young and awkward, he had more interest in Legos and Fortnite than girls.

As the least acknowledged and youngest of Michael's children, Kieran found solace in his mother's deep conviction that he was the best of the four. Of course, being Nikki's only child, she was somewhat biased. He certainly loved his half-siblings immensely but found his mother soured against them in almost every aspect. He couldn't see the moodiness of Mike, or the sullenness of Addison, or the silliness of Harris. To him, they were a delight, and he enjoyed any time spent with them. He couldn't find much value in being better than them anyway, if, in her opinion, they were not worth anything.

Eight years younger than Harris, Kieran had been a compromise on Michael's behalf. He'd agreed to one more child only to keep Nikki happy. By the time he was born, any joy Michael took in fatherhood had long vanished. Michael simply smiled at the boy and patted him on the head and went right on back to work. He hadn't stopped to give the boy much attention or direction. Michael figured he'd done his duty with the first three; that was more than enough to carry on his legacy. Kieran was superfluous. But he made Nikki happy, which made his life easier.

* * *

Kieran had spent the majority of his summer practicing archery, his favorite hobby. His mother had gotten him into it at a young age and he was quite good. He'd won some competitions. His father had not come to see any of them. When he wasn't shooting arrows, Kieran was playing Fortnite or swimming in the large pool at his home. He thought back to the beginning of the summer when he'd asked his father if he could help out around the office.

"No, the office is no place for a child. We do serious work there. Why don't you stay home and help your mother out?"

But his mother was never home. He was usually alone or with the maid or the chef, looking for almost any opportunity to socialize.

A black Ford Escort pulled into Kieran's driveway.

"Kieran?" the driver said out the window.

"Yup," Kieran said, climbing into the back seat.

"Heading to Fellini's pizza on Howell Mill?"

"Yes, sir, I'm meeting my brother."

"Is their pizza good? I've never been there."

"Oh yeah, it's great. You should grab a slice when you drop me off."

"Maybe I will."

Kieran was happy that his brother Harris had invited him to meet for lunch. He'd always gotten along with both his brothers and his sister, but he'd always had a special affinity for Harris. He was the only one in the family who didn't take everything so seriously. Kieran admired the way he could manage the same boring dinners as everyone else with a smile and enthusiasm.

When he arrived at Fellini's, he chose a table inside because of the heat and watched the door for Harris.

Harris arrived a few minutes later.

"Hey, bud!" he exclaimed as he threw his arms around his brother, who had stood to greet him. "I hope I didn't keep you waiting too long. I came straight from work. Dad made us all sit in on a meeting. Snooze fest."

"Not me," Kieran said.

"Consider yourself lucky."

The two got in line to order their food at the counter and then sat back down at the table Kieran had chosen.

"Check out what my mom gave me," Kieran said, pulling a Swiss Army knife from his pocket.

"Cool. I can't believe your mom gave you that. I don't think my mom let me cut my own steak until I was in high school."

"Yeah, she said it's a tough world out there and I might as well prepare for it."

"Yikes. Your mom can be a bit intense."

A waitress came out with a tray.

"I've got two slices of pepperoni," she said. Kieran raised his hand, and she set them down in front of him.

"The other two are mine," Harris offered.

"Okay, that's one sausage and onion, and one pepperoni, green peppers, and mushrooms.

"Thanks."

They were halfway through their pizza when Harris got to the point. He looked around to make sure no one could hear them.

"Listen, Kieran, I've gotten a heads-up that Dad is taking us all out of his will. He has a meeting Monday morning with his estate lawyer. He's going to cut us all out of it."

"How do you know that?"

"He was bragging about it at the office, and word got around to me. I don't think I would do well being poor."

"That's terrible."

"Yeah, it is. We've done everything he ever asked. I gave up that swimming scholarship at UGA to study business at Emory. And

Addison works like a dog to take care of him and go to school. It's not fair."

"No, it's not."

"Maybe something should be done," Harris said, looking down at his pizza and glancing up at Kieran.

"Like what?"

"I don't know. He's a horrible man, and if he dies after Monday, we all end up with nothing. But if he dies before Monday—"

"You don't mean—"

"No, no, not really. Besides, if I were to get caught, it would be life in prison. In fact, Mike and Addison would also get life in prison. Money is not much use if you're spending the rest of your life in prison."

"Okay."

"Now, say, if you were to be the one to do it—just hypothetically—well, you'd only get a couple of years in juvenile detention."

Kieran looked at his brother, dumbfounded. He swallowed.

"You mean . . . you want me to . . . to . . . to kill him?"

Harris looked around to make sure no one was listening. "Hypothetically. I'm just brainstorming. Kieran, don't think of it like killing him. It's more of helping death to find him. I'll come by the house before Mike's party tomorrow and we can talk more."

LIZA

Liza had been better suited to Michael in age and, for a few years, they'd been quite happy together. Partly because it didn't bother her that Michael always chose the restaurant or the movie or the house. She could be happy with almost anything. And he was only happy when he got his way. Then the children came along and distracted her from many of the problems with the relationship. She loved her kids and wanted to make it work for their sake, but after the third affair that she knew about, she'd left him.

Liza and Addison walked across Emory campus to Everybody's Pizza. Her daughter had moved into her student housing for the year, and Liza had come to check it out. They slid into a booth.

Liza sat across from her daughter in silence. She studied the appearance of her only daughter. Her long dark hair was frizzy and unbrushed. Black circles lay under her eyes. Addison studied the menu and had not made eye contact with her yet.

The waitress approached. "Can I get you something to drink?"

"Just water please and a side salad with light vinaigrette and a slice of cheese pizza. Mom, you're ready to order, right?"

"Oh, sure, I'll just have a slice of sausage. Would it be too much trouble to get some crackers while we wait?"

"Certainly," the waitress said and disappeared.

"You look so tired, honey. Are you sure you're not wearing yourself too thin?" Liza asked. To her immense surprise, her very logical, very analytical, very practical daughter burst into tears. Addison reached under her glasses, wiped at the tears, and looked at her mother.

"I feel like my life is slipping through my fingers," she said. "I worked so hard to complete my undergraduate degree and take care of Dad. Now I'm supposed to start medical school, and I don't know if I should."

"What do you mean?"

"Dad's getting worse. I spend so much time taking care of him. I don't know if I'll be able to do both. I think I'm going to have to defer for a year. But I don't think anything with Dad will get easier. If I don't go to medical school now, maybe I never will."

"No. You need to go now. Medical school takes so long. Don't put it off."

"I know. But Mom, something has changed."

"What? What has changed? Nothing could be that important."

"I can't say. But there is no end in sight. I don't want to waste my life."

"So, don't. Tell your father to go pee up a rope, and do what's best for you."

"You don't understand. He'll cut me off. I'll have no money for school. I'll have to leave my apartment, and he'll take my car. I'll have nothing."

"You can live with me. There are worse things than no money."

"But now he needs me. He really needs me."

"Your father has enough money to hire anything he needs."

"He's too ashamed. He doesn't want anyone to know."

"What is it?"

"You can't ever tell another soul, not even Mike or Harris."

"I won't."

"He has dementia. He's going to need me to be with him more and more and more as his decline increases. He won't tell anyone."

"Well, sooner or later, people will know. They will figure it out if nothing else. It's your life; you can't let him take it. I already gave him too many good years. I won't let you do the same. You'll start school next week as planned. We'll figure something out."

SLOAN

Sloan entered Michael's office and shut the door behind him.

He threw the glossy photos onto the desk and sat down across from Michael, who looked at the photos for a fraction of a second. His jaw set as he looked up at Sloan.

"I've tried to reason with you. I've talked logically and rationally, but you refuse to let me have a seat at the table. You insist on selling my company without my consent."

"Technically, it is my company, as I own the controlling share. I understand that it is your baby, but like all babies, eventually they grow up and you have to let them go."

"Like you've let any of your kids go? They all work here even though they hate it."

"Enough. I'm selling. You will be well compensated. You have no reason to complain. The numbers on the ice cream are like nothing I've ever seen. The numbers are almost too good to be true," Michael said, looking Sloan in the eye. "Is there anything you want to tell me? Is there a reason the numbers are SO good?"

"Of course not. What are you implying?"

"Just making sure."

"We can't sell."

"We can and we will. Do people really like ice cream that much?"

"Everyone loves ice cream," Sloan said.

"There isn't anything fishy going on with those numbers, is there? Before we sell, everything will be gone through with a fine-tooth comb by the Nestle people. Tell me now if they are going to find anything."

"Of course not. But if you insist on selling, I will show those pictures to Nikki."

"I don't think you will. You're more scared of her than I am."

"If she sees those pictures, she will probably kill you."

"So, I guess you'd better keep them to yourself then."

BETSY

Betsy followed the detective to the interview room. A pair of her colleagues, fellow detectives, stood outside the room talking.

"What do you have her on?"

"Suspicion of prostitution. To be honest, we don't have enough to hold her. And she knows it."

"She's not old enough. Shouldn't we find her parents?"

"She says she's twenty-one. But we're checking missing persons now."

"That girl is nowhere near twenty-one. Can I ask her a few questions?"

"Be my guest," the detective said.

Betsy entered the small interview room and sat across the table from the girl. She wore a tight, thin purple halter dress and high-heeled shoes. Her hair had been dyed blonde, but her eyebrows had a hint of red. She had a small mole high on her cheek, under her eye. Her face was plastered with makeup. Betsy put her between fourteen and sixteen. Wherever she came from, she had not been well taken care of. She was skinny, and her hair, although curled and sprayed, lacked the shine that came from a healthy lifestyle.

"Hi, I'm Betsy. What's your name?" The girl stared at her. She didn't speak but looked at Betsy as if she was bored. "I'd like to help you. If you tell me about yourself."

"We both know the charges won't stick."

"Do you really want to go back? I can help you get a new life."

A brief crack in the facade crossed the girl's face. She wanted out. But she didn't believe that it was possible. At least not yet.

"What can you tell me about that tattoo on your arm?" Betsy asked. The girl looked at the inside of her wrist and ran her hand over it. "Someone made you get that, didn't they? Who was it?"

She didn't answer and held one hand over the tattoo, looking out the window at the sky and the nearby windows of other office buildings.

Betsy placed a file on the desk. She opened it to a headshot of Jane Doe from the morgue. She took the picture and slid it across the table to the girl, who stared at the picture. A tear rolled off her cheek and landed on the photo.

"Sorry," she said, wiping her eyes.

Betsy slid the box of tissues on the table toward her.

"What's her name?"

The girl opened her mouth to speak and then shook her head.

The door opened, and a man in an expensive suit with shiny hair and shoes entered.

"I'm Miss Smith's lawyer. Please give me a minute to talk to my client."

He was too fancy a lawyer for the girl to afford, someone her pimp most likely had hired. She knew that whoever hired this guy did not have her best interest in mind.

"Miss Smith. You don't have to talk to him. I can protect you."

The girl stared at the floor and shook her head. She was done talking to Betsy. This guy would make sure of that.

Betsy left the interview room and found the arresting detective outside the doors.

"Do me a favor and keep her overnight. Don't send her back yet. We need to find out who she is first."

"The lawyer had all the proper identification."

"Yeah, I'm not sure that is legit. I'm concerned she may be connected to my Jane Doe, the DOA in the park. They have the same tattoo. I'm starting to think there may be a human trafficking link."

"Okay. I think she's just another working girl. But we'll hold her overnight. She'll be arraigned and probably released in the morning."

"Okay, thanks. I owe you one," Betsy said. "Make sure to get her something to eat. She looks hungry."

Betsy grabbed her phone. Tara had not come by as they'd discussed earlier in the day. Betsy had called and texted but received no answer. She had a bad feeling, but she shook it off. She'd hear from Tara in the morning. She didn't have time to worry about her. She was too busy trying to save her sister. Only a day and a half left.

CHAPTER 5

FRIDAY MORNING

BETSY

Henry returned to the police station with two frosted coffees and two chicken biscuits from Chick-fil-A. He and Betsy had worked all night scouring missing persons cases from across the country, hoping to find the identity of Miss Smith, as she called herself. The tattoo made her the only lead in identifying her or finding Cara.

"Any luck?" Henry asked.

"No. We only have one more day if Jane Doe was right about Saturday at midnight."

"That's assuming she meant Saturday night at midnight, and not Saturday morning at midnight."

Betsy looked at him. "But midnight tonight would be Friday at midnight."

"I'm just saying, she's young, and she was very ill, so she may have meant midnight between Friday and Saturday. It's a possibility."

"Not a possibility I like. Either way, we don't have much time. I'm convinced that tattoo has to do with human traffickers. We're close to something. I don't want to let Miss Smith go back into the hands of the traffickers. We have to find her real identity and her real age. There's no way she's twenty-one like the driver's license the lawyer provided said. She's being arraigned at eleven. We've got until then to find out who she is and where she came from."

NIKKI

Nikki held her white and brown King Charles spaniel, Coco, as she came downstairs to inspect the work of the team cleaning for the party. She paused to look at the wedding picture of her and Michael, which hung on the wall. She looked fantastic in her lace bodice dress with a plunging neckline. Nikki had married Michael for the money, a choice she was content with. She'd grown up poor in Colombia and knew what it was to be hungry. To her, Michael's home was an impossible dream.

Sloan had introduced them. He knew she was just his type. She didn't care Michael was a creep. All men were creeps as far as she could tell. She'd never met one who didn't stare at her and treat her like an amusement or property. At least with Michael she'd have money, security, and a green card. She'd come here illegally, but Michael had the kind of money and contacts that made those kinds of problems little more than a nuisance.

Michael loved her too, well, as much as he was capable of loving anyone, probably because she was gorgeous. He always told her she was the prettiest woman he had ever seen. Her dark brown hair, mocha skin, womanly body, which had been enhanced since her marriage to Michael, drew attention from men wherever she went.

She gained immense satisfaction from being a desired object that they could not have. She was a jealous woman though and told Michael the only thing that would ruin her happiness with him was if he ever cheated on her. Her pride would not stand for anyone to be her equal in her husband's eyes. She couldn't imagine it would ever be a problem, for few women could compete with her beauty.

Michael had cheated on his first wife, Liza, nearly constantly. Nikki felt sorry for Liza and her clear inability to keep her husband happy. She sighed as she thought of Liza who was invited to the party tonight. It was Mike's request that his mother be there. Nikki had hoped Liza would have had the grace to decline the invitation. But she'd agreed to come. How Michael had ever loved that woman was beyond her. She certainly never found anything to talk to her about. Oh well, there would be enough people there that she could avoid talking to her for any length of time.

Nikki spent her days tending to Kieran as well as participating in a number of hobbies, including yoga, that kept her away from home. These activities seemed to fill up her time most days. In fact, today was the first day she had spent at home in quite a while. The cleaning crew was moving from one room to the next. Nikki found them in Michael's office.

"Have you started in here?" she asked.

"Yes, Miss Nikki. We have already done the rest of the downstairs. We will move up after this room."

"You mean to tell me the dining room is clean? Ha, I guess my definition of clean is different than yours. Do you think it is clean to leave a layer of dust on the windowsill?"

"No, Miss Nikki. Sorry, Miss Nikki. Please show me and allow me to correct it."

Nikki pointed out the error to her. During the morning, she found fault with the cleaning in almost every room. The team of three ladies smiled and fixed the problems, but when they left, they grumbled and called her names.

It wasn't just the cleaning ladies Nikki spoke to harshly. She challenged the florist on his inability to procure heather for the arrangements for the party. Her belief was that he was lazy or had not heeded her instructions.

"I'm sure I had them last year around this time," she'd said.

He had apologized. Nikki had graciously accepted the beautiful and rare arrangements he had procured for her. He barely noticed the evil stare she gave him as he left.

Even though it was well before noon, arranging everything and doing everyone's job for them had exhausted her. She took a nap, as she didn't want bags under her eyes for the party.

BETSY

The clock read 10:45. Betsy had not found anything on Miss Smith, who would be released in just a few moments back into the hands of what were probably human traffickers. She pushed her chair away from the computer.

"That's it, Henry. It's too late."

Henry looked up from his computer. "I'm sorry, Betsy. We tried."

Betsy nodded and stretched. One of the other officers entered the room holding a mug that said, *Canada is for Lovers*. Betsy sat back down at the computer. It was worth one last attempt. She pulled up the missing persons database for Canada.

After filling in the appropriate fields into the search parameters, Betsy stood and looked Henry in the eye. The first picture that popped up was of a ten-year-old girl with red hair and a small mole on her cheek, just below her eye. She'd been missing for four years. Her name was Tori Fontaine.

Henry walked around the desk to look at the screen.

"Let's go," he said.

When they reached the courthouse, Henry let Betsy out in front of the building. Betsy took the wide steps up to the courthouse two at a time. She quickly maneuvered the metal detectors and found her way to the courtroom. Inside, Tori, as she now knew her, stood before the judge.

"Wait," Betsy cried out. Everyone in the courtroom turned to look at her.

ADDISON

The brilliance of Addison's plan was typical of her general character. Her logic allowed her to see the clearest path and to take it. Although she loved research, she knew better than to research rare poisons, leaving a trail of evidence to her dirty deed. She was too smart for that. Better to kill Michael with something she could readily get, and something that involved no further research than what she already had on hand.

Addison was going to simply inject her father with an air bubble from an empty syringe instead of his nightly insulin shot. He never paid much attention to what she was doing. Once done, he would be dead within hours.

It was a mercy killing in a way. She didn't want him to spend the next few years of his life sinking into a deeper and deeper state of confusion. At least that's what she told herself.

TARA

Tara's phone chirped, another missed call from Betsy. That made fourteen today. She pressed decline. Tara wasn't going to talk to the detective until she had the proof she needed. If everything went to plan, she was just a few hours away from the truth. A pang of guilt hit Tara's stomach. She'd lived with these pains for the last few days. But she pushed it down. It didn't matter now. She hoped she'd find answers tonight because tomorrow would be too late. Once she had solid evidence to stand on, she'd let the police take over. She set her alarm and lay down to take a nap. There was nothing more to do now but wait.

MIKE

The dream of living the life of a painter haunted Mike constantly, ever since he met Yvette. They could survive on love alone. Why should he continue to work at a job he hated? Was his only motive money? Should he sell his life away for money? He had stayed up late again last night painting, inspired by her, his muse.

Tonight, she would meet his family. He knew they would adore her, as he did. But he worried his father would be difficult. His father was always difficult, and he always got what he wanted. Mike had gotten the impression since he was a teenager that his father wanted to use his marriage to advance his company. Michael had never said as much, but he'd hinted at it. When he had been looking into the airline industry last year, he had suggested that Mike date the daughter of a company he was trying to acquire. There'd been a similar discussion a few years before for a tech start-up that Michael had missed out on investing in. It felt like a Hail Mary, and Mike had ignored it. Addison had mentioned feeling the same way over the years. She was convinced that one day she'd come home to find a marriage had been arranged for her. Not that she would have gone along with it. Addison was not a people pleaser.

But Yvette, although perfect, brought no big-power connections to the table. Mike worried that his father would not accept her easily.

In the back of his mind, Mike worried this threat would hang over his head for every major decision for the rest of his life. If his father didn't like Yvette, would he threaten, once again, to cut him off? If he did, Mike knew what he would do. He'd choose her. A life with Yvette, even a poor life, was priceless to him. But maybe it wouldn't come to that.

BETSY

The judge had released Tori into Betsy's custody until she could be reunited with her family. Betsy returned her to the police station, the girl's eyes nervously darting toward the door every few seconds.

"Are you sure they're not coming back for me?" she asked.

"No, the court gave you to me. They won't mess with that. You are no good to them anymore. I called your parents. They got on the first flight. They should be here at seven."

Betsy slid a picture of Tori's parents across the table to her. She picked it up and began to cry. "It feels like a lifetime ago."

Henry arrived, carrying a brown paper bag with grease stains on the side.

"Conference room," he said.

Betsy led Tori to the large table in the middle of the room. Henry slid a cheeseburger, a chili dog, and a pile of fries in front of Tori. She grabbed the burger and bit off nearly a third of it, followed by a handful of fries. Henry put the drink in front of her.

"I got you a chocolate shake. I hope you like it," Henry said. "And one for you as well," he said, placing one in front of Betsy. "I know you'll like it."

After Tori finished eating, Betsy began asking questions.

"What else can you tell me about the traffickers?"

Tori looked around. "I just don't think I can say much. They could still get to me. They'll kill me if I say anything."

YVETTE

Yvette pulled on a lilac tulle maxi skirt with a metallic belted waistline, paired it with a white blouse, and examined herself in the mirror. She looked confident but felt anything but. She held her hands in front of her. They were visibly shaking. She looked at herself again. Although the white and the lilac looked good together, she felt the white was a bit too transparent, even with a camisole. She turned to her closet and found a black silk top.

"Perfect."

The black top slipped over her head. She glanced in the mirror. *Much better.* Her hair went through several styles before ending up clipped back loosely on the sides, out of her face, the rest down and curly. She took a deep breath, grabbed her bag, and glanced inside, doing a quick eyeball over the contents.

SLOAN

Sloan sat at the small desk in his high-rise downtown apartment with a view of the city. Storm clouds had been building all day. They were thick and heavy as the wind propelled them quickly across the sky. They were in for one heck of a storm. Hurricane Maude had hit the Gulf of Mexico as a category four and devastated the panhandle. It was now making its way toward them.

The laptop beeped as a new email came in. It was from Ted Mullaney, a private eye Sloan had hired to investigate Mike's new girlfriend, who'd been added last minute to the guest list for tonight.

He quickly read the email and slammed the computer shut. He grabbed his phone and dialed Nikki. No one picked up. He sent a quick text. Well, if nothing else, tonight would prove to be interesting.

CHAPTER 6

THE DINNER PARTY

CHEF JOE

Rain pounded on the roof and ran down the windows as Chef Joe looked over his timeline for the evening. He had written up exactly when to attend to each of the dishes. Working as a chef was a bit like conducting a symphony. There were many parts to integrate, and the timing of each was critical.

Kieran stood adjacent to him at the large marble island, cutting cucumbers. He always wanted to help. Joe felt that he was really just looking for the attention that he didn't get from his parents, neither of whom were around much. Joe liked the kid and always found a job for him. Although tonight he would not serve the chunky irregular cucumber pieces; he'd cut them properly once Kieran left. The clock read 6:20. The guests would be arriving soon. He pulled the lamb chops out of the fridge, allowing them to rest at room temp before it was time to cook them.

Nikki entered wearing a knee-length, tight, red dress.

"This rain is unbelievable. I hope it doesn't delay the arrivals. If so, be prepared to push dinner back," she said.

"Yes, ma'am," Joe replied. The chef was used to the daily opinions from Nikki and had begun to expect them. He could not cook a single dish without it being challenged by the woman. He went over the party menu and, as usual, she made a few changes. "There, isn't that better?" He never disagreed.

"You're not starting the lamb chops now?" Nikki asked.

"No, ma'am. Just allowing them to rest at room temperature. It allows for a more—"

"Is that sanitary?" Nikki interrupted.

"Yes. It—"

"Please put them back in the fridge. I won't have you poisoning the meal with bad meat."

Joe left the lamb chops on the counter. In his mind, food followed a strict set of rules that, if obeyed, led to perfection on a plate.

"Kieran, how many times have I told you that you do not need to help Joe? He is perfectly capable."

"I know, Mom. But I just thought I could give him a hand. I'm not doing anything else. Besides, I'm learning so much from him. Did you know he always removes the seeds from the cucumbers to keep the salad from getting soggy?"

"Fascinating. Now please go upstairs and change. The guests will be here soon."

"Nobody's here yet," Kieran said.

Nikki raised an eyebrow and stared at the boy.

"Yes, ma'am," he said, wiping his hands on a dishcloth.

"Thanks for the help," Joe said.

As soon as Kieran left, Joe swept the cucumbers he'd been cutting off the counter into the trash can.

"He is getting better, but not quite good enough to serve yet. Don't tell him."

Nikki looked into the trash can and saw the discarded package for the lamb chops. She pulled it out to examine the label.

"You bought this organic free-range crap again? How many times do I have to tell you not to waste my money on that? It's all the same thing."

"It wasn't much more expensive, and the way they slaughter is so much more humane."

"It is my money, and I won't have it wasted. Understood?"

"Yes, ma'am," Joe said as he began to chop the remaining cucumber in perfectly equivalent slices.

"Are we still on schedule for dinner at seven, starting with salad, then soup, and the entree promptly at seven-thirty?"

"Yes, ma'am," Chef Joe said.

Nikki heard the front door open.

"If you'll excuse me. Oh, and do make sure to feed Coco," Nikki said as she ducked out of the kitchen.

Joe wiped his hands on his apron and leaned down to rub the King Charles spaniel's head and ruffle her ears. Coco spent most of her time in the kitchen at his ankles. Maybe because he was the only one who gave her any attention. Or more likely because he cooked special food for her instead of the processed kibble that lived in the pantry. He tossed a couple of the frozen meatballs he'd made for her into a pan to warm them up. Coco sat patiently next to his feet, tail wagging as she awaited her dinner.

NIKKI

On her way to the front door, Nikki stopped to check her reflection in a large, framed wall mirror. The nearby grandfather clock showed 6:30. She smoothed out her dress and smooshed her hair before walking to the foyer.

Addison stood by the front door, shaking out her umbrella, creating a puddle on the floor. Michael's first batch of kids were not as refined as her Kieran. Standing there dripping water all over the floor, Addison wore a gray sleeveless shirt dress and black Hunter rain boots, which she removed. Her hair was, as always, pulled into a messy knot at the top of her head. She pushed her brown square glasses up her nose as she put her umbrella in the stand by the door.

She forced a smile. "Good evening, Addison. Nasty weather."

Addison looked at Nikki as if she were slow and replied, "Yes, it is." Nikki went to the front door to close it behind Addison as she disappeared into the house. A bright yellow Corvette pulled up the drive and backed between Addison's navy-blue Porsche Taycan and Chef Joe's white Prius. The driver door opened, followed by a metallic gold umbrella. Sloan Peterson stepped out under the umbrella wearing a custom tan suit and a red-and-white bowtie.

"Nikki!" he called as he approached. "Didn't you remember to order better weather for this party?"

"If only," Nikki said, offering him her cheek to kiss as he crossed the porch. He shook out his umbrella before stepping inside.

Sloan looked around the foyer for anyone. "I need to speak to you, alone," he said.

"Not now," Nikki said forcefully. She wasn't going to talk to him about business, not tonight.

"It's important. You are aware of the—" Sloan began just as Kieran came downstairs in a gray suit with a black skinny tie.

"Hello, Mr. Sloan," he said as he ran down the stairs to hug him. Sloan embraced the boy and then held him by the shoulders and looked into his eyes.

"You're getting taller! It won't be long before you pass your mother."

"Never!" Nikki said, smiling at him.

"Oh. I almost forgot. Sorry it's all wet." Sloan handed a bag to Nikki. "It's your favorite flavors, Scarlett's Red Raspberry and Washington Carver's Delight and a pint of Butler Pecan for Michael too."

"Awesome, thanks!" Kieran said.

"Go put these in the freezer, Kieran," Nikki said. Kieran took the bags and headed for the kitchen. "Would you like a drink?"

"Certainly," Sloan said.

Sloan followed Nikki from the foyer to the adjacent parlor. Sloan plopped himself down on one of two red couches.

"Listen, I've got to talk to you," Sloan whispered to Nikki.

"Not now . . . not here."

"But you need to know—" Sloan said in a gritted-teeth whisper.

DING DONG. The doorbell rang.

"I've got to get that. No more of this tonight," Nikki said. She walked to the foyer hoping that was the end of it.

Nikki pulled the door open to find Harris looking like a drowned rat on the other side.

"Good evening, Harris."

"I forgot my umbrella," Harris said. His brown hair hung over a puma sweatband on his forehead. He wore athletic shorts and a sports league shirt, typical. "I just came from my Spikeball league. We made it to the playoffs."

"You played in this weather?"

"Yeah, why not?"

"It's pouring rain!"

"Eh, we're not scared of a little rain. There wasn't any lightning." A significant puddle formed under Harris.

"Close the door behind you for once while I get some towels," Nikki said.

Harris looked behind him at the open door and pushed it closed. "Oh, so that's how it closes."

"Ha ha," Nikki mocked.

Kieran returned from the kitchen.

"Hey, bud!" Harris said.

"Kieran, go grab some towels for Harris."

"Hi! Sure, Mom. Be right back." Kieran bounded up the stairs and returned with a pile of towels and handed one to Harris, who dried his hair and tried to dry out his clothes a bit. Kieran kneeled on the floor with a towel to clean up the pooling water.

"Be careful not to get your suit wet," Nikki said.

"How ya doing, step monster?" Harris asked.

"I told you not to call me that," Nikki said, shaking her head and smiling very slightly. Harris always knew how to push her buttons.

"Kidding," he said, backing away, hands upturned in a gesture of innocence.

Harris threw the wet towel into the corner and wrapped one arm around Nikki's shoulders, pulling her into a side hug. She pulled away.

"You'll get me wet."

"Ah, you'll dry."

Kieran, finished with the cleanup, stood and threw his arms around Harris.

"Kieran, your suit! Go stand by the fire, the both of you, and dry yourselves out," Nikki said. "Harris, can I get you a drink?"

"Nah, I just chugged a Red Bull."

"Can I get a Coke, Mom?" Kieran asked.

"Yes, but only one."

"Yes, ma'am," Kieran said, darting in the direction of the kitchen.

"Do you have some clothes to change into?" Nikki asked Harris.

"No, I forgot them. Looks like I'm stuck with this." *Not on my watch,* Nikki thought as she led him into the parlor.

"Good evening, Harris," Sloan said.

"Hey, Sloan. How's it going?"

Lightning flashed brightly outside, lighting up the world like daylight briefly. Thunder sounded low a few seconds later.

"Some storm out there," Harris said.

"It's only going to get worse overnight," Sloan said. "Did you see any pictures from the Gulf where it hit?" Harris and Sloan talked weather while Nikki watched the rain out the window.

"Nikki, pour me a drink." Michael's voice boomed down the stairs as he made his way to the parlor.

Annoyance flashed on Nikki's face. She quickly recovered and plastered on the smile of a hostess as she made her husband a drink.

"Harris, I see you've changed out of your business attire. Did you get the impression that this was an informal affair?" Michael asked.

"Spikeball tournament."

"I hope you brought a change of clothes."

"Sorry, sir. My sincerest apologies. I will remember to dress to impress next time." Harris flashed a bright, winning smile. Michael didn't return the gesture but walked past him to Sloan.

"Go upstairs and find something. Surely you have something in your old room. If not, you can find something in my closet."

Nikki smiled to herself. Michael never let his kids walk all over him, and she respected that. Even if there wasn't love between them, she loved seeing him take control. If nothing else, Michael was no-nonsense. She had worked hard to make sure everything was perfect; the least Harris could do was wear something respectable.

"Yes, sir. I'll head up in a minute," Harris said.

ADDISON

Addison never much liked her father's new house, the one he'd had built with Nikki. It was too big. How does one feel at home in such a huge space? He'd even put secret passageways inside, which she found ridiculous.

Addison pulled the candlestick forward to reveal the secret passage from the upstairs hallway bedroom down to the kitchen. If she had overseen building the house, she would have put a second staircase at the back of each hallway instead of these secret chambers. It was juvenile, and she hated using them, as they were a bit spooky. But she needed to talk to Chef Joe about Daddy's meal, and this was the most direct route.

She followed the spiral staircase down to the kitchen and exited through the pantry. Chef Joe was alone in the kitchen prepping the meals.

"Joe. Daddy is going to need the low-sodium dinner option we discussed. His blood pressure is too high. If we can, let's get him to avoid the chocolate cake as well. His diabetes numbers are up again. It's like he isn't even trying."

"Yes, ma'am."

She exited the kitchen, walked through the dining room, into the parlor and past everyone, and poured herself a glass of wine.

"Hey, Addi," Harris said, walking up behind her and picking her up.

"Hello, Harris." He put her down, and she turned to face him. "Did you get the article I sent you about energy drinks and the effects they have on your heart? They gave rats energy drinks and found an increase in—"

"Yeah, yeah, I got it." He wasn't taking her seriously. She knew he wouldn't, but the information was so powerful, she wanted him to know the facts.

Kieran entered from the kitchen holding a glass of Coke. "I'm sure it's not any worse than this stuff," Kieran said, hugging Addison.

"Yeah, he's got a point," Harris said.

He clearly hadn't read the article. "Actually, according to the research, the incidence of heart attack—"

"Okay, I'll read it," Harris relented.

Addison sighed; she doubted it.

"Kieran, have you thought more about where you want to go to college?" Addison asked.

"Yeah, some. I mean, I'm only in seventh grade, so there's still time."

"What do you think you'll want to study?" Addison asked.

"I don't know. Maybe medicine, like you. I think I'd enjoy being a doctor."

"Don't you have to go to business school at Emory like Mike and I had to?" Harris asked.

"No. Dad thinks the company is fine with Mike and you. I'm free to do what I want."

"No fair," Harris said.

"Yeah, I guess. I mean, it would be nice to be needed, too, but maybe freedom is better."

"Trust me, it's way better. The company is snoresville. I take a nap under my desk every day. Don't tell anyone," Harris said.

"Everyone knows," Sloan interjected from across the room.

LIZA

Liza stood on the porch of her ex-husband's new home. He'd been rich when they were married, but they had kept a modest house of 4,500 square feet. This monstrosity must have been four or five times that size. But humility was never Michael's strong suit, and it clearly wasn't part of Nikki's vocabulary. It was a regal Southern-style brick home with a wide front porch, potted ferns, and a large double door.

Liza knew it annoyed Nikki that she had accepted the invitation to her son's birthday party. Liza found Nikki to be high-strung and disagreeable, so she planned to stay out of her way.

She shook out her umbrella and rang the doorbell. One of the two ornate beveled doors opened. Kieran stood on the other side. She was surprised by the change in him.

"Good evening, Kieran," she said. "Look at you. You're so tall. You must have grown a foot since I saw you last," Liza said.

"Yeah," Kieran said, smiling. Liza gave the boy a big hug and ruffled his hair. Despite her strong dislike of the boy's parents, she found love in her heart for him. He was a good kid and easy to be around.

Liza found herself in a two-story foyer with double oak staircases with wrought iron railings that switched back on themselves and rose to a balcony that looked down from above. Beyond the staircase and opposite the front door, there was a wall of windows, beveled with black lead that looked out onto a pool area. She followed Kieran to the left into the parlor where she found her two youngest kids already engaged in a conversation.

"Hey, Mom," Harris said.

"You should've seen this guy in his Spikeball tournament today," Liza said. "You've always been gifted athletically. Hey, honey," she said, giving Addison a hug that her daughter leaned into.

"Next time, I'll come watch, too," Addison said, "if it's not raining."

"Good evening, Liza," Michael said, coming over to his ex-wife. Liza's hand reflexively went to her pocket, where she ran her thumb over a small pill bottle.

"Hello, Michael. Our kids are turning into wonderful people, aren't they?"

"You always did have low standards," Michael said, walking away.

"Yeah, I guess that's why I married you," she whispered. Harris and Addison giggled quietly.

Liza walked over to the bar. "Anyone need a drink? Michael?"

"No, I got one."

"Okay, maybe later then," Liza said.

"I've got to go change," Harris said. "Hey, Kieran, want to help me find something? We may be getting close to the same size." He wasn't wrong. Kieran was only a few inches shy of Harris, but he still had the slim body of a boy.

"Sure," Kieran said. The two headed up the stairs.

KIERAN

Kieran didn't want to be alone with Harris. He told himself that Harris had been kidding the other day and just venting, surely, about killing their father.

At the top of the stairs, Harris grabbed Kieran's shoulder and steered him into the playroom to the left of the stairs.

"What'll it be? Air hockey? FIFA?" Kieran said.

"Legos," Harris replied.

"Legos? Sure! I made a bot last week, but I couldn't get it to move like I'd hoped."

"Wow. That's cool, bud. But first, I want to show you my plan."

Kieran didn't like the sound of that. Harris walked to the corner of the room where a large low table held several Lego projects. Mostly they were from kits, the Hogwarts Castle, the Death Star. But Kieran had also made a few of his own creations. Harris knelt next to the nearly exact replica of the Higgins Estate that Kieran had made. It had taken him months of work and a fortune in Lego pieces.

"Okay, so here's the plan I've been working on," Harris said as he gathered a couple of miniature figures.

So, he's serious. He actually wants to go through with it. Kieran's heart sunk into his toes.

"This will be Dad," Harris said, picking up a minifigure. He adjusted the piece to add a scowling face and a bowler hat. "Dad will go for his nightly after-dinner cigar, like always. Luckily for us, he goes rain or shine." He moved the minifigure to the back exit of his father's office. "He leaves from the back door to his study. Then you," he said, picking up a minifigure with brown wavy hair and a Jurassic Park T-shirt. He pulled open a drawer and added a bow and arrow to the minifig. "You'll wait here, along the trees lining the driveway, where you'll have a good view of the covered patio. One good shot should do it. He'll be dead before he feels anything, as long as you shoot your best."

"Harris, is it really necessary? I mean, isn't there another way?"

"I wish there was, buddy. You're the only one who can do this and not spend your whole life in jail."

"Yeah, but he probably isn't leaving me any money anyway."

"All the better! You'd have no motive. So, the police would have no reason to suspect you."

"Except the fact that I'm the only one with awards in archery."

"Like it's that hard. Any of us could have taken your weapon. Don't worry, it's a good plan," Harris said as he stood. "I've got to go find something to wear." Harris left the room.

Kieran looked at the Legos mapping out the murder scene of his father. It was the first time in his life that Legos brought him any feeling other than joy. He picked up a nearby Lego rocket ship and threw it across the room, smashing it into a thousand pieces.

HARRIS

In his old dresser, Harris found a short sleeve black polo shirt and a pair of dark jeans. It was still more causal than his father would want, but it was dry and it fit. He kept the black Puma sweatband on his head as a rebellious statement. Harris bounded down the stairs and found everyone in the parlor. Kieran had returned as well and was sitting alone looking out the window at the rain. *Maybe I'm asking too much of my brother.* He shook his head to clear the thought and then made his way over to the bar to fix himself a drink.

YVETTE

An inch of running water covered Riverside Drive as the rain continued to pour. Water splashed onto the windshield of Mike's blue sports car as they drove through a deepening puddle.

"What kind of car is this? I like it," Yvette said.

"A Shelby Mustang GT500, 1967. Why? Are you into cars?"

"No. But I like this one. It's cool."

"Thanks."

Mike turned off the road onto a drive flanked by high ivy-covered walls. She looked at the brick building and got a vague idea of the size of the home.

Mike pulled into a cobblestone parking area. It looked like a luxury used car lot. Lined up neatly were a blue Porsche Taycan, a yellow Corvette, an orange Mercedes G-class, a gray BMW Sedan, and a white Prius. They parked next to the BMW.

Yvette looked out the rain covered window at the grand Southern home. The butterflies seemed to turn on each other, warring in her stomach.

"Don't be nervous. They're just people," Mike said.

Yvette fussed with her skirt. "Do I look like a hussy?" She blurted out, rethinking her outfit.

Mike smiled at the question. "Do you look like a what?"

"A hussy? Come on, I'm serious. I'm nervous."

"No, you look beautiful and most un-hussy like."

Mike exited the car with a large golf umbrella and ran over to Yvette's side. He opened the door for her and held the umbrella over both of them. She put her feet down into standing water.

"Oh no, your shoes. Want me to carry you?" Mike said.

"It's just water. It's fine," she said. Mike smiled at her. "What?"

"I like you," he said.

"I like you, too," she replied, faking an approving smile. Too bad she'd have to betray him.

He grabbed her hips and pulled her close with his free hand as they walked toward the house.

Water gushed out of the gutters, creating a stream across the driveway that they walked through on the way to the front door. They reached the safety of the wide front porch and shook the water off their shoes and umbrella.

"Ready?" Mike said, taking Yvette's hand.

She nodded at him and gulped.

Mike reached up and rang the bell. The door opened a moment later. The woman who opened the door wore a tight red dress and had the body for it. She was slender and beautiful. She had thick, long, shiny black hair that went well past her shoulders.

"Good evening, Mike. This must be the mystery woman you added at the last minute. I'm Nikki. Please come in."

"Hi, Nikki, this is Yvette," Mike said. "Yvette, this is my dad's wife, Nikki."

"Thank you for inviting me. I hope it wasn't too much trouble. Your home is lovely," Yvette said.

"Oh, anything for Mike. Please come in," Nikki said. "What terrible weather." She led them through a wide archway into the parlor. Yvette's apartment would easily fit into the long room. There were two sitting areas, one around a large fireplace and the other near a bar. Each side had its own grand chandelier.

Mike introduced Yvette to everyone, and she tried to tie faces to the names.

"The man of the hour!" said Sloan, who was just pouring himself a drink at a bar in the back of the room. "Happy birthday!" There was something familiar about Sloan. She felt she had seen him before but couldn't place where.

The chef entered with a tray of tall champagne glasses. He served Michael first and then the rest of the group, starting with the ladies.

"Now that everyone is here, I'd like to make a toast," Michael said. "To my son on his twenty-fifth birthday. May all your endeavors in business and in life be successful. To many more."

"To many more," the group repeated.

All the glasses toasted to Mike.

"I just want to say how moved I am that you would each come here tonight to celebrate me," Mike said. "Each of you has touched my life in a profound way."

"Here, here," said Harris, and all drank again.

"Now, before we sit down to dinner," Michael began, "you know how I feel about phones at the table. So, if you wouldn't mind, please give them to me, and I'll put them in the safe until after dinner."

Chef Joe carried around the now empty tray on which he'd brought out the champagne and collected the phones.

Yvette looked at Mike a bit wary. "Do I have to?"

"It's silly. We're being punished for using our cell phones at the table as teenagers. He enacted this law and seems to plan on continuing it in perpetuity." He smiled at her. "Nothing to worry about. We can always get them back if we need them."

Yvette reluctantly placed her phone on the tray.

Michael walked over to meet his eldest son's new love interest.

"This is my father, Michael Higgins. Dad, this is Yvette."

She reached her hand out to his and hoped he didn't notice it shaking. She looked him in the eye for a split second before tearing her eyes away.

"Your home is lovely," she said, dropping his hand as quickly as possible without being rude and turning to look around the house instead of at his face. "It's so big. I almost feel like I need a map of the fire exits."

"Yes, well it's twenty-two-thousand square feet, so one can certainly get lost in it. Now if you'll excuse me," Michael said, taking the tray of phones from Chef Joe and carrying them upstairs.

A shiver ran through Yvette.

"Are you cold?" Mike said. He led her to the grand stone fireplace, where a fire crackled. It was too warm a night for a fire, but Yvette was grateful for it because she was wet from the rain, which had given her a chill. She walked over to dry her skirt out. Harris and Sloan were sitting on a red couch near the fire.

"So let me see if I remember," she said. "You're Harris, Mike's brother."

"That's right," Harris said. "It's nice to meet you."

"Likewise. Mike mentioned that you are into a few extreme hobbies."

"Yeah, I'm always trying to talk him into joining me."

"I know he mentioned mountain climbing, scuba diving, heli-skiing."

"Guilty as charged. Don't forget, skydiving and flying airplanes. I'm thinking of learning to fly a helicopter next."

"You fly? Do you have your pilot's license?"

"Yeah. I recently got a small plane to zip around in."

"If you can call it that," Sloan said.

"It's a small, little one-seater job," Harris said. "I don't even have to store it. I can keep it here in the garage. It doesn't need a runway, just a large lawn to take off."

"That doesn't sound safe," Yvette said.

"Safety isn't really Harris's strong suit," Sloan said. "How many broken bones have you had?"

"Twenty-one," Harris said, smiling. "If you'll excuse me." Harris walked toward the bar.

"And you're Sloan. You work with Michael?" Yvette asked.

"Well, I work with Mike and Harris, too, but mostly I deal with Michael. He's a partner in my little ice-cream shop, Butler's," Sloan said.

"Oh, I love Butler's," Yvette said. "Georgia Peachy Keen is my absolute favorite."

"Oh, that's a popular one," Sloan said. "You want to know the secret? Fresh peaches. We make the ice cream in peach season with fresh peaches. We capture all the juicy goodness of the fresh Georgia peaches as they mix in with the cream. Most commercial ice creameries use frozen peaches that were probably as hard as rocks when they were picked and have no real flavor. With fresh peaches, the juice is infused into the cream itself."

"Stop, you're making me hungry," Yvette said, smiling.

"I'm passionate about ice cream. Sometimes I get carried away."

Nikki approached. "Can I get you a drink? A whiskey? Wine?"

"Yes, wine would be lovely," Yvette said.

Mike looked a little surprised. "I thought you didn't drink."

"Well, it is a special occasion," Yvette said. In reality, she needed it to calm her nerves.

"In that case, I'll take one as well, Nikki," Mike said.

"Sloan, I don't know what I'm going to do with that chef you recommended to us," Nikki said as she poured the drinks.

"Why? I thought his food was divine," Sloan said.

"Yes, it is. But he insists on buying that hippie-dippie organic free-range meat. I told him that it's all the same thing, but he seems hell-bent on wasting my money on it. If his food wasn't so good, I would've already fired him."

"Actually, Nikki," Addison began from where she sat nearby on the couch, "while there is some debate about the legitimacy of the organic label, free-range is widely accepted as a more humane way to raise and process animals for human consumption. Further studies—"

"But if it's my money and I don't care, then shouldn't it be spent the way I want, regardless of his opinions?" Nikki said, cutting Addison off.

"Anybody want a tour of the house?" Harris intervened.

"Ooooh me, please. I've always wanted to see the other rooms," Liza said.

"I'm not sure that's entirely appropriate, Harris," Nikki said.

"Oh, come on. I'm sure the staff cleaned every inch of this place. All that hard work should be appreciated."

"Very well," Nikki said.

"We're in," Mike said, taking Yvette's hand. Her heart raced. She wanted to get a look around this place. This was perfect.

• • •

Harris led them from the parlor to the dining room. The stone fireplace that divided the rooms was two-sided and opened onto the dining room as well. Yvette turned to see the fire crackling and gasped when she saw what hung above the roaring fire. She looked at Mike, who just looked down and shook his head.

"Should we talk about the elephant in the room?" Harris said.

"Isn't it illegal? To own—" Yvette asked.

"Not sure about the legality," Harris said. "Most would agree it's morally reprehensible. But not good old Dad. Dad likes hunting and has branched out from duck and deer to African animals. This is Ellie, although the tusks point to it being a he. Somehow the name Ellie just stuck."

"Actually, in African elephants, both females and males can have tusks," Addison said.

"Really? Huh," Harris said.

"We all hate it," Mike said. "We've begged him to get rid of it. He says he's honoring the animal by displaying it."

"It would have honored the animal more not to shoot it in the first place," Liza said.

Yvette found herself staring into the dark dead eyes of a large, mounted elephant head complete with trunk and tusks. A shiver ran down her spine.

"He loves to hunt. He's supposed to go again next week. I just hope he doesn't come back with anything else to display," Harris said. "On to the next room."

They walked past a large wooden dining table with an ornately carved edge where nine places were set. Two hurricane lamps decorated either end, and a floral arrangement in a long, low wooden oval bowl stretched across the center. They walked along a hallway lined with dome-shaped leaded glass windows. Outside the windows and through the driving rain, she could see a pool and across to an identical wall of windows on the opposite wing. She could now see that the house was U-shaped with two long wings, the entrance being the connecting piece. At the end of the wide hallway, the chef was working in the kitchen.

"Excuse us, Joe. We're just taking a tour," Harris said. "Let's just look in from the hallway and not interrupt the master at work."

"Of course. Good evening," Joe said.

Even though quite large, the kitchen was still homey with off-white cabinets and barstools. The chef moved about the space prepping plates and stirring sauces.

"It smells wonderful in here," said Liza.

"Joe has turned out to be a better chef than I expected," Nikki said. "Even if he does buy free-range meat." Nikki looked at him meaningfully. "He came with very few references, as he hasn't been a chef that long. In fact, it was Sloan who referred him. But Michael let the food speak for itself and hired him over a cheeseburger. I thought he'd last a week, but he has proven himself more than acceptable. Except for the night of the corn chowder, but we won't speak of it."

"Thank you, Miss Nikki," Chef Joe said.

"Wow, the rain is really coming down out there," Liza said, ending the awkward silence.

"If you'll step outside into the covered eating area, I'll show you—"

"No," Nikki said, grabbing Harris's arm on the doorknob. "There's no need to go out there tonight."

"But I was going to show them the—"

"I know. It's not a good idea in this weather," Nikki insisted. "You don't need to bother with the other wing; you can see from here," Nikki said, pointing out the window at the opposite wing. "There's Michael's office at the end, next to that is a billiard room, and at the front of the house is a large library."

"Come on, I'll show you the upstairs too," Harris said.

"Harris, I hardly think it's appropriate to continue the tour upstairs," Nikki said. "Besides, it's almost time for dinner, right, Chef?"

"Yes, ma'am."

"Let's all take our seats in the dining room," Nikki said. The group wandered back to the dining room.

"If you'll excuse me, I just need to use the powder room," Yvette said, walking away from the group in the direction of Michael's office.

JOE

Chef Joe knew not to serve the salad course until everyone was seated. Mike's girlfriend was not back at the table. He checked his watch, 7:04—already four minutes behind schedule. The salad course could be rushed a bit, but the lamb chops were time sensitive.

He peeked into the dining room. Nikki was getting antsy. Her jaw was set, a fake smile pasted on. Movement caught his eye from the other wing of the house. *Thank God, maybe she was on her way back.* But no, Yvette was in Michael's office. She was rifling through the papers on his desk.

What was she doing snooping in Michael's office? He stared at her through the rain. Should he go and fetch her before dinner was ruined?

YVETTE

Nikki had said Michael's office was at the end of the hallway on the opposite wing. Yvette didn't have much time. Dinner was about to be served. She wasn't sure but thought this was the kind of family that would sit staring at their plates, not eating until she returned.

She reached the end of the hallway where Nikki had pointed out Michael's office. She looked behind her to make sure no one was coming before turning the doorknob and slipping inside. She closed the door most of the way in case anyone came looking for her.

A solid wooden desk in the middle of the room dominated the space. The wall behind the desk was lined with built-in bookcases. She heard a strange rattling sound and saw to her left a medium-sized terrarium sitting on a long table. Inside, a brown patterned rattlesnake shook his tail and waved his tongue in the air. She shrunk away from the tank, walked to the desk, and began to thumb through the papers on top, not seeing anything particularly meaningful.

She felt eyes on her and looked up. Out the window and through the rain, she saw Chef Joe watching her from across the courtyard in the kitchen. She dropped the papers and pretended to be lost, confused, and generally blond before exiting the office and returning to the parlor. She'd have to come back. She just hoped she could sneak away again.

NIKKI

The salad was nearly ten minutes late. Where was Yvette? The salad and soup courses would be rushed. *What's taking her so long?* Maybe she should send Mike to find her. Maybe she got lost.

Chef Joe peeked into the dining room and looked at Nikki, who stood to excuse herself and find that damned girl. As she did so, Yvette returned. Nikki gave Chef Joe a slight nod as Yvette slid into her seat next to Mike.

"I'm so sorry to have kept you waiting," Yvette said. "I got a bit turned around."

The table was now in order as it should be. Nikki had created the seating chart. She looked around approving her choices. Michael Sr.

was seated at the head of the table. No one sat at the other end. To his right were, in order—Mike, Yvette, Addison, and Liza. On the left side of the table sat Nikki, Sloan, Harris, and finally Kieran. The flames in the hurricane lamps danced and flickered, casting a warm light over the table. Rain pounded on the windows outside.

"Nikki, are you still volunteering with that camp for young girls?" Liza asked.

"Yes, in a behind-the-scenes way. I helped to throw a fundraiser for the camp, it's called Pleasure Island, in the spring. It was a big success."

"What does the camp do again?"

"It's just a camp for troubled girls to build their confidence. I wish I had more time to volunteer with the kids. But it's hard to get away."

"It's near the lake house, right?" Harris asked. "Speaking of the lake house, I want to go up there next weekend with some friends. Would that be alright?"

"I'm sure it can be arranged."

"Can I come with you?" Kieran asked.

"If it's okay with your mom," Harris said, shrugging.

"And that's on Lake Rabun?" Liza asked.

"Yes," Nikki replied.

"I've always loved that area," Liza said.

"We don't seem to get up there much anymore," Michael said.

"It's hard to get away with Kieran's activities," Nikki said.

Chef Joe emerged from the kitchen with the soup course. Nikki checked her watch, 7:20. Dinner would still be served on time, a relief.

"Maybe you should get a place up there, Sloan. After we sell Butler's, you can leave that high-rise apartment and live at the lake."

"Your selling Butler's?" Mike asked, shocked.

"Yeah, Nestle wants it. They're giving us more than I think it's worth," Michael said.

"Sloan, you're okay with that?" Mike asked.

Sloan faked a smile. "I'd rather keep it, but it's ultimately Michael's decision."

"Dad. You can't sell Butler's," Mike said. "Sloan loves that place."

"Well, I own the controlling share, so I guess I can do whatever I want."

Nikki cut her eyes to Sloan. *This isn't going to work. This isn't going to work at all.*

SLOAN

Sloan dug into his soup and looked around the room. He had a feeling tonight was going to be interesting, but it was starting out slow. He had tried to tell Nikki about Michael agreeing to sell Butler's and what he had learned about Mike's new friend, Yvette, but Nikki hadn't answered his calls.

Sloan would just sit back and watch the drama unfold as it surely would sooner or later.

"I'm looking forward to my hunting trip next week," Michael said. "I'm heading to Tanzania. We're going after rhino."

Michael was so obtuse. He'd never been good at reading a room. This group did not want to talk about exotic animal hunting. Not that many groups did. Most people were horrified by the idea of it. It was morally questionable, but he had no room to judge. Morality was not his strength.

"Oh, I know you don't approve," Michael said. "But I don't care. See that beauty I got three years ago?" Michael gestured to the elephant on the wall.

"Isn't it illegal to own ivory?"

"Yes, Yvette, it is. It's also illegal to speed, and everyone here is guilty of that. So, get off your high horses."

The room became bright as daylight as lightning flashed outside. Thunder boomed almost instantaneously, shaking the house. The lights in the house flickered and went black. Sloan's eyes flashed to the other faces at the table in rapid succession. There was enough light from the fire and the hurricane lamps to see. Within seconds, they heard tree limbs snapping and popping, followed by a loud whoosh and thump. Yvette grabbed Mike's hand under the table.

"That sounded like a tree going down," Addison said.

Clever girl. Nothing gets past her, Sloan thought.

"Maybe now would be a good time to get our phones back," Harris suggested.

"After dinner," Michael said, controlling everyone for no reason. It was appalling that his family put up with all his nonsense.

Joe returned and gathered the soup plates. "Dinner will not be affected. I'll have it out momentarily."

"Thank you, Joe," Nikki said.

JOE

Joe returned to the kitchen, which had very little light. The gas-powered oven was still cooking the pork chops. He felt his way to the drawer where long lighters were kept for the outdoor grill. He flicked one on and looked around. There were two decorative candles on the kitchen table. He lit them both and carried one over to the marble island so he could continue working.

He tossed the dirty dishes into a sink full of hot soapy water and washed his hands.

He pulled eight lamb chops and one chicken breast out of the gas oven and began to plate them. He piped mashed potatoes into neat piles and garnished them with parsley. He scooped exactly five Brussel sprouts garnished with bacon next to the potatoes. He turned to the nine plated dinners, eight lamb chops and one of chicken with a mushroom sauce for Michael. His hands shook as he picked up the first two plates. He put them down, took a steadying breath, and picked them up again. He slid the chicken plate into his hand, careful not to touch the surface, and grabbed another. He carried the plates in two at a time to serve the guests.

Michael picked up his fork to eat when he looked down and realized his plate contained a chicken breast while everyone else had a lamb chop.

"Addison, what is the meaning of this?" Michael bellowed.

"Daddy, your numbers are too high," Addison said.

"You disappoint me. Tonight is a night of celebration. I will celebrate, but not with this garbage. Coco . . . come here, girl." The dog trotted over, tail wagging.

Joe stepped forward and gasped. "Don't!"

Michael put the plate on the floor for the dog, who sniffed it and walked away. Joe leaned over and picked up the dog.

"Ha, you see, even the dog won't eat it, Chef Joe!"

"Yes," Joe said, sweat dripping down his spine.

"Don't listen to my daughter anymore. Bring me a lamb chop."

"But sir . . . I didn't prepare another."

Michael stared silently at the chef, his disgust apparent.

"I'll have a lamb chop out in just a moment. Please excuse me," Joe said, taking the dog with him to the kitchen.

"Make sure you wash your hands after touching that animal," Michael called after him.

In the kitchen, Joe set the dog on the floor before opening the door to the outside covered patio. He stepped out into the rain, closed the door behind him, and screamed. The sound was lost completely in the rain and wind.

COCO

The dog had second thoughts about eating the food left on the floor. Luckily, the door was left just ajar enough for her slim body to slip through. She followed the scent back to the plate and began to gobble up the contents.

SLOAN

Addison really should have known better than to try to give her father something other than what he expected. Not that she was put in an easy position. Health was low on his list of priorities.

"Addison, I'll take yours, and you can wait on the new one since it was your idea to trick me with that garbage."

"Sorry, Daddy, just trying to save your life," Addison said as she stood up and served him her plate.

Now that Michael had his own lamb chop, Sloan figured he could start eating. He waited to see Michael take a bite and then dug in.

Joe entered the dining room a few moments later to collect the chicken plate from the floor. "I'll be right out with another lamb chop," he said.

"Thank you, Joe. Sorry for the confusion," Addison said.

"Certainly," Joe said. He leaned down to pick up the plate of chicken off the floor.

"Why is some of it gone? Did . . . did . . . Coco eat it?" Joe said a bit panicky.

The dog sat a few feet away licking her lips. A look of horror flashed over Joe's face briefly. He looked quite ill, turning a bit greenish. Suddenly, the contents of Joe's stomach, accompanied by a loud throaty kind of cawing sound, erupted, wet and chunky from his throat. It splattered and ricocheted on the wooden floor. Sloan slid away from the table, his hunger forgotten. In this exact moment, Coco, the beloved family dog, keeled over, dead.

Silence hung in the air before Nikki let out a scream.

"I do believe this man has tried to poison me," Michael said, pointing at the chef.

"I doubt it, Daddy," Addison said.

"Coco?" Nikki said. "Coco!" She kneeled next to the limp dead dog. "Call an ambulance!" She scooped Coco's lifeless body up into her arms.

"For the dog? Or for Dad?" Harris asked.

"The dog, you fool!" Nikki said.

Michael cut a look at her.

"What? You're fine," Nikki said.

"An attempt has been made on my life and all you seem to care about is that dog."

"Daddy, I'm sure Joe didn't try to poison you. There must have been something in the food that dogs can't eat."

Joe nodded. "Yes. It was the mushrooms. They can be toxic to dogs. I didn't think . . . I didn't plan for her to have them."

"Coco is dead. And he poisoned her," Nikki said, standing and pointing at Joe. "We trusted you! Forget the ambulance. Call the police."

Chef Joe fell to his knees, landing right in the foul congealing puddle of vomit, and began to sob.

"How could you?" Nikki said. "You . . . you . . . you, monster! You killed Coco! Get out! Get out of my house!"

"It was an accident. . . . I never would have hurt her on purpose. It was the mushrooms. Oh, Coco," Joe said as tears poured down his face.

"Shall we retire to the parlor?" Liza suggested. She never had the stomach for difficulties.

BETSY

Betsy sipped coffee at her desk. Tori, who hadn't been more than a few feet from her since this morning, sat in a desk chair, sleeping next to an empty pizza box on Betsy's desk. Tori had probably had more to eat today than she had all week. Henry worked across from them at his desk.

The week had been long, and answers had been slow in coming. Rain pounded on the windows and the roof of the old factory that was now the police precinct as the storm pummeled the city. Thunder boomed, the old windows rattled, and the power flickered before the backup generator kicked on. Tori looked up in alarm.

"Are they here for me?" she asked.

"No. It was just the storm," Betsy said, putting a hand on her arm. Betsy's desk phone rang.

"Hello. Oh, no. Okay. Yes. I understand. She's right here. Let me put her on." Betsy held the phone out to Tori. "It's your parents."

"Hello," Tori said warily into the phone. "Mom?" Tears streaming, she nodded but formed no more words before handing the phone back to Betsy.

"We'll see you soon," Betsy said and hung up. "Their flight was rerouted due to the storm. They were forced to land in Nashville. They've rented a car and will be here soon."

"How long will that take?"

"It's about a three-hour drive, but the weather may slow them down."

"It feels more real now," Tori said. "That it really is over and I'm going home."

"You are going home. You've been so brave, but it's over now."

"Thank God. I was supposed to be sold tonight as a substitute for the one who died. Along with another girl."

Betsy looked at Henry, who whipped out his iPad and stylus and began to write.

"Sold to who?"

"They just call him Mr. Green. I don't think that's his real name. They say he gets new girls every few months and they never come back. They just disappear."

"Before Jane Doe died, she said the name O'Hara. Was that her name?"

"No," Tori said, looking around. "It's someone else. Someone bad. But I don't want to talk about it."

"Okay, well let's start with something easier then. Where did they keep you?"

LIZA

In the parlor, a somber mood hung over the party guests.

"Shall I go serve the cake?" Liza offered. No one responded. Liza walked to the kitchen. She passed Joe cleaning up his mess and sobbing in the dining room. She pretended not to notice, unsure of the right thing to say.

In the kitchen, Liza found the cake, a large chocolate affair sitting on an elevated cake stand. It was almost too pretty to cut. Nine plates sat stacked next to the cake. Liza grabbed the knife and stabbed the perfect cake, scarring its beauty and revealing the delicate soft center. She cut one tall thin piece and placed it on the top plate. A small silver cylinder of toothpicks stood on the counter. She took one and stuck it into this piece of cake. She looked over her shoulder; no one was around. With a shaky hand, Liza reached into her pocket and took out a small pill bottle. She struggled, briefly cursing the inventor of child lock bottles under her breath. She had just enough time to conduct her business before young Kieran entered the kitchen.

She didn't think he noticed as she slipped the pill bottle back into her pocket.

"I can help," the boy offered.

"Wonderful, will you go ask who wants a piece of cake?"

"I'm sure everyone does."

"You're probably right, dear, but go ask, to be sure."

"Okay."

Liza put the piece with the toothpick on the far side of the cake and cut eight more slices.

Nine plates of chocolate cake sat waiting to be served, one with a toothpick, when Chef Joe entered, crying.

"That poor creature, and it's all my fault. You know I've always been an advocate for animal rights. Now I'm just a hypocrite," Joe said.

"Oh, Joe, it was an accident," Liza said. "You can't blame yourself. How were you to know that Michael would feed it to the dog?"

"I should've been more careful. What was I thinking? There are always unforeseen consequences."

"You get on home. Try not to blame yourself."

Glassy-eyed, Joe looked at her and nodded. Grabbing his personal effects, he glanced once more around the kitchen before slipping out the back door.

Kieran returned announcing, "Everyone wants cake."

Liza and Kieran entered the parlor. Kieran carried three pieces of cake and Liza just the one with the toothpick. She placed hers in front of Michael and returned to the kitchen, a drop of sweat appearing on her brow. She leaned both hands against the cool counter and took a few deep breaths.

ADDISON

Addison studied the room. Her father was in a leather chair by the fire, alone. Everyone else was gathered around the bar talking. This was her moment. She approached her father carrying the piece of cake that Kieran had given her.

"Hey, Daddy, can I check your blood sugar before you consume this massive amount of sugar?"

"Fine, honey, but make it quick. That looks delicious."

She kneeled in front of him, placing her cake right next to his on the side table. She checked his pulse, and his sugar numbers, which were slightly high but not alarming. She touched her pocket and pulled out a syringe.

"Daddy, you need a bit of insulin."

"Not here," Michael said, looking around.

"I'll be discreet. No one's looking." Which of course was part of the reason she wanted to do it now, because no one would see her. She uncapped the needle while the other guests talked and paid them no attention.

The sound of brakes screeching against wet tires, exploding glass, and crunching metal followed by an unrelating car horn filled the house. Addison looked up, startled. Her father was out of his chair, at the window, as were the others, looking into the rainy night for the cause of the sound.

Addison took a deep breath, recapped the syringe, and placed it back inside her pocket. She picked up the piece of cake, not noticing the toothpick in it. Absentmindedly, she ate a few bites of cake as the others looked out into the dark night. She knew there wasn't anything to see and didn't waste time walking over to look. Instead, she stood here thinking that a car must have crashed outside. If she had her phone, she would call 911, but her father had taken her phone. She sighed and took another bite of cake.

A wave of sleepiness washed over her that was quite unexpected. She sat on the closest couch shaking her head and blinking her eyes. Her head began to droop, and she couldn't fight the pull of exhaustion that gripped her. She collapsed onto the couch.

JOE

Pain, hot and deep but unpinpointable, took over Joe's mind. The windshield wipers continued in their rhythmic clearing, although they no longer touched the shattered windshield. The car horn sounded loud, inescapable, and constant. He reached down to unclick his seat belt, leaving red smudges from his bloody hands. He tried to stand but fell out of the car onto his knees. The rain soaked through his clothes in seconds. He tried to assess his injuries, but it was too dark. The pain was everywhere at once. He crawled away from the car into the grassy yard, one arm held to his chest uselessly. He sat in the grass to assess his injuries. The light from the headlights allowed him to see more clearly in the dark, rainy night. An open, gaping wound marked his arm. A strange, sharp, white dagger sticking up. It was his bone. His stomach heaved, but there was nothing left to come up. The world faded before his eyes, and he passed out in the grass.

MIKE

As far as birthdays went, this one was not going to make the top-ten list. And poor Yvette. His family was hard on a regular night, but this night, their acrimony had been on steroids. She probably regretted agreeing to come. He looked across the room at her and smiled over his cake. She smiled back politely but guarded.

A loud crash interrupted his thoughts, and he ran to the window to see what had caused it. Rain splattered against the windows, making it hard to see outside. But a pair of headlights illuminated a large, downed tree at the end of the driveway.

"It's got to be Joe," Mike said. "I'm going out there."

"But it's raining," Nikki said.

"I'll go with you," Harris said.

"Me too," Kieran said.

"Kieran, honey, you stay here. It's really storming out there."

"Mom, it's just rain. I'll be fine."

The boys ran toward the front door.

"Wait," Kieran said, stopping at a credenza near the front door. He opened a drawer and pulled out three flashlights and tossed one to Mike and one to Harris. Mike clicked the light on and stepped outside.

The headlights of the crashed car illuminated a massive old oak that had stood on the edge of the property. The storm had brought it down across the driveway so that no one would be able to exit or enter until it was cleared. Joe's Prius must have skidded into it as it was sideways, with branches reaching through broken windows into the car. The driver side door stood open. Joe was not inside.

"Joe, JOE!" Mike called out. Mike reached the car and looked inside; there was blood everywhere. He aimed his flashlight around and saw Joe unconscious in the grass. He ran to him and kneeled next to him. Joe's face was scratched up, his glasses broken and askew on his bloody face. His arm clutched to his chest, the bone protruded out.

"He must have hydroplaned," Harris said. "He skidded right into the tree."

"We need to get him back up to the house. Maybe Addison can help him until the paramedics arrive," Mike said.

"How will an ambulance get here? They can't get past that tree," Harris said.

"Yeah, and we don't have our phones," Kieran said.

"Harris, you and I will carry him in," Mike said. "Kieran, you find Dad and get the phones from him. We need to call 911."

"Got it," Kieran said. He picked up the discarded flashlights and ran ahead to open the door for them.

"I'll get his arms," Mike said as he hooked his hands under Joe's armpits. Harris grabbed his feet.

"We can't take him back inside. Nikki might kill him," Harris said.

"No, she won't," Mike said. "Well . . . probably not."

LIZA

Liza watched with pride as her sons ran out to rescue Chef Joe. She had raised them right, or they'd gone the right way despite their controlling father. She turned away from the window to the parlor. Addison rested on the couch, exhausted no doubt by all the drama from the evening. Tending to her father while attending school was too much for anyone.

Yvette stood leaning against the bar but not participating in the conversation with Nikki, Sloan, and Michael. She looked to be lost in thought, staring out into the rain. Liza looked for signs of weariness from Michael but saw none. It didn't make sense. She ran her hand over the vial in her pocket once more. Michael excused himself from the group and walked upstairs. Was he getting tired and heading to bed early?

"Excuse me," Yvette said. "I'm going to find the powder room."

"Take a flashlight," Sloan said, handing her a slim black one.

"Thanks," she said as she walked out of the parlor and through the foyer.

"There's a closer one this way," Nikki said, but evidently Yvette didn't hear as she kept walking away.

Moments later, the front doors flew open as the boys carried Joe inside. Liza rushed to help them.

"This way," Liza said. "Let's take him to the couch in the parlor."

"Get Addison," Mike said. "She may be able to help."

"What are you doing?" Nikki asked. "You can't bring him in here! I want him out of my house!"

"He's in bad shape, Mom. We need to help him," Kieran said.

"I don't care if he's on death's door. It looks to me like karma. Leave that worm out in the rain where he belongs," Nikki said.

"We can't do that," Mike said. "We're going to help him."

"I want no part of this!" Nikki said. "As long as he is here, I'll be somewhere else." Nikki left the parlor.

Liza ran to fetch her daughter. "Addison," Liza said, gently touching her arm to rouse her. "Addison, wake up."

Addison did not move. Liza shook her with increasing vigor. Her body only shook in reaction to her mother's shaking. "Addison! Addison!" Liza called, getting frantic. Her eyes caught sight of the half-eaten piece of cake that sat next to Addison on the couch, a slender toothpick in it. Liza let go of her daughter as both hands flew to her mouth. "Oh no! No! No!"

YVETTE

Yvette slipped away from the group and clicked on the flashlight. She grabbed her bag from the front entryway before heading down the hallway and past the bathroom toward Michael's office. She closed the door behind her and walked over to his wooden desk in the middle of the room. The papers on top were nothing of interest, so she turned her attention to the drawers. The small top drawer on the left held office supplies, pens, pencils, sticky notes. She pulled open the bottom drawer and saw a black Glock sitting alone in the bottom of the deep drawer. She closed it quickly and then opened the drawer again, considering. She thought about tucking it into her waistband but couldn't bring herself to do it. Shivers ran down her spine as she closed the drawer again. Footsteps echoed from outside the room. They didn't sound like they came from the hallway. Yvette ducked under the desk, holding her bag in her lap, and clicked off the flashlight. The sound of something sliding across the rug came from behind her, inside the room.

The bookcase behind the desk groaned. Carefully, she peeped her eyes out enough to see the bookcase opening like a door. She slid back into the shadow of the desk. Michael stepped out from behind the bookcase.

She tried not to move or breathe. He walked over to the desk and stood there, his knees only inches away from her.

HARRIS

"What's wrong with Addison?" Harris asked.

Liza shook her head. "It's . . . I . . . I don't know."

"Okay, well, both Joe and Addison need medical attention," Mike said.

Harris looked at Joe, his arm battered and blood pouring down toward the floor and his unconscious sister. Things were unraveling fast.

Why is Mom crying so much? Harris thought as Liza sat next to Addison, clutching her hand and sobbing into the couch.

"I'll go find the phones," Sloan said.

"Dad put them in the safe. Get the combination from him," Mike said. "Oh, crap, he may have already gone out for his nightly cigar."

"Surely he won't go out in this weather?" Sloan said.

"He's pretty stubborn about that eight o'clock cigar. He has the covered patio right by his office. He might be there," Mike said.

"I'll see what I can do," Sloan said, leaving the parlor.

"Kieran, bring me some towels," Mike said.

"Yeah," Kieran said as he darted out of the room.

Harris checked his watch. It was just past eight.

Kieran returned with the towels.

"But how will an ambulance get to us?" Kieran asked. "With the tree blocking the driveway."

"One thing at a time," Mike said.

"Mom. Are you okay?" Harris asked.

Liza picked her head up and nodded.

Harris walked over to Kieran and whispered in his ear, "If Dad is heading out now, you need to get in place."

Kieran looked at Harris in shock and whispered back. "We can't do it now. Look at what's happened."

"It makes it all the better. Everything is so chaotic. Come on, let's go get you ready."

"But I need to help Joe."

"We'll handle that," Harris said. "Trust me." Harris put his hand on Kieran's shoulder. He turned and announced to the room, "Kieran and I are going to help Sloan with the phones."

"Okay," Mike said. "Hurry back."

"You got it," Harris said.

KIERAN

Harris opened the closet in Kieran's bedroom and pulled out a bow and arrow case and handed it to him. Kieran refused it. He looked at his big brother with pleading eyes.

"Harris, I don't think I can."

"Don't worry, bud," Harris said. "I've got it all planned out."

Kieran's hands shook as he took the case. He pulled on his raincoat and a billed ball cap.

"I'll head back down and tell everyone you went to bed. That's your alibi, and I'll make sure I'm with everyone, so no one will suspect me."

"Okay," Kieran said, his voice quivering.

Harris put his hand on Kieran's shoulder. "It's for the best. I wouldn't ask if I didn't think you could handle it."

Kieran nodded, afraid to speak, afraid to unfurl emotion that threatened to burst out. Harris turned and left.

Kieran looked into the hallway before walking quietly out of his room and down the east wing, away from the main staircase. As instructed, he took a secret passage from the hallway downstairs to the kitchen. He checked to make sure the kitchen was empty before he climbed out from behind a secret panel in the pantry. He was able to slip unnoticed out onto the lawn. His feet splashed across the soggy lawn, soaked through almost instantaneously. The ball cap kept some of the water out of his eyes, but it was still hard to see. He sprinted across the open lawn to the tree line at the edge of the driveway. He found a spot to hunker down and sat on the wet earth.

His hands pulled the long bow from its case and tested the tightness of the string. He put a few arrows in his quiver, although he would only need one. He took one arrow out and had it in his hand ready to load and fire. He wiped tears from his eyes with his wet sleeve and took a deep breath.

Thoughts of his father ran through his mind. The man clearly didn't care much about Kieran, a superfluous fourth child and third son. He'd never gone to see Kieran in sports or any of his archery tournaments. He barely even went out of his way to say hello to him when passing in the hallway. Kieran longed for the man to love him, but it was never going to happen. All the same, he didn't want to kill him.

But Harris needed him. Harris and Mike had been more like a father to him than Michael. And if Harris said it was necessary, it must be. He would do anything for Harris, apparently even murder.

YVETTE

Michael's legs stood in front of the desk. Yvette squished herself as far into the back of the cubby under the desk as possible and held her bag tightly. She couldn't get caught. Not yet. She hadn't found anything. She was suddenly aware of how loud her breathing was. As she focused on breathing quietly, she felt a tickle rise in her throat and the deep need to cough. She clapped a hand over her mouth and tried to swallow spit to soothe her throat. It didn't help.

The legs stepped away from the desk. She peeked out to see Michael, an unlit cigar in his mouth, grab a fedora off a hook by the door before pulling the office door open. Her eyes watered as the sound of soft rain filled the room until he closed the door behind him.

Yvette coughed until her throat was soothed. She needed to search this room quickly before he returned.

She clicked on the flashlight again as she opened the top drawer on the right side of the desk. It was full of files lined up neatly and alphabetized. She rifled through them quickly. They appeared to be regular paperwork, titles for cars, electric bills, mortgage papers, that sort of thing.

She opened the second drawer. It was more of the same alphabetized files filled with routine paperwork. Then she noticed the section for *Y* was gaping open with a file labeled *Yvette* siting in plain view. She slid it out of the drawer and flipped it open. Inside was a picture of her with brown hair and glasses, accompanied by a letter.

Mr. Higgins:

I looked into the matter we discussed. I was unable to complete a background check on Yvette Smith, as she doesn't exist. It's a fake name. I discovered her true identity. Her real name is Tara Sharp. Her sister Cara went missing last May. You may remember her from the news.

I'm not sure why she's using a fake name, but I would be very careful if I were you.

Sincerely,

Ted Mullaney

Private Investigator

NIKKI

Nikki closed the door to her bedroom—her bedroom, not hers and Michael's. She figured in such a big house, they might as well each have their own room. She'd never had her own room and had talked Michael into letting her sleep on her own three times a week. Everything in the room—the walls, the curtains, the tufted headboard—was a creamy white. The only exception was the silk bedding, which was bright red.

She slumped onto the rich, cool comforter. Michael's family was exhausting. She hated playing the little wife, meek and submissive. She sat up on her bed and removed her earrings. She turned to place them on her bedside table. That's when she saw it.

A manila envelope on the bedside table, with *Nikki* written on it in black Sharpie. It hadn't been there when she'd come down for dinner. She opened it and found glossy 8x10 color photos of Michael with some blond. They were kissing familiarly. First in a restaurant and then out on the street in plain view for the world to see.

Anger rose inside her. She imagined how it would feel to visit Michael at work, pull a knife, and lodge it in his spinal column. Not that she entered into this relationship blindly. She was no dummy. She knew Michael was a creep. She'd known when she married him that he was only a half-step above pond scum. But he had turned her into something she could not accept, a jilted woman, a Liza, someone to pity.

She cracked her neck from side to side, stood, and removed a dagger from the drawer in her nightstand. She pulled the ruby-encrusted handle from its matching sheath and ran it along her finger. A small drop of blood escaped the skin. She slammed the knife back into the sheath.

No one cheats on Nikki. She didn't care if he was a jerk, if he killed endangered species for fun, or even if he was a sexist, racist, selfish pig. The only unforgiveable sin in her mind was cheating. And her husband was doing so openly. That was it for Nikki. She would not allow it.

She was more than enough woman for any man. He was just greedy and sick. Her thoughts turned back to how much easier her life would be without him. She knew that he was splitting his money four ways when he died. The will left her the house and two million dollars. The rest of his nearly two hundred million would be split between his four kids equally. Kieran would never have to worry about money.

KIERAN

Kieran sat on the cold, wet mulch, rain dripping off his hat into his face. His bottom was soaked through and starting to feel numb. The bow and arrow were in his hands, ready to be used within seconds.

Right on schedule, the door opened, and his father stepped out onto the covered patio and lit his cigar. Kieran's eyes had adjusted to the blackness of the night. Even so, he could only see the silhouette of his father, lighting his cigar, the small flame illuminating part of his face.

Kieran took a steadying breath just as he did in every archery competition. He put the arrow onto the bow, sliding the string into the notch at the back. He lined up the shot and pulled back, then adjusting his aim a few feet to the right to compensate for the wind. He pulled the string tight and took another deep breath. The bow began to quiver in his hand. His eyes dropped from the target. He lowered the weapon. *I can't do it. I won't.*

A moment later, the dark figure stepped behind the outdoor brick fireplace, making a shot impossible. Tears spilled out onto Kiernan's cheeks. He felt relieved. All the pressure put on him released and poured out of him. As the tears flowed, he found himself smiling, and he began to laugh to himself at the absurdity of it all.

TARA

Tara dropped the file on the desk and slumped down into the leather office chair. *So he knows.* The blond hair hadn't fooled Michael. Tara had dyed it because she looked so much like her sister, Cara. Yet, Michael knew her identity the whole time and he hadn't said anything. *Did he tell anyone else? Surely not Mike.* He hadn't acted any differently toward her. But why had Michael kept her secret? Was he just playing with her? There had to be an answer somewhere in his office, proof that Michael had Cara, and where she could be found.

Tara opened the bottom drawer of the left side of the desk again and picked up the gun. As she did so, she noticed the bottom of the drawer moved slightly. She looked closer, putting the gun down on the desk. It was a false bottom. She popped it open and found a thick file. She pulled it out and drew in a deep breath. Inside were pictures of girls, lots of girls, each given a number. Each page read like a bill of sale. *Number 494 sold for 130k, to client B-76. Cash.*

She had him! This was it! Proof!

She had to get these papers to the police. But how? She couldn't leave with the tree blocking the driveway, and she couldn't call or take a picture without her phone.

Lightning lit up the night sky and a few seconds later as a clap of thunder shook the house. Tara thought she heard someone scream. She picked the gun up off the desk and slid it into her bag.

NIKKI

Nikki tore out the back door through the rain to find Michael standing under the covered patio smoking his cigar. The inflexible bastard insisted on a cigar at eight no matter what was going on, including a typhoon or a murdered dog.

"I warned you," Nikki said, stepping onto the covered patio.

Michael flinched back from the surprise appearance of his wife. "What are you doing out here?"

She held up the manila envelope, protecting it mostly from the rain by holding it under her chest, and waved it in the air. "Do you know what I have here?"

"Yes, and I can explain," Michael said.

"I don't think so. You can't explain this away."

"I'm going to kill Sloan," Michael said.

"Not if you're dead," Nikki said as she lunged at him, the knife in her hand. She held it to his neck.

"Nikki," he said, busting out his most charming and disarming smile. "I've made mistakes. I'll admit it. But—"

"No. You don't charm you're way out of this one. I only asked one thing of you. Be loyal. Don't cheat on me. I thought we had a pretty good thing going here," Nikki said.

"You're still the most beautiful woman I've ever seen. But you don't love me. You love this life, but you don't even really need me. You certainly don't adore me. And these women do. They worship me and treat me like a king. And I'm not sorry."

"I've never given you reason to complain or look outside of our marriage to have your needs met. I've lived up to my part of the bargain. And you have not."

Lightning flashed across the sky. Michael grabbed her arms and pushed them away from his throat. He pulled the knife from her grasp. As thunder crashed loudly, Nikki let out a loud scream. The smile left Michael's face and was replaced by a glare reserved for those who had crossed him. He placed the knife in his pocket.

"Nice try," Michael said.

"You won't know when, you won't know where, but you will pay for this," Nikki screamed.

"Are you quite finished?" Michael said before entering the house and closing the door behind him.

TARA

A shadow appeared on the outside door to the office. Tara didn't have time to get out of the room. She saw the open bookcase. She had no choice; there was no time. She had to duck inside. She grabbed the file and shoved it into her leather tote, then slid into a tight, dark passage with spiral stairs. She heard the door to the office open from the outside. She quickly decided to head down, flicking off her flashlight. Michael entered above her head and took the stairs up and away from her. A moment later, she heard the office door open again. She peeked up over the edge of the stairs and into the office. She saw Nikki look into the passage before shutting the secret door, leaving Tara in complete darkness.

She waited to be sure Michael had left before clicking on her flashlight again and heading down. The stairs ended in a long stone hallway that led into the darkness. Tara's heart began to beat rapidly. *What if Cara is here?* What if he hid the girls somewhere inside this giant house? She had to investigate. Tara put one hand on the cool, cold stone and followed the tunnel. After about twenty paces, the stone on one side ended in a long-arched opening into another room. Tara shined her flashlight into the space and found a large wine cellar, the walls filled with wine in square cubbies. In the middle of the room was a long table, and in the corner, a safe embedded in the wall.

She left the wine cellar and walked down the dark passage. She followed it on until she came to another spiral staircase and an elevator leading upstairs.

There was a door under the stairs. Tara pulled it open. Inside were pool supplies, nothing more. Not what she expected.

Tara walked back to the wine cellar and sat at the table. She would take a few minutes in this place alone to read the file she had found. She opened the file and thumbed through it. Inside page after page of girls, their sale date and their price were listed in chronological order. There was also a deposit slip stapled to each page. Tara did the math in her head. Fifty percent of the sale went to an account at the Grand Cayman Bank, twenty-five percent went into the Butler's ice-cream account, and twenty-five percent went into Michael Higgins's personal account. She had him. He was tied to the sales directly. She flipped through the pages of girls to the end of the file. That's when she saw it.

In the dim light, Cara's face smiled back at her. She gasped and it echoed around the chamber.

Below Cara's picture, the paper read:

Cara Sharp # 587—Sold
Price: $347,000

The date of exchange was listed as tonight at twelve midnight. But it didn't say where. *Midnight.* She thought she'd had one more day, but the sale was tonight.

Tara checked her watch; it was 8:15. She was running out of time. And so was Cara.

MIKE

"Did you hear something?" Liza asked, looking away from Addison briefly.

"Just the storm, I think," Mike said. He was beginning to worry about Yvette. "Mom, did you say Yvette went to the bathroom? I'm starting to worry."

"Yes. That's what she said."

"Maybe I should go look for her," Mike said.

"I can hold the pressure on Joe for you," Harris said.

"What is taking Sloan so long with the phones?"

"Maybe he can't find Dad," Harris said.

"I'll try to find them and Yvette. You guys stay here," Mike said.

"You got it," Harris said, taking the blood-soaked towels and holding pressure on Joe's arm with one hand and giving Mike a thumbs up with the other.

Mike walked to the foyer. He debated where to start. He decided to head for his father's office. The phones might be in there.

TARA

Tara closed the file and tucked it back into her bag. She followed the tunnel back the way she came and up the stairs to Michael's office. She heard a noise beyond the door in the office, bringing her back to herself. She quickly flicked off her flashlight. A shadow passed the crack under the door.

The door popped abruptly open. A dark figure loomed over her.

"Sneaking around? Let's cut to the chase, Tara," Michael said. "You didn't think I knew? Of course, I knew. When it comes to my family, I know everything."

"I feel the same way. And now I know your secret," Tara said as Michael grabbed her by the arm and pulled her into the room. He tossed her into a chair opposite his desk.

"I know you have no interest in Mike," he said. "You came here with other intentions. What those are, I'm not sure. But you're going to tell me," Michael said.

"You know why I'm here. I'm here for Cara." She pulled a picture out of her bag, the photo that proved Michael's nefarious scheme. She held it up.

"Your sister?" Michael looked around. "I haven't seen her."

"This was the last picture taken of her the night she disappeared. She was at the fair. Do you recognize what she's holding?"

"Yeah, an ice-cream cone."

"Not just any ice-cream cone. Look at the color of the chocolate, the ribbon of light brown running through it. That's Washington Carver's Delight. I checked. One of your ice-cream trucks was there at the fair."

"That doesn't prove anything!"

"No, it doesn't, and I would never have made the connection if it hadn't been for the other girl—the girl who died of hypothermia. That's how you're transporting them, isn't it? With ice-cream trucks?"

"You have a wild imagination."

"No, I have proof. I did some digging and found the name *O'Hara* is tied to large deposits from Butler's. They received over three million this year alone from Butler's. He's the mastermind behind the whole operation, and he is you!"

"No. He's not," Michael said smugly.

"Liar! Where is she? Where is my sister? I won't turn you in. Just give her back. Please. I love her, and she's still so young. I just want her back."

"I have no idea where your sister is. I don't know anything about her. Why would I?"

"Sex trafficking is a very lucrative business, not to mention a handy side hobby if you happen to be a sicko."

"Now you're out of line. This is insanity. I have no knowledge of any of this."

"I came here to find out where my sister is, and you're going to tell me."

"Or what? What's your plan, Tara?"

Tara reached for her bag. Before she could grab it, Michael kicked it away with his foot. He picked it up and looked inside. He pulled out her taser and pushed the button, causing it to zap and crackle at the air.

"So now that I have your bag of tricks, what's your plan?"

Tara's face turned red. She was out of options. She had come this far only to be thwarted by this idiot.

"Where is my sister?" she screamed.

"How would I know?"

"You can stop playing dumb. I found everything. All the proof I need," Tara said. "Check the file in my bag."

"What are you talking about?" Michael said. He reached into the bag, pulled out the file, and opened it on his desk. Michael's eyes grew large. "Where did you get this?"

"Oh, uh, like you don't know. From your desk drawer. Under the false bottom." Tara stood and pulled the top piece of paper off the stack. "Okay, so explain this," she said as she read the paper. "Lilly Newton, age fourteen, date of sale March 2016, price one hundred seventy-six thousand dollars." She grabbed the next page. "Anna Riviera, age eleven, date of sale July 2018, price two hundred twenty-one thousand dollars. Should I continue?"

Michael's mouth hung open as he took in the information. He shook his head and sat down in the desk chair. He flipped through the pages. "This isn't me, I swear," he said.

"A quarter of each sale goes into an account for O'Hara, which ties into your personal account, scumbag. Explain that."

Michael's face turned white. His mouth hung open. He looked at Tara. Her resolve wavered briefly.

"I think I've been set up," he said, sitting down in his desk chair as he took in the information.

"It was in your desk. This is the only one I'm interested in, you sick piece of garbage." She held up the picture of Cara. "The sale happens tonight. Tell me where, and I'll leave you alone. I won't tell the cops what I know, and I'll leave Mike alone. I'll never contact him again." Her heart hurt as she said it. But she would walk away from Mike, from the beginnings of love. For Cara, she'd sacrifice anything.

"I can't tell you where she is. I don't know. This is the first time I'm seeing any of this."

"So, it's just a coincidence that six new Butler's Ice Cream trucks were recently purchased. That seems excessive for ice cream, but not if you're trying to move girls around the country unnoticed."

Michael looked at her. "How do you know that?"

"I've been looking into it."

"Tell me more," Michael said.

"And the profits on the store far exceed the number of sales you could have had based on the amount of supplies you guys used. It's a front."

"I knew it was too good to be true. It's far exceeding the projections we had on it. That's one of the reasons I wanted to sell. Numbers don't lie," Michael said. "I assumed he was just overcharging or padding the numbers, and I didn't want any part of it." Michael stared at the floor, his mind working through these new facts. "I'm being set up," he said as much to himself as to her. "I didn't do any of that. I was more of a silent partner."

"I've seen the purchase orders. Your signature is on all of them."

"Show me," he said.

Tara pulled the papers out of her bag, the information she had discovered before she came here. She showed him the papers, the trucks he purchased, the signed bills of sale, the money from each sale going into his personal account. It all pointed to him.

"It's a setup," he said, convinced.

"I don't believe you!" Tara said.

"Knock knock," a voice said as someone knocked on the door. Michael and Tara turned to watch as the door opened.

NIKKI

Calming down wasn't something Nikki had ever quite mastered. She could not put on a happy face and the appearance of tranquility when she was a rolling ball of anger and resentment on the inside. Michael had dared to cheat on her, and she would not forgive or forget the offense. But for now, she needed to prepare for all the houseguests to stay overnight. No one was leaving with the tree across the driveway.

Even the vile chef would have to stay here, after what he did to Coco. She thought he was taking a risk to stay here after that. She could not be blamed for her anger over such a completely heinous crime against her.

She took deep breaths and forced a smile as she checked each of the bedrooms to make sure they had fresh linens and plenty of pillows.

HARRIS

Harris looked over his shoulder toward the stairs. What was taking Sloan so long? They needed to get Joe and Addison medical attention. Joe had lost a lot of blood. He must have hit his head pretty hard. He was still unconscious.

"Maybe I should go find some bandages and Tylenol," Liza said. She stood up from her place next to Addison and walked toward the kitchen.

Joe's breathing changed slightly. His eyes fluttered and opened.

"That a boy, Joe!" Harris said.

"My arm . . . it hurts."

"Yeah, I bet it does. You're just going to have to hang in there with me. My mom went to get some pain medicine. As soon as we get the phones, we're going to call an ambulance to come and set this arm for you."

He moaned. "It's karma. I deserve so much worse than this for taking the life of Coco."

"It was an accident. You can't hold onto it. It wasn't your fault."

Joe looked into Harris's eyes. He opened his mouth to speak but no words came out, only tears. "I've taken an innocent life. I'm stained. I'm irredeemable. I'm worthless. I'll never escape what I have done."

"Wow, Joe, calm down. It's okay."

"The cost of taking a life is a heavy burden. Too heavy to carry. I'll never escape what I've done." Joe's head fell back against the pillow, tears streaming down his cheeks. Harris had a sinking feeling in his gut. He tried to push it away, but it invaded his mind.

The guilt over taking a life had messed with Joe. And he had asked

Kieran to do more than that. He'd asked him to murder his own father. Kieran would never be the same again. He'd asked too much of him. He could see that now. Murder wasn't something you ever fully escaped. The guilt of it would haunt him, like it was haunting Joe.

MIKE

Mike pushed the door open. Yvette and his father looked at him in shock, and he felt tension and mistrust emanating. Quiet Yvette, sweet Yvette, stood over his father, both looking at some papers on his desk.

"Hey, there you are. I got turned around," she said, smiling and stepping away from the desk.

"Dad?" Mike said. "What's going on here?"

"You want the truth?" Michael said. Yvette's eyes flashed to Michael. "Come on. There's no point in keeping up the lie. There's nothing else for you to find here."

"What's going on? Yvette?"

"Your girlfriend is a fraud . . . sorry, sonny," Michael said. "Her real name is Tara Sharp." Michael slid the note from the PI about Yvette across the desk to Mike.

"Yvette, what's he talking about?" Mike said.

Tara's face flushed. She looked into Mike's eyes and then down at the floor.

"I had her background checked," Michael said.

"Of course, you did," Mike said as he picked up the file. He flipped it open and saw a picture of Yvette. Her hair color was brown, and she wore glasses, but it was definitely her. He read the letter from the PI.

Yvette hung her head, her face beet red.

"What are you saying? Yvette?" Mike asked, teary-eyed.

"Her name is Tara," Michael said.

"Yvette, tell me the truth right now. Was it all an act? Did you just want to get close to my dad?"

"What we had . . . I've never felt about anyone the way I feel about you. And I'm sorry I broke that. I wish we'd met under different circumstances," Tara said.

"Oh, please, you've only known each other a few days," Michael said.

"Sometimes that's all it takes," Tara said.

"She's not here for you," Michael said.

"So, what's she here for?"

"I'm so sorry, Mike," Tara said. "I didn't mean for any of this to happen. I didn't mean for you to get caught up in the middle of this."

"In the middle of what?" Mike asked.

"Your father knows the truth about my missing sister, and I need him to tell me."

"Your girlfriend is confused. I don't know anything about her sister. She's crazy."

"He kidnapped my sister," Tara said, pointing at Michael. "He runs a sex trafficking ring out of Butler's Ice Cream."

Mouth agape, Mike stood speechless.

"Obviously that's not true," Michael said.

"Well then explain all this evidence," Tara said, pointing to the file on the desk.

"Give me a minute. Let me look at these documents," Michael said. He opened the folder and sat down in the chair behind his desk. He slipped on his glasses and began to scrutinize the papers from the file. "There has to be a trail here," he mumbled.

"I don't have time for this," Tara said. "Tell me where Cara is."

"I don't know!"

Tears rolled down Tara's face. "Please." Her voice was quiet now, softer. "Please, tell me."

Mike saw the pain in her eyes and felt a connection to it. What if Kieran had been taken? He would go to the ends of the earth to find whoever did it. He thought about his father, about his childhood of fear and obedience and not much love. In an instant, he knew that despite the history or the blood they shared, he trusted Yvette more, even if that wasn't her real name.

Mike crossed the room to the long bookshelf on top of which stood Zeus's terrarium. He picked it up, ripping the heat lamp cord from the wall, and held the snake tank out threateningly toward his father.

"Tell her what she wants to know, or I'll set Zeus free."

"Mike, no," Tara said.

"Put that down, you insolent child," Michael said.

"Tell the truth for once in your life."

"I am telling the truth. I know nothing. Someone set me up."

"You're a monster," Mike said. He raised the terrarium over Michael's head, ready to smash it open on the ground at Michael's feet.

"Did you kidnap my sister? Or do you know who did?" Tara pressed.

"I honestly don't know. Someone is framing me," Michael said. "The answer is here. We can find it."

Mike walked over to the desk and studied the papers. He lowered the snake's tank and set it on the desk. "Is this . . . is this true? All these girls? Dad?" He looked at his father pleadingly.

"I have no idea. Tara found the papers. She was showing them to me just now. I've never seen them before."

"But it has your name all over it," Mike said.

"You work with me. What do you think that means?" Michael asked his son.

Mike flipped through the pages of girls. He looked at the bank statements. He thought about how careful his father was. He paid himself a paycheck from the company, but he never intermingled his own money with the businesses. This wasn't like him. If he was involved in something illegal, there's no way he would link it to his personal accounts.

"It's not you. It's a setup," Mike said, looking up at his father.

"What?" Tara said. "It's as plain as day, there on the papers."

"Yvette, I mean Tara, hear me out," Mike said. "It can't be him. He knows better than to have his name and his bank account linked to anything illegal. He has offshore accounts and LLCs to hide money . . . for tax purposes. Unethical? Yes. Illegal? No. Someone is setting him up," Mike said.

"Who? My sister, Cara, is going to be sold at midnight, and I need to find her."

"Okay, let's think this through," Mike said.

"Who do you think framed you?" Tara asked Michael.

"Let me look at the papers again." Michael studied the papers and slowly stood up. "That son of a—"

"What? What is it?" Mike asked.

"He set me up to take the fall in case he ever got caught. I should have paid more attention. But he was my friend. Son of a bitch. I invest in his company, and he's been setting me up from day one."

"Who?" Mike pleaded.

Just then, the door to the office opened. Sloan stood, taking in the scene.

SLOAN

"Oh, excuse me. Am I interrupting?" Sloan asked, smiling.

"Is this you?" Michael said, holding up the picture of Cara. "Have you made me the patsy in some sick world you're involved in?"

Sloan sneered. "You're not going to believe some silly little girl? She's got no real proof of anything."

"Proof of what?"

"Anything," Sloan huffed.

"Oh, I've got proof and plenty of it," Tara said, holding up the file. "You framed him, didn't you?"

The snake began to rattle its tail in the commotion.

Tara pulled the gun from her bag and aimed it at Sloan. "I have some questions." Sloan's smirk disappeared as he pulled a gun from a holster inside his jacket and aimed it at Tara. "Drop it," he said.

"You drop it," Tara said.

"That's cute," Sloan said. He stepped forward, put his elbow against her neck, pulled the gun out of her hand, and tucked it into his pocket.

"Stop!" Mike screamed.

"Finally putting it together?" Sloan asked.

"I should've known. I didn't see it," Michael said. "I let my guard down."

"I guess the gig is up," Sloan said. "It's been fun. Actually, that's a lie, you have been most unpleasant to work for. Although the money certainly helped. We've been able to smuggle a lot of girls with you on board as the patsy. We took bigger risks knowing it would all land in your lap."

"We?" Michael asked.

Mike grabbed the terrarium off the desk and held it close to Sloan.

"What are you doing?" Sloan asked.

"My girlfriend wants answers, and you're going to give them to her."

"Or what? You'll throw a snake at me?"

"Yup," Mike said.

"Well, you should know she is a fraud. Her name isn't even Yvette," Sloan said.

"You knew the whole time?" Mike said. "Did everyone but me know?"

"I was going to tell you," Sloan said. "I only found out this afternoon. Put the snake down. She's the enemy here. She's trying to turn us against each other."

"You just admitted to smuggling girls. I think I'll trust her," Mike scolded.

"You can't be serious? This is madness. She lied to you! Think with your brain, not your groin! You don't even know her real name."

"Yes, I do. It's Tara. Tara Sharp. And that doesn't matter," Mike said. "Her name doesn't change who she is or what we have."

Tears rolled down Tara's face.

"You fool. She's using you. Can't you see that?" Sloan said. He cocked the gun and aimed it at Tara. "Last chance. Put down the snake, or you get a firsthand view of what a bad guy I can be."

Mike lowered the cage onto the desk and lifted his hands into the air. "Good boy, now——" But the tank had been set down too close to the edge. It slowly tilted forward, crashing to the floor. Zeus coiled among the shards, making his characteristic rattle sound.

Tara jumped onto the desk. Mike quickly joined her.

"You've always been klutzy, even as a boy," Michael said. The snake slithered under the desk. Michael quickly got up from the chair, grabbed the files off the desk, and pulled open the passage behind the bookshelf. "I'm calling the authorities. I've got enough here to prove you framed me. Mike, handle the snake."

Michael slipped into the secret passage. Sloan sidestepped around the desk, cautiously, one eye on Zeus, and followed Michael up the secret passage.

HARRIS

"Mom, I don't know what's taking Sloan so long, but we need to find a phone. Can you handle these two?" Harris asked.

"Yes. Good idea, honey," Liza said.

Harris knew his father had a safe in the basement. It wasn't a secret that Harris had been known to sneak down on occasion to help himself to a bottle of wine. In his wanderings, he'd seen a safe embedded in the wall on the far side of the cellar. He took the secret passage from the kitchen down to the basement, shining his flashlight as he went. Even as a grown man, Harris found the basement creepy. He walked down the dungeon-like hallway to the wine cellar. He stood and stared at the combination pad. Let the guessing begin. He tried a few birthdays, his own and that of his siblings. Although he had to enter Addison's twice because he could never remember if she was April third or fourth. But his father wouldn't use a birthday. He wasn't sentimental like that. Harris walked to the cache of wine and grabbed a bottle off the shelf. Using the corkscrew on the table, he opened the bottle and took a long pull.

MIKE

"Wait! Where's Cara?" Tara called as Michael and Sloan fled.

"It's okay. We'll get him. He can't leave," Mike said.

"That's not good. I have to get out of here. The paper said Cara was being sold tonight."

"Okay, we'll make a plan," Mike said. He looked down at the snake, rattling his tail, his eyes locked on the pair of them where they still stood on top of the desk. "But first, we need to get past the snake. I think I'll need to capture him."

Tara turned to Mike. "I'm so sorry. Truly. I didn't want to lie to you. I've felt like the worst person lying to you. And worst of all, I couldn't keep my heart from falling for you. Which just made me feel awful. You are such an amazing person. Passionate and deep and honest. And your art is an inspiration. You are an artist. Don't let working with your father change your identity. You're an artist whether you spend eight hours a day on it or not. I'm so, so sorry. I hope, with time, you'll be able to forgive me."

Mike didn't need time. He figured she had more guts in one pinky than he did in his whole body. He'd never been able to stand up to his own father, to tell him this wasn't what he wanted for his life. He let that man push him around his entire life, and for what? For money? It made him sick. His father was probably incapable of loving another human being. He'd known that for a long time. Not that anyone ever gives up on trying to earn the love of their father, even if it is unattainable.

"I don't need time. You're forgiven. You did all the things you did to save your sister. You are the bravest person I know. You faced these people, knowing what they are capable of, to save her. You are courageous. I see your heart and I can't help but love you."

"You are too good to be true," Tara said. "How can you just overlook the lies?"

"I saw you. You can't hide your soul. I'm not sure how much of you was the real you and how much was Yvette, but I'd like to find out."

Tara threw her arms round Mike. He pulled her back, looked into her teary eyes, swept a stray hair out of her face, and kissed her as Zeus rattled away beneath them.

BETSY

Once Tori had started talking, she became a fountain of information. Henry took vigilant notes and Betsy had listened calmly, not interrupting the flow of information, only interjecting when necessary.

"They kept us in a white two-story house. It looked like a dollhouse, with fancy railings and a big porch," Tori said.

"Sounds like a Victorian-style. Did you see the street name?"

"No, but I could smell waffles sometimes. And the symbol on my wrist, it was on the front door, like in stained glass."

"That's very helpful. Were there any other girls there?" Betsy asked.

"There were about four mattresses on the floor. I was there for a few months at least. I kept track of all the girls that came and went. I made a list," she said.

"Where is it?"

"In my head."

Betsy handed her a notebook and pen. "Can you write it?"

"Yeah."

SLOAN

Sloan had known that there were hidden passages in Michael's home, but he had never been in them before. He followed Michael behind the bookcase and up metal circular stairs, exiting into the master bedroom. Michael walked across the barrel-vaulted room and sat down on one of a pair of gray wingback chairs. He stood when he saw Sloan by the secret passage.

"What are you doing here? You need to stay away from me," Michael said. "I'm calling the police."

"You'll be dead before they get here," Sloan said. He pulled the gun from his pocket and aimed it at Michael.

"You're going to kill me? Over ice cream? You're pathetic."

"No, I'm not going to. There's no need. I've given motives to nearly everyone in the house. One of them will do it for me, leaving me free to continue my business. Butler's won't be sold, and the sex trafficking can continue."

"No one here will kill me. They are my family. They need me."

"Do you really believe that? You've put them all through hell doing whatever you asked and never having a chance to live their own lives. Well, except for Nikki. But she's as likely to kill you as any of them now that she's seen the photos of you and that blond."

"Yeah, thanks for that. She already came close, but she didn't. Neither will any of the others."

"We'll see," Sloan mocked.

"Just answer a question for me. You had a daughter, Sloan. How can you buy and sell other girls? I know you loved Cindy. I saw you with her even at the end when she was so sick and hard to look at."

"What's your point?"

"How can you make other girls suffer? How can you take them away from their families?"

"You think the girls I sell are suffering? They don't know what suffering is. They don't live with constant agonizing pain. They don't have to poison their bodies in order to try to buy time. They don't suffer. They, like almost everyone on this planet, have never experienced real suffering."

"But you steal them from their families."

"Usually no one wants them. They're just throwaway kids. So, we feed them and make their life easier in a lot of ways."

"I doubt that. You're sick," Michael said.

"Oh, I'm sick. That's rich coming from you!"

"I never hurt anyone."

"That's all you do," Sloan said. "You hurt everyone all the time, constantly, with your selfishness."

"Hmm what's worse, a self-serving lifestyle or the abduction and selling of little girls? I win. As usual. Maybe it's for the best that Cindy died. She never had to see what you've become."

Sloan lurched and slammed Michael into the wall, creating a divot in the drywall. He put both his hands on Michael's throat. Michael, stunned by the sudden blow, took a moment to react. He began to scratch at Sloan's arms, causing red lines to appear on Sloan's forearms. Sloan saw the marks and immediately let go of Michael, who slumped to the floor, rubbing his neck.

Sloan stepped away from Michael and dusted off his coat. "You almost made me do something stupid. But give it time. Someone else will do it for me. Good riddance," he said as he turned and left the room.

CHAPTER 7

THE MURDER

The next ten minutes proved life-changing or rather life-ending for Michael Higgins. He went from alive to dead, from in his bedroom to on the pavement in the rain. Michael Higgins's murder took place at exactly 8:46.

No one would admit to seeing Michael Higgins alive again after 8:40, when Sloan left him in his bedroom. Of course, one person did. The murderer. As of 8:40, the whereabouts of those in the house were as follows:

In the parlor, Liza sat watching and praying over Addison, who had yet to regain consciousness, and Joe, who was in a lot of pain, slipping in and out of consciousness.

In Michael's office, Mike and Tara stood on top of Michael's desk as they planned out how to recapture Zeus without getting bitten. Sloan had just left Michael's room after having an altercation. He stood angrily in the hidden passage between Michael's bedroom and the office.

Nikki was trying to regain her composure while she prepared the house for the unexpected onslaught of overnight guests.

Luckily, the beds were all freshly made, but she carried towels into all the bathrooms and made sure to restock the toiletries and toilet paper.

Kieran was sitting cold and miserable in the rain. He didn't have the guts to face Harris and tell him he hadn't gone through with it.

Harris sat in front of the safe in the basement, staring at the numbers, a half-full bottle of wine in his hand. He'd already entered a ridiculous number of combinations. What would his father use? What numbers meant anything to him? Harris sat contemplating this in the moments before his father was murdered.

The events of the night, starting at 8:40, left a ten-minute window in which someone lost their innocence and became a murderer.

CHAPTER 8

THE AFTER PARTY

MIKE

Mike stood on top of the desk, holding Tara and watching the snake.

"If I can just grab him by the head, he won't be able to bite us," Mike said.

"And then we'll need somewhere to put him," Tara said, looking around the room. "What I wouldn't give for some Tupperware right about now."

"Once I have him, I can hold him while you run down to the kitchen and look for something like that to put him in. Just make sure the lid is strong."

"But how are you going to grab him by the head without him biting you?"

"I've had practice. Ready? Okay, here goes nothing."

Mike looked the snake in the eye and Zeus looked right back at him. He took three steadying breaths, preparing to leap off the table and grab the snake's head from behind. But before he could, the sound of footsteps banging down the metal spiral staircase caused them to break eye contact.

SLOAN

Sloan took the secret passage back down to Michael's office. He pushed the door open and saw Tara and Mike still standing on the desk, the snake still loose, curled, and rattling on the floor. Could nothing be accomplished without his involvement?

"You haven't gotten that snake yet?" Sloan asked accusingly.

Then it happened. Zeus lunged and planted his teeth into Sloan's leg. Pain erupted and he screamed. A wave of heat and nausea washed over him as the poison traveled up his leg and throughout his body. He reached down and grabbed the blasted thing. He pulled open the bottom desk drawer and threw the snake in, slamming it closed. He slumped down onto the desk chair and pulled up his pant leg to investigate the wound.

Tara hopped off the table, followed by Mike.

"Quick, we need to suck out the venom," Mike said, leaning down toward the wound.

"Get away from me. You're not putting your lips on me," Sloan said.

"But the poison could kill you."

"I've survived worse. Sit down," Sloan said as he pulled the gun once again from his pocket and pointed it at Tara.

"This is your fault."

"I just want my sister. I'll pay for her. I'll double the sale you have now."

"Really? That'll be about seven hundred grand. Want to Venmo it to me?"

"I can get it," Tara said.

"No, you can't. Let's not lie to each other. The only way you'll see your sister again is if I take you, to be sold as well. You're a bit older than I usually deal in, but the quality is there."

"What are you talking about?" Mike said. "You're not taking her."

"You should be more careful about what kind of answers you look for," Sloan said.

"Where is she?" Tara pressed. "Where is she?" She took a step toward him. "WHERE IS SHE?"

"Please, I'd rather not shoot you."

"I'd rather die than leave here without answers."

"Well, now that would be a waste. I might not be able to make top dollar off you, but you are certainly worth something."

"You're not taking Yvette, I mean, Tara," Mike said.

"What? You're going to stop me?" Sloan said. He saw Tara's tote bag and dumped it out on the desk, grabbing zip ties and duct tape, keeping the gun aimed at them.

"You do come prepared," Sloan said. He grabbed her hands, attaching them in front of her. He took another and attached Mike's hands behind his back.

"WHERE IS SHE?" Tara demanded once more as he ripped a piece of duct tape off the roll and slapped it over her mouth.

"Sit down," he said, gesturing to one of the chairs. Mike sat down, awkwardly leaning a bit forward to make room for his hands. Sloan took two more zip ties and attached both of his feet to the legs of the chair.

Tara sat in the chair next to Mike.

"No, you're coming with me," Sloan said. He grabbed her zip-tied arms and pulled her to her feet.

"Where are you going?" Mike asked. "You can't leave. The tree is blocking the driveway."

"I'm sure we can get around it," Sloan said, wincing in pain and taking a gasping breath.

"Not likely, especially with that snakebite. You need a doctor."

"Well, there ain't one here. I guess leaving is my best option. You stay here and keep quiet," Sloan said as he pulled more duct tape from the roll and covered Mike's mouth.

Sloan pulled Tara to the back door. Before going outside, he took Michael's fedora off the hook and placed it on his head. He opened the door and led her out into the pouring rain and onto the sloping lawn.

KIERAN

Kieran was soaked through, his clothes heavy with water, his fingers wrinkled prunes. He still did not go inside. He couldn't face the disappointment of his brother, Harris. But he was cold and uncomfortable. The time had come to go inside.

As Kieran began to pack up his bow and arrow, the office door opened once again, and Michael stepped out onto the lawn. But he wasn't alone. He was pulling someone. From the silhouette, Kieran thought it must be Yvette. She had her hands tied in front of her. He was pulling her forward as she struggled to break free. Something nagged at Kieran, something about his father wasn't right.

The sound of her screams carried on the wind. She fell backward, fighting Michael.

Michael leaned over her. From where he stood, Kieran heard the loud crack of his dad's hand on her face. Michael pulled a gun from his waistband and pointed it at her. Kieran grabbed his bow and arrow off the wet ground.

TARA

The face slap surprised Tara. Sloan had been a charming enough person just an hour or so before. Now, he was an evil, abusive abductor.

"Listen up, honey. The amount I could get for you isn't worth this much trouble. So, make it easy on me, or I will shoot you."

She nodded at him as rain poured down her face, into her eyes. As she stood, she heard a strange whistling sound. An arrow pierced the fedora on Sloan's head, sticking halfway through the hat. Sloan pulled the hat off and, seeing the damage, began to panic. He turned and aimed his weapon toward the tree line along the edge of the property. He grabbed Tara and pulled her to him like a human shield. He put the cold gun barrel against her temple.

"Who's out there? Show yourself," Sloan screamed out into the darkness.

MIKE

Mike studied the ties, tight around his ankles. There was no way he'd be able to pull his feet through, even if he removed his shoes. But then he saw the obvious solution. He stood and, with his hands behind his back, lifted the chair behind him. The legs of the chair lifted right out of the zip ties. Mike sat and wiggled his tied hands underneath him and pulled his legs through so his zip-tied hands were in front of him.

He ran out the back door into the rain, wiping the water from his face as he ran toward Sloan and Tara. Sloan held Tara with a gun to her head, an arrow in his hat, like Robin Hood.

"Tara!" Mike called.

Sloan and Tara looked up at him.

KIERAN

Kieran had missed. Maybe it was the wind or nerves, or maybe deep down he didn't want to hit him. But now his father held the gun to Yvette's head. Kieran loaded a second arrow and took aim, adjusting to strike lower. He couldn't shoot though, not with Michael using Yvette as a shield. He couldn't take the chance he would miss and hit Yvette. This wind couldn't be trusted. He'd have to wait for a better shot.

SLOAN

Sloan held Tara tight as he looked around the property for the source of the shot. He clamped her to his body with one arm while aiming toward the edge of the yard with the other. She wiggled in his arm.

"Tara!" Mike called as he ran toward them from the house. "Tara!"

Great! Now I'll have to shoot him, too, Sloan thought. He'd always liked Mike. Not as much as Harris, who was always fun to be around. Mike sometimes had a somber, moody air that rubbed Sloan the wrong way. But still he was a nice enough guy. He pointed the gun at Mike. As he did, in that moment of distraction, Tara wiggled free and fell to the ground.

Sloan took a breath and pulled the trigger.

TARA

Tara felt the change in Sloan. When he'd aimed the gun at Mike, something about his whole body tensed. She knew he was going to shoot Mike.

It was her fault Mike was involved, and she wouldn't let him die. She ran for Mike, through the soggy grass. But she didn't have time to reach him. She turned and jumped in front of Mike just as Sloan pulled the trigger.

SLOAN

Two things happened in that one second. An arrow whizzed by and hit Sloan in the shoulder, and Tara was thrown to the ground by the impact of the bullet. Pain exploded in Sloan's upper arm. He felt the second arrow rip through his body like a marble of molten lava. He screamed out in pain and looked to see an arrow sticking clean through his shoulder. He dropped the gun and clasped his hand on the arrow. Sloan collapsed onto his back with the sound of the crack of the arrow breaking under this weight.

KIERAN

Kieran had seen the bullet hit her in the chest. He had seen her body suddenly thrown backward by the impact of the bullet. Beautiful Yvette had been shot. He dropped everything and ran flat out as fast as he could toward Yvette, where she lay on the ground.

MIKE

Mike sprinted to Tara. He dropped to his knees next to her and ran his hands over her to find the wound and stop the bleeding. "Tara, Tara! Wake up! No! Nooooo!" Mike had seen the bullet hit her in the chest. He had seen her body catapult as she'd jumped in front of him, suddenly thrown backward by the impact of the bullet.

TARA

Tara could hear Mike calling her as if from the other side of a foggy chasm. Her head throbbed, and her eyes were so heavy. She looked through the fog and saw Cara in her baseball tee, her freckly face smiling. The fog grew thicker, enveloping Cara. Tara was slipping away.

"You know the answer, you can do this," Cara said as she disappeared into the fog.

Everything Tara had learned over the last few weeks swirled in her head. Jane Doe dying from hypothermia; the bill of sale for Cara; the words of Sloan. *Sloan!* Suddenly she knew where she recognized him from. He'd said at dinner that he lived in a high-rise, but she had seen his home. She'd staked it out. Twenty-Nine Pasadena. She saw him go in with groceries, too many groceries for a single man, and tampons.

Tara's eyes popped open. "I know where we have to go." Tara sat up and shook her head to clear it.

"Tara? Please be okay," Mike said. "Selfless, loyal, you've proven yourself to me no matter what your name is. You shouldn't have taken that bullet for me. Please don't die. I can't lose you."

"I'm not going to die," Tara said.

"He shot you!" Kieran said, running up the lawn to where Tara lay in the grass. "I can't believe he shot you!"

"Kieran, get out of here. It's dangerous," Mike said.

"Where were you hit?" Kieran said.

"We just need to get out of here before you guys get shot too," Tara said.

"Huh?" Kieran said.

"Someone is shooting arrows at people."

"Yes, me. I only did it because he was hurting you. And he was going to shoot Mike. I'm sorry I didn't stop him," Kieran said.

Tara looked at him and grabbed his face with her hands. She kissed him on top of the head. "Thank you!"

"But how are you okay? I saw him shoot you." Kieran said.

"I don't see any blood," Mike said, his eyes pleading for answers.

She pulled up her black top, revealing the slim, black vest underneath. She knocked on it with her fist. "Bulletproof," she said.

"Thank God," Mike said, hugging her.

"Why are you wearing that?" Kieran asked. "Is our family that scary?"

"Apparently," Mike said.

They heard a groan coming from Sloan.

"Should we help him?" Kieran asked, looking for the first time at the wounded, unconscious man. He gasped.

"That's . . . that's not Dad. It's Sloan!"

BETSY

Betsy stared at the list of names Tori had given her.

Cara Sharp
Jen Brooks
Olivia Garrison
Ellie Aronson
Samantha Jenkins . . .

Nearly thirty names. But right at the top of the list—Cara.

"Are all these girls still at the house?" the detective asked.

"Some of them. Some of them were moved to Pleasure Island," Tori said.

"What's Pleasure Island?"

"I don't know much. It's just a camp, I think. The girls that went there never came back."

A couple entered the police station. They held hands as they looked around the large space. The woman's eyes found Tori first. Her hand flew to her mouth as she ran the short distance between them. She grabbed her daughter and sobbed. Tori's father was right behind her. He leaned down and held Tori's face in his hands before pulling them both into a hug.

Tori looked over her shoulder at Betsy. She slowly pulled away from her parents, ran back to Betsy, and hugged her.

"Thank you! You saved my life."

"Thank you. Your information may save more than one life."

The parents walked arm in arm with Tori between them to the elevators.

Betsy had to find that flophouse, where they were keeping the girls, and find it before midnight. She didn't have much to go on. She looked at her notes.

Two-story, Victorian, white, wrought iron fence, stained glass window, near a waffle shop.

"I guess I'll start looking for Victorian neighborhoods near Waffle Houses?" Betsy said.

"There's got to be a hundred Waffle Houses, not to mention other places that make waffles in Atlanta. That's not much to go on," Henry said.

"It's all we've got."

Betsy's phone rang.

"Hello," she said.

"Hey, it's Tori. I just remembered that the guards always had ice cream from Butler's. Sometimes they'd give us some. I thought that might help."

"Yes. It does. Thank you!"

"If I think of anything else, I'll call."

"Please do."

She clicked off the phone. "Butler's," Betsy said. "That could explain the waffle smell. They make their own waffle cones."

"Well, that's easier to check. There's only five of those in the city," Henry said.

TARA

Tara took Kieran by the shoulders and looked into his eyes. "Kieran, you saved my life, you saved Mike's life, and if we're lucky, you may have even helped to save the life of my sister, if I can get out of here. You did the right thing."

"Why do you want to get out of here?"

"It's a long story, but thanks to you, I have a chance now," Tara said.

Tara turned to Mike. "I have to get to my sister. I know where she is. It's not too far."

"How are we going to leave with the tree blocking the driveway?" Mike asked.

"I don't know," Tara said.

"Harris could take you," Kieran said.

"No one can drive out with the tree down," Tara said.

"I didn't say anything about driving. I'll get him. Meet us in the garage."

Kieran ran off in the direction of the house. Tara heard a low moan behind her. Sloan lay bleeding on the ground; his gun had fallen from his hand a few feet away from him. Tara ran over to it and picked it up. She pointed it at him.

"My sister is at the house, right? The one on Pasadena Avenue?" A look of disgust passed over Sloan's face. "I saw you there, but I didn't make the connection."

"If you know so much, go get her and leave me out of it. We both know you're not going to shoot me," Sloan said.

"Like hell I won't," she fired the weapon, hitting a patch of grass next to Sloan's backside.

"It's too late. She's been sold. I got a good amount too. Virgin, you know."

"Of course, she's a virgin! She's eleven! She wasn't yours to sell. You don't own her!"

"I took her, and thus I owned her." Sloan checked his watch. "She's being sold at midnight. Tick, tock. You'll never make it in time. The guy that bought her, he's a nasty one. He even gives me the creeps. He'll make her disappear. I've sold him a half dozen girls over the years, and I've never seen one of them again."

Tara picked up her foot and brought it down hard on his groin. Sloan moaned out loudly, took a deep, raggedy breath, and slipped out of consciousness again.

KIERAN

Inside, Kieran found Liza in the parlor, wrapping Joe's arm with some gauze.

"That should hold it until the paramedics get here," she said.

"Where's Harris?" Kieran asked.

"He went to the basement to try to get the phones from the safe," Liza said.

Kieran darted out of the room, toward the kitchen. He grabbed a flashlight off the kitchen table and took the metal stairs into the basement two at a time. He found Harris on the floor in front of the safe.

Harris looked up. Tears welled as he ran to his baby brother and threw his arms around him. "I'm sorry, I'm so sorry. I never should have asked you to—" Harris said.

"It's okay."

"No, it's not. I'm so sorry. My sweet, innocent brother. I don't know what I was thinking."

"I didn't do it."

Relief washed over Harris. He pulled Kieran in for a hug. "Thank God. Let's never speak of it again."

"Deal. Oh, but I did shoot Sloan."

Harris looked at his brother for signs that he was joking.

"Wait. You shot Sloan?"

"Yeah, in the shoulder. It's a long story. He'll probably live, but I need to call an ambulance. Any luck with the safe?"

"No, not yet."

"Mike's outside with Yvette. She needs your help."

"Is she hurt?" Harris asked.

"No. She has to get out of here, but the driveway is blocked. You still have your plane here, right? In the garage?"

Harris smiled. "Indeed, I do." He turned toward the stairs; Kieran followed.

"Wait, Kieran, why don't you stay here and see if you can unlock the phones?"

"Sure," Kieran said.

Harris darted upstairs and out into the rain, not bothering to close the door behind him.

TARA

Tara followed Mike out of the rain into the five-car garage. Inside, a black Rolls Royce, a Porsche Spyder, and a red Mercedes filled the space. In front of them, a gray tarp covered a large, irregular shape. She grabbed the tarp and pulled it off, unveiling a small, metal, framed contraption. It had a blue cone nose, a seat, steering with a control panel behind it, and a canvas-covered tail fin. It rested on three wheels, one in the front and two toward the rear. Two canvas-covered wings sat nearby. She was looking at an airplane, a one-seat, tiny airplane.

"Harris bought it a while ago. He flies it around the city sometimes, another one of his hobbies."

Tara gulped. Images of the contraption on fire plummeting to the ground filled her head.

The garage bay door rolled open behind her. Harris stepped inside.

"So, you need a ride?" Harris asked.

"Yeah," Tara said, eyeing the small death trap.

"It's really only made for one, but in an emergency, we can make it work. How much do you weigh?"

"Uhhh—"

"Not to be rude, but we can't fly with more than three hundred pounds. I'm one eighty-four; that means you need to be one sixteen or under."

"I'm one twenty-five."

"Close enough."

"What?"

"I'm sure they've built in some wiggle room. Besides"—Harris took off a small electric box, held it in his hands, judging the weight, and placed it on the ground—"that's the emergency radio. It should counter the extra few pounds."

"Should?" Tara asked, gulping. "Don't we need an emergency radio?"

"Only if there's an emergency."

"But—"

"It's fine. I know what I'm doing. There is one problem though."

"You mean one more problem," Tara said.

"Yeah. It can't fly in heavy rain."

They all turned to the open bay door and the pouring rain outside.

JOE

Chef Joe lay in the parlor, watching what was left of the fire in the fireplace in a state of self-pity. He'd never taken the life of an innocent creature before and was stricken with guilt. He listened to the rain and watched as it ran down the windowpanes. *Poor Coco.*

The small clock on the mantelpiece showed ten minutes after nine o'clock. He couldn't lie here for another minute. Addison was asleep on the opposite couch. He warily sat up, his head swimming with the movement.

Joe stood, cradling his bandaged arm. He walked into the dining room. Coco's body lay on the wide hearth next to the dying fire. Tears rolled as he rubbed her still, soft form. Her floppy ears moved under his hands. He looked up and saw the other soul in the room. *Ellie.* He'd give them both a proper burial. They deserved that much at least. He went to the kitchen and opened the utility closet. He grabbed a crowbar and returned to the dining room. He'd start with Ellie the elephant. He slid a chair over to the large beast. He patted her trunk, slipped the crowbar with one hand behind the wooden mount, and pried it. His arm throbbed with the effort. He heard a loud crack and the beast swung free, broke loose from the wall, and crashed to the ground. At the same time he felt light headed and collapsed into a chair.

TARA

Tara paced near the open garage door. The cooler air from the rainy night calmed her. While they waited out the rain, Tara explained her sister's disappearance and her research that led her to Butler's and Michael Higgins. She explained how she wore a disguise and came to Michael Higgins Industries to try to get to the files there, but that she'd met Mike and thought that might be as good a way as any to get to Michael. She told them that it had never been Michael, but Sloan, framing him all along, and about staking out the house on Pasadena Avenue. It wasn't until a moment ago that she realized it wasn't his house at all but a place where he kept girls.

"What time is it?" Tara asked.

Mike checked his Rolex. "Nine-fifteen."

Tara nodded as a single tear slid down her face. "She's running out of time," Tara said. "If this rain doesn't stop, I'll never see my sister again."

Mike grabbed her and pulled her into his arms. They held each other for a few minutes.

"Well, would you look at that," Harris said. "The rain is letting up."

Tara slipped out of Mike's arms and looked outside. The rain was much lighter now than it had been. She ran out into it and looked up at the sky. "It is slowing down."

Within five minutes the rain had stopped. Harris pushed the machine out of the garage onto the driveway. He took a few minutes to set up. Tara bounced on her heels, nervous about getting into the machine but knowing she had to. Even leaving now, she might still be too late. She was also a bit chilly, being wet from the rain and the temperature having plummeted from the nineties to the high seventies.

"Climb aboard," Harris said.

Tara sighed as she sat on Harris's lap. He adjusted the straps to fit across them both and buckled them in.

"Are you sure it's tight enough?" Tara asked.

"It's just to keep us from falling off the seat. If we go down, it won't matter what kind of seat belt we are wearing."

"I can't do this." She was breathing erratically and waving her hands. "I can't do this."

"It's all right. I've been up hundreds of times. It is actually quite safe," Harris said.

Mike walked over to Tara and put her face in his hands and locked eyes with her. "Breathe . . . you can do this. I just saw you take a bullet. You can do this . . . for Cara."

The thought of Cara emboldened her. She exhaled deeply and nodded. "Okay, let's go," Tara said.

Tara held her breath as Harris drove the contraption down the driveway. Muddy water sprayed up from the cobblestones, covering them in brown speckles. The speed increased as they headed toward the tree line. *Not enough room. We're going to crash full speed into the trees and the high wall.* Tara closed her eyes and braced for impact. She felt a gentle lifting in her belly. She opened her eyes, and they were up. She flinched as they brushed the tops of the trees and rose above the estate and off across the steamy city.

MIKE

Mike stood in the driveway at exactly 9:30, watching two of the people he cared about most rise into the air and barely clear the trees. He watched until they were out of sight. He smiled, hoping they'd find Cara and that it wouldn't start raining again. He also hoped he could work things out with Tara.

Mike walked toward the garage and saw a shadow out of the corner of his eye. He turned.

"Oh, you scared me," Mike said as someone approached him from the house carrying a cast-iron skillet.

"I'm sorry."

"For what?" Mike asked.

"For this."

The last thing Mike saw was the heavy skillet crashing into the side of his face. He was unconscious before he hit the cobblestone driveway.

TARA

Harris's arms wrapped around her to reach the control panel. She leaned to one side slightly so he could see them, but not too much because there was nothing but empty sky and eventually the ground below. She clutched the bottom of the seat so tightly that she lost feeling in her fingertips. The city rose out of a blanket of green treetops and steam. She tried not to look down and instead across at the tall buildings of downtown Atlanta.

They skirted the edge of the city, and she found it strange to see skyscrapers from this perspective.

"Which way?" Harris asked.

Tara got her bearings and pointed in the direction they needed to go. After a few minutes, the cool wind began to make her cheeks tingle. Her fingers, too, were getting cold, but she couldn't release them from their death grip on the seat. Once she was confident that they were close, she pointed at the ground and Harris circled, looking for a place to land.

Harris lowered the flying machine onto a flat, empty road and rolled to a stop.

"Thank you, Harris. You are a literal lifesaver."

He unbuckled the seat belt. Tara hopped out a little too eagerly, ready to be back on the ground.

"It's not for everybody, but I sure do love it."

"It was beautiful, and we didn't crash! Thanks a million!" Tara turned toward the house. Harris got out and followed along.

"Oh, you don't have to come. You've done enough already, Harris."

"I might as well. You may need a ride home after this."

"Oh, I hope not," Tara said.

"I told Mike I would come with you. You know, I've never seen him so smitten before. Are you going to break his heart?"

"I hope not. I mean, I did lie to him for the entirety of our relationship, but I really do love him."

"Okay, so what's the plan?"

"Sneak into the house and find my sister without being noticed."

"Gotcha, lead the way."

Tara and Harris ran down the street to the address and looked up at the two-story Victorian house. The house was white with a navy-blue door. She elbowed Harris and nodded toward the door. Set into the wooden door was a stained glass window with the black outline of a triangle and a semicircle on top of it, an ice-cream cone.

"We're in the right place," she said.

The lights were on inside, and she could see men sitting around watching TV in the front room. Tara walked up the front steps onto the front porch.

"Wait," Harris said, "what's your plan?"

Tara peeked in the front window. "She's here. I can feel it. But how do I get to her?" She stepped off the front porch and out into the grass. There was a low roof over the porch with the second-story windows just above it. "She must be upstairs. Maybe I could sneak into one of those windows. Can you boost me up?"

"Sure."

"If the windows are unlocked, I can sneak in."

"And if they're not?"

"Maybe if I knock, the girls will let me in? I've got to try."

"I know. Go ahead. I'll keep an eye out down here." Harris knelt. "Climb up onto my shoulders, like a cheerleader."

"What?"

"Don't worry, I won't let you fall."

Tara stepped onto his back and held his shoulders with her hands. She placed one foot on one shoulder and hesitated.

"I can't."

Harris put his hand firmly on the foot on his shoulder. "I did some cheerleading in high school."

"Okay, but I didn't—"

"You can do this."

Tara shut her eyes and put the other foot on his shoulder and slowly stood up halfway. Harris held both her feet with his hands and rose from the ground.

"Stand tall. It will be easier for me," Harris said.

Tara straightened out her body and reached for the edge of the porch roof. She was just able to grab it. She swung one leg up onto the roof and then the other. She turned to Harris and gave him a thumbs up before approaching the windows. She tried each of the three, and all were locked. Dark curtains kept her from being able to see what was inside the rooms. She decided to tap lightly on the window, but nothing happened. She tried to pull the window open, but it held fast. *Damn! Probably locked.* She crawled back to the edge of the roof.

"I think I need to break one of the windows," she whispered. "Throw me a rock or something."

Harris disappeared and returned with a rock a moment later. He tossed it up to her. "Let me try to distract them."

Harris approached the door and knocked.

HARRIS

A large man with a tattoo of a tiger climbing from his cheek onto his eyebrow, tail wrapping up and around his ear, answered the door.

"Hello. Harris Higgins. Sloan asked me to come and inspect the operation here and report back to him."

"At this hour?"

"He wanted me to come when you wouldn't suspect anything. How many men do you have here?"

"I don't believe you. Get out of here," Tiger Tattoo said, pulling a gun.

"Whoa. Put that away. A little quick on the draw there. Let's say I was some innocent bystander you've just let on that something is wrong here. We can't have that. Now put that away before someone sees it," Harris said, looking around him as if the neighbors could be watching. "Do you know who I am? My father is Michael Higgins, Sloan's business partner. Sloan has asked me to run this operation for him, but I'm not sure this outfit is up to my standards."

"Wait, run the operation for Sloan?"

"That's right. And if you'd kindly show me inside."

"Okay, sure, right away." He led Harris inside to the living room, where three tough guys looked up from the television.

"Hey, guys, this is Harris. He says he's taking over the business for Sloan."

Harris smiled and tried to look like a serious businessman. The man closest to him began to laugh, and so did the others.

"Taking over for Sloan, are you?" one of them mocked.

"That's right."

"Okay, enough joking around," Tiger Tattoo said. He raised his gun again and put it to Harris's head. "Who are you, and why are you here?"

"I told you. When Sloan finds out about this—"

They all began to laugh again. "Nice try, but Sloan doesn't run this operation."

Harris looked up, confused. "But he was the one smuggling the girls."

"He works here. He's indebted to the boss. He's more of a lackey, running errands, that sort of thing."

A loud crash sounded above them.

"You're not alone, are you?" Tiger Tattoo said. He nodded at the others, who pulled guns and went upstairs.

TARA

Tara wasn't sure what Harris was doing inside, but it had been a few minutes. She had no way to know what was going on inside. She couldn't stand doing nothing, knowing that Cara may be only a few feet away. She took the rock and smashed the window. She tried to knock the big pieces of glass loose before scurrying inside, carefully avoiding the sharp edges.

Inside, she saw mattresses on the floor with girls lying on them. There were five in the first room. She studied their faces.

"Cara? Is Cara here?"

They all stared at her blankly. She heard footsteps on the stairs. She slipped into the hallway and saw the shadows of men coming upstairs.

"Get out!" Harris screamed from downstairs.

Unable to get back to the window, she opened a closet door and pulled it shut to hide.

She heard the men inspecting the rooms upstairs, feet running past the closet.

"You think they left? Go check outside," a voice said just outside the door.

Tara sighed with relief as she heard footfalls descending the steps. She waited a minute before she continued her search for Cara. She heard one more pair of footsteps walking slowly along the hall. They stopped right in front of the door. The shadow of two feet shone beneath the door. She held her breath.

"Gotcha," the man said as he ripped open the door and pulled her out by her hair.

MIKE

A slow scraping sound roused Mike. He opened his eyes, but there was nothing to see. It was pitch-black. His arms and ankles were bound and his mouth taped. The floor he lay on was cold, like concrete. The scraping sound continued. His heart raced. He didn't know what the sound was, or who was making it, or what they wanted with him.

As the sound got louder, a bit of light slipped through a crack under a door. He was in some kind of file room, not much bigger than his closet at home, which, granted, was large for a closet. The light grew brighter as the sound got closer. He didn't dare make a sound.

Then the sound stopped, and the light faded away. He was alone in the dark.

HARRIS

Harris hadn't expected the kick. He'd been watching them drag Tara down the stairs by her hair when he'd felt the pain erupt in his stomach. He couldn't breathe.

"You've caused me a lot of extra work," Tiger Tattoo said.

Harris inhaled deeply. It hurt. Maybe a broken rib.

Tiger Tattoo pulled Harris's sweatband down over his mouth, ripped a piece of duct tape off a spool, and taped the sweatband there. "You're lucky the boss said not to shoot you. Your little girlfriend may not be as lucky."

Tiger Tattoo pulled a long piece of duct tape from the roll, ripping it with his teeth. He wrapped Harris's arms together in front of him and bound his feet.

Tiger Tattoo grabbed Tara from the other guard. He pulled a hard eyeglass case from his pocket, flipped it open, and pulled a syringe out. He looked at Harris and winked as he jabbed it into Tara's neck.

"MMMMMRRPH . . . MMMMRPH!" Harris screamed as he tried to stand. One of the guards put a booted foot on him, holding him to the ground.

Tara looked at Harris with panic and tried to wiggle free of Tiger Tattoo's grasp. Her eyes lost focus and fluttered closed. She slowly slumped forward, slipping from the guard's arms to the floor.

"MMMMMRRPH . . . MMMMRPH!" It was no use. He saw Tiger Tattoo roll his eyes before pulling out a second syringe.

He kneeled down next to Harris. "Next time, know who you are messing with." He felt a sharp sting as the syringe hit him in the neck. A wave of heat washed through his body as his eyelids grew impossibly heavy. The last thing he saw before he lost the battle to keep them open was the guard pick Tara up, throw her over his shoulder, and carry her out the back door.

O'HARA

It was time the safe with the phones was opened. Afterall, there was an important sale tonight.

O'Hara entered the code into the safe, which popped open compliantly. The pile of cell phones sat glowing with various notifications.

O'Hara grabbed the one on top and dialed. It was answered in just one ring. They knew not to make O'Hara wait.

"Is everything on track for the sale?" O'Hara asked.

"No, I'm sorry. We had to postpone until tomorrow. The client couldn't fly in with the storm. He'll be at Pleasure Island tomorrow."

"Be sure that he is. I'll be there to greet him."

O'Hara hung up the phone with the same hand that held a small hourglass keychain.

CHAPTER 9

SATURDAY

BETSY

Betsy took a deep breath as she stood in the dark street outside a two-story Victorian house with a porch swing and navy-blue front door. There was a small glass window inset into the door. Clear beveled glass surrounded the black outline of a triangle with a semicircle on top of it. A shiver ran down the detective's spine at the thought of what could, at this very moment, be happening inside.

Betsy had used Google Maps's street view to find houses matching the description Tori gave them. They had hit the jackpot and found the house that Tori had described, right down to the door with their symbol, a triangle with a semicircle on top, an ice-cream cone.

Betsy looked up and down the street. The line of Victorian-style houses sat innocently, projecting an air of perfection and calm. No one was around at this hour, nearly 1 a.m. No matter how lovely each house on this road was, inner problems existed, a creaky stair, a leaky roof, a termite infestation, human trafficking. There was no such thing as perfection. Betsy had learned it the hard way. Unfortunately, this wasn't just true of real estate but also of people. Just like this row of houses with their shiny exteriors and hidden depravity, people were full of hidden darkness. She used to think people were generally well meaning and good, but she'd learned that everyone, without exception, had their own inner decay, to varying degrees, of course. Her years as a police officer had reinforced this truth. Everyone, every single person you pass on the street or share an elevator with, has some inner darkness. Maybe it's an affair or an addiction or vanity or any number of other vices.

A strong wind caught a trash can and knocked it over with a bang. All eyes and a number of guns turned toward it briefly. The remnants of Maude, a category-four hurricane down in the Gulf, had worked its way inland and wreaked havoc in Atlanta. Trees and cars lay cracked and overturned, strewn about as if the whole world had tipped. All that remained of the powerful storm was the gusty wind and scattered power outages.

The wind blew Betsy's long dark hair into her eyes and mouth. She breathed in the cool, wet air deep into her lungs. She pulled her hair back into a messy bun with a rubber band.

"You ready?" asked Henry, her police partner. He stood next to her, across the street from the house.

Betsy nodded. "Always."

A line of officers circled the house. Betsy pulled her gun from the arm holster she wore over a white T-shirt.

She darted across the road, Henry with her as they got in line behind the officers at the front door. The head officer banged rapidly on the door.

"Police," he hollered and kicked the door in. The team filed steadily in behind. It took about five seconds for Betsy and Henry to reach the front door. The sound of boots echoed eerily throughout the house. She waited to hear some reaction from those inside but heard nothing, no screaming, no commotion, nothing. She held her gun to her chest and raced through the interior. But it was obvious they had cleared out. No one was home. She had missed them.

Betsy wandered through the living room and into the kitchen where a half-eaten bowl of spaghetti sat on the table. She ran her hand above it. It was still warm.

"We didn't miss them by much," Henry said, entering the kitchen after her.

"That's comforting," she said.

"Up here," an officer called down from above.

Betsy looked at Henry and headed for the stairs. She took them two at a time as Henry followed. In an upstairs bedroom, they found a man, early twenties, with a Puma sweatband duct taped over his mouth, his head lolled to one side. His hands were tied in front of him with duct tape. His body was taped to a kitchen chair, the only furniture in the room besides four mattresses on the floor. Henry pulled a Swiss Army knife from his pocket and began cutting the bindings loose.

"Get the paramedics up here," Betsy called as she took his pulse. It was steady, though a tad slow. "Sir, can you hear me?" The man's head raised, and his eyes opened briefly. "I'm not going to lie. This is going to hurt," she said. Without a moment's hesitation, she grabbed the corner of the duct tape by prying it up with her fingernail and ripping it off quickly.

"Son of a—" the man said, his eyes popping open as he looked frantically about himself.

"I'm Detective Betsy Turner. Can you tell me your name?" she said. "What are you doing here?"

"Long story."

HARRIS

Harris woke up unsure if minutes or hours had passed. His head felt heavy, and he was worried but not immediately sure what he was worried about. He tried to pry his eyes open, but they felt so heavy.

Pain erupted as duct tape was ripped off his face.

"Son of a—" Harris said opening his eyes in panic. It all came back to him, Tiger Tattoo carrying Tara away, drugging him in the neck. What did they want with him? Were they going to kill him after all?

Someone was leaning over him. A woman. She had a badge.

"I'm Detective Betsy Turner. Can you tell me your name?" the voice asked. "What are you doing here?"

She was with the police. He wasn't in imminent danger. He could go back to sleep.

But . . . she was talking. . . . She wanted to know his name . . . how he got here. He tried to form the words but couldn't. He shook his head to clear it.

"Long story," he managed to say. Just the idea of retelling it exhausted him. He gave in and let sleep carry him away again.

BETSY

"Sir . . . sir, what's your name?" Betsy asked as they loaded the man onto the stretcher.

"This will have to wait," the paramedic said. "He can't help you until he's been treated."

"Call me as soon as he's awake," Betsy said.

She sighed, her brain foggy, her emotions raw from lack of sleep. She'd been up for over forty hours. And for what? Something deep inside her brain called for her attention. She stared into the gray horizon and thought it out. There had been girls here. And those girls had been connected to ice cream, to Butler's.

Henry walked over to her. "Come on, I'll drive you home. You can catch a few hours of sleep before he's ready to talk."

"No," she said. "I can't sleep, not while Cara is still out there."

"We've missed the deadline. There's nothing more we can do."

"We don't know that. We can't stop now. We're so close."

"What do you have in mind?"

"Let's go talk to the owner of Butler's. Let's go talk to Michael Higgins. Can you get me his address?"

As they drove across the city, they passed a Waffle House. Betsy parked while Henry ran in and got two coffees. They drove toward the address, 901 Riverside Dr. Betsy had to swerve to avoid the occasional downed limb.

Betsy looked at the homes along Riverside as they drove by. It was *the* street in Atlanta. Every house was huge, beautiful with immaculate lawns. Each bigger, grander than the last, at least the ones you could see from the street. Many had huge privacy walls surrounding the property. The 901 address proved to be one of them. Large ivy-covered walls hid the home from view.

They pulled up to the gate and got out. A large tree blocked the driveway. Betsy moved closer. A massive oak had fallen just inside the ivy-covered walls, making it impassable either by car or by foot.

The large tree had probably been standing for a century or more. The trunk was at least five feet in diameter. The trunk was not what blocked the driveway but rather the thick top of the tree, which had cracked on its descent and now lay like a round ball of broken limbs, some sticking straight up into the air twenty feet high.

"I'll call it in and see if we can get someone out here to clear the tree."

Betsy tried to find a way to get around the tree, but it was impassible. They had no choice but to wait for the city to come and clear it. Betsy looked past the tree at the large brick home. No lights on, not inside, not outside; it was pitch-black. She looked at the houses on either side and the one across the street, and they were equally black. The storm must have knocked out their power.

Betsy climbed into the passenger side of the police car and waited for the city to come clear the tree.

When she awoke, the sky had turned from black to a pre-dawn grayish pink.

"Morning," Henry said.

"How long was I asleep?"

"About four hours. It's almost six o'clock."

"What?"

"You needed it. Besides, it was just a waiting game anyway."

"Did you sleep?"

"Yeah. For a couple of hours. They've just about cleared a path for us to walk through."

Betsy followed Henry through the slim cut in the limbs and up the driveway. The lot was wider than it was long. The house was situated sideways on the lot with the front door facing the right side of the lot.

"Illogical madness," Henry said.

It was eerily dark and quiet as they approached. As they reached the front door, they saw a parking pad on the far side of the house. Henry whipped out his iPad. Betsy made a mental note of the cars parked there.

A blue Porsche Taycan, a yellow Corvette, an orange Mercedes G-class, a gray BMW sedan, and a blue 1967 Shelby Mustang GT500.

"I like that one," Henry said, gesturing to the Shelby.

"I like them all," Betsy said.

They turned to the house, Georgian-style with soft-red brick and a wide, white front porch with ceiling fans and potted ferns. The wooden double front door, inset with beveled glass, stood open.

"Thank God you are here!" a woman with a Latina accent said, running out of the house. "Please come quickly." The gorgeous woman with long shiny black hair and tan skin wore a red silk robe. She led them through the foyer and pushed open the French doors. She pointed toward a man-shaped mound next to the pool.

"I found him; he was already . . . there was nothing I could do. . . . He was gone when I found him."

"Can you identify the body for us?" Henry asked.

"It's my husband, Michael Higgins Sr. Oh, how could this have happened?"

Betsy looked at the rain-soaked body. She looked up at the balcony above the body. She saw out of the corner of her eye three faces peering down at them from an upstairs window.

"Could you please gather everyone downstairs?" Betsy asked the new widow.

"I'll call it in," Henry said.

Betsy walked onto the pool deck. The pool chairs were all overturned, and a large red umbrella had blown up against the house.

Betsy kneeled next to the body. Glassy eyes stared up at the sky. Part of his forehead was caved inward. She knew before she took his pulse that he was dead.

Henry was taking notes, looking at the body from various angles.

"It could have been a fall," Betsy said, looking up at the small Juliet balcony above their heads.

"From one story up? That's unlikely. We'll know more after Aja gets here."

"There's no way this is not connected to Cara," Betsy said to Henry. "Something here will point us to her. I just hope it's not too late."

The faint sound of a man moaning carried on the wind. Betsy pointed her light toward the lawn. The sun was beginning to rise, and she could just make out the shape of a man lying on the grass.

"There's someone out there," Betsy said.

"Police! Identify yourself," Henry said as they ran toward him.

"Help," came the feeble reply from the grass.

Even from a distance, Betsy could see he was in bad shape. An arrow protruded from his upper torso. She ran toward him and knelt next to him, skidding a bit on the grass. Beads of perspiration covered his face, and his clothes were soaked in rain and sweat. He had been sick in the grass as a puddle of congealed vomit sat next to and on his face.

"We're going to help you, sir," Betsy said. "Henry, call it in. Tell them to get the tree fully cleared so we can get an ambulance up here."

She turned back to the man and began examining the arrow.

"No, the arrow is okay, it's the snake bite," Sloan said, pointing to his leg while holding his breath and wincing. Two red puncture wounds marked the center of a large red swollen lump on Sloan's leg.

Nikki ran toward them, down the lawn, her red robe flapping in the wind.

"You need to go inside," Betsy said. But she just stood staring at the man.

They heard approaching sirens. "The ambulance is on its way," Betsy said. "Do you know who did this to you?" she asked Sloan.

"I have a pretty good idea."

"He's delirious. Don't listen to him," Nikki said, approaching despite Betsy's order not to.

"Nikki, they're going to figure it out," Sloan said. "They're detectives. There's only one person in that house with awards for archery."

"Stop talking," Nikki said. "Now!"

TARA

Tara was aware of penetrating cold even before she woke up. She had dreamed of treading water and fighting to stay afloat in a pool-sized churning vat of ice cream. Girls were lined up on a diving board, stepping blindly off the edge into the swirling vortex along with chocolate chips and caramel ribbons. They screamed as they spun around until they were finally swallowed by the dense cold concoction. Cara was next in line. She stepped to the edge of the diving board. Tara tried to scream out her name, but her voice was gone. She was powerless as she watched Cara step off.

Tara's eyes flew open. Her lungs heaved. It was pitch-black and so cold as she lay on a hard metal floor. Her limbs were heavy and awkward. She didn't try to move them. The drugs were pulling her back under. Her eyes were so heavy. The cold floor embraced her as she fell back into a drugged sleep.

BETSY

"What's your name?" Betsy asked as she kneeled next to the man with the arrow in his chest.

"Sloan Peterson."

"Sloan Peterson? You are a partial owner of Butler's? Is that correct?"

"Yes."

"Do you know anything about a missing girl named Cara?"

"No! Why are you asking? Can't you see I've been shot! I'm the victim here."

"Anything you can think of could prove useful."

Two paramedics rolled a stretcher toward where Sloan lay on the grass.

"Can you tell me the name of the man who shot you?" Betsy asked.

"Don't say anything, Sloan. I'm getting a lawyer," Nikki called.

"No. I didn't see anything," Sloan said.

"A lawyer?" Betsy said. "But he's the victim. Sloan, you said earlier that someone in the house had won awards for archery. Who?"

The paramedics worked to stabilize the arrow, to prevent further injury en route to the hospital.

"The kid, Kieran. I really liked that kid too," Sloan said.

"This is madness! Don't say another word Sloan!" Nikki yelled.

"You think a kid shot you?" Betsy asked.

"Maybe not. I don't know. You're the detective," Sloan said.

"If Michael had been hiding girls, where would he have hidden them?" the detective asked Nikki.

"Oh, this is absurd!" she snapped.

The stretcher jostled and Sloan bumped around as the paramedics rolled over the uneven lawn.

"I don't want to tell you how to do your job," Sloan said. "But a little pain medicine might be called for in this instance."

"Let's get you to the ambulance, and then we'll worry about that," the paramedic responded.

"Well, mind the bumps then, would you?" Sloan said.

Inside, a second set of paramedics were at work. "She won't wake up," Liza said.

"What's her name?" Henry asked.

"Addison."

"Do you know what's wrong with Addison?"

"I—" Her eyes darted up to meet Betsy's and then flashed back to the paramedic. "She took some sleeping pills."

The paramedics looked at each other.

"Ma'am," Betsy said, "could you step over here for a moment?"

"I want to stay with my daughter."

"She's in good hands now. I just want to ask you some more questions so we can get a better feel of how best to help Addison. Do you know how many sleeping pills she took?"

"Not more than three, at the most."

"Does she do that a lot?"

"No, never."

"So why did she tonight?"

Liza looked at her daughter. "I just . . . I don't think she meant to."

"What does that mean?"

"I don't know."

As they loaded Addison from the couch onto the stretcher, an empty syringe rolled out of her pocket and onto the floor. Betsy leaned down and carefully picked up the syringe with a gloved hand before sliding it into an evidence bag. She handed it to a nearby uniformed officer. "Have that tested."

"Does your daughter have a history of drug use?" the paramedic asked Liza.

"No. Nothing like that. Addison did not do drugs," Liza insisted. "It was probably just something for Michael. Addison was working as his nurse."

Betsy looked at Henry and nodded to the uniformed officer. "Put a rush on that."

"You don't think she hurt him? Anyway, he didn't die from drugs or anything. Didn't he die from falling off the balcony?" Liza asked.

"We don't know anything yet. Right now, we just want to gather as much evidence as possible so we can have a clear picture of the events that transpired here last night. If you could wait here, we'll want to ask you some questions in a few minutes."

Betsy followed the stretcher into the driveway, where it was loaded into one of two waiting ambulances. The wind swept through the breezeway between the house and the tall wall surrounding the property.

A car pulled up the driveway and parked out of the way of the ambulance. Aja Patel, the medical examiner, climbed out.

"Good morning," she said to Betsy.

"I'll take you to the deceased," Betsy said.

HENRY

Henry paced the crime scene, studying it from various angles. Occasionally, he leaned his head to the side for a few seconds before scribbling something down. Rain-diluted blood had pooled up on one tile that was marginally lower than its neighbor.

Aja pulled on gloves and crouched down next to the body of Michael Higgins.

Henry pulled his phone from his pocket and held it toward the balcony above the deceased. Using an app, he measured the distance from the balcony to the ground—fifteen feet.

"I doubt he died from the fall," Henry said.

"The fall is irrelevant. He was already dead before he left that balcony," Aja said. "I'll have to run some more tests to prove it."

"Even if he jumped?" Betsy asked.

"He landed headfirst, so I think jumping is extremely unlikely. No one commits suicide jumping off a first-story balcony, headfirst. In fact, a fall from that height is easily survivable. Furthermore, if he had died from the fall, his skull would be flat and even from hitting the solid ground, like a ball of Play-Doh hitting the ground. But his injuries were concave, as if an object went into his head in one spot, causing the bone to bend inward. I believe he was hit in the head before being pushed out the window. I'll run tests to see if I can find any evidence of what he may have been hit in the head with prior to going over the side."

"Good work. Anything else?" Betsy said.

"You're looking at a time of death between eight and ten, based on the body temps, factoring in the rain, which would have cooled him off more quickly. There are a few other noteworthy things. Look at his neck." She pointed. "Do you see the bruise there?"

"Yeah."

"It looks almost like a handprint, like someone tried to choke him. But he did not die of strangulation. There are a few pieces of skin under his nails as well. They will be tested for DNA, of course, and I'll let you know once that's back."

"He may have gotten a piece of his killer before he went down," Betsy said.

"It looks that way."

"So, are you ruling this a homicide?"

"Yes."

"With that tree falling last night that means the killer is still here."

BETSY

Betsy and Henry entered the home and found four people gathered in various stages of mourning seated in a grand living room. Betsy studied them. She'd entered hundreds of houses in the moments and hours after a death and learned to read the faces of those left behind.

Nikki, the new widow, stood at an oak bar at the back of the room, still wearing her red robe. She was drinking coffee. Given the morning she was having, there was probably a splash of something in it. She held a handkerchief and dabbed at her dry eyes. Betsy reasoned that Nikki's grief was an act. There was no substance to it.

A man with curly hair and glasses in a white chef's jacket sat in a leather chair next to the window, being attended by a paramedic. The chef would be the least biased in a case like this. His version of events would likely hold the truth.

Henry had taken out his iPad and was taking notes.

Addison's mother sat on a red couch consoling a teenage boy.

"I'm Detective Turner. This is Detective Sanders. We'll be looking into the matter of Michael Higgins's death. Could you all please introduce yourselves?"

"As you know, I'm Nikki Higgins. I live here with my husband, Michael." Nikki wiped her eyes, although there was no moisture there, and took a deep breath. "Our son Kieran lives here with us," she said, gesturing to the boy on the couch, who looked strikingly like his mother. He was adorable, with dark-brown hair and piercingly green eyes that were red and swollen. Betsy sensed real pain in the child's green-gold eyes that simultaneously asked for help and spoke to a guilty conscious. He couldn't have been much more than thirteen, and she hoped to God she wouldn't have to prosecute him for murdering his father or shooting Sloan. "This is Michael's ex-wife, Liza," Nikki said, gesturing toward the woman who sat holding Kieran. Liza's face did not grieve, nor did it celebrate. Heartsick was the emotion that came to Betsy's mind. It was odd that Nikki wasn't the one comforting her son.

"I'm Chef Joe," the curly-haired man by the window said. It was clear that Nikki had no intention of introducing him. A paramedic was inspecting his arm that hung in a homemade sling.

"We never had an any trouble with him until last night," Nikki said. "He killed Coco."

Henry stopped writing, and everyone in the room looked at Chef Joe.

"Who is Coco?" Betsy asked.

"My dog, a King Charles spaniel and a rare beauty, and now she's dead." Real tears sprang to Nikki's eyes.

"Joe, is there something you want to tell me?" Betsy asked.

He looked around at all the eyes staring at him and rubbed his hands together.

"It was an accident," Joe said.

"It was no accident! That man killed my Coco!" Nikki yelled.

"I hoped to never see him again, but that damn tree fell, and he was forced to stay here. I should have let him sleep outside in the rain."

"We need to take him to the hospital," the paramedic said as he loaded the chef onto a third stretcher and wheeled him out of the room.

"Just wait a second before you go. I want to ask him some questions," Betsy said.

"We'll be outside."

"I'll be right out," Betsy said.

"Good riddance!" Nikki yelled after him.

"The death of Michael Higgins has been ruled a homicide," Henry announced.

Nikki gasped and put her hand to her mouth. Liza looked at the floor and clutched her purse tightly. Kieran looked around in bewilderment.

A police officer returned from searching the house. "There's no one else here," he said.

"But that's . . . impossible," Liza said. "Where are they?"

"Where are who?" Betsy asked.

"There were more of us here," Liza said. "My sons, Mike and Harris, are missing. And Mike's new girlfriend, Yvette. All three of them were here."

"I'm sure they are around here somewhere," Nikki said. "They couldn't have left with the tree blocking the driveway."

"Actually—" Kieran said.

"Let the police ask their questions, Kieran," Nikki interrupted.

"Go ahead, Kieran," Betsy said.

"Never mind," Kieran said.

"Maybe they're sleeping," Liza said. "Kieran, can you go check on them?"

"No, we'll have an officer do that," Henry said. He nodded to an officer who went upstairs to check for the others.

"I don't know about Mike, but Harris and Yvette aren't here," Kieran said.

Everyone looked at him, waiting for him to continue.

"They left, last night after . . ."—his face flushed red, and he looked at the floor—"after dinner."

"Before the tree fell down, you mean? What time was that?" Betsy asked.

"No, after the tree," Kieran said.

"How did they leave if the tree was blocking the driveway?" Henry asked.

"They flew," Kieran said.

Betsy's jaw dropped. "Kieran, did you say they flew?"

"Yes. Harris—" Kieran started to say.

"Kieran, don't say anymore," Nikki again interrupted. "I'm sorry, but now that it is a murder investigation, we are going to have to have a lawyer before we talk with you any further."

"But Kieran, they may be in danger. Please tell the detectives what you know," Liza said.

"No, they were fine when they left. Don't worry. And Mike must be around here somewhere," Kieran said.

"Not another word, Kieran," Nikki scolded.

"I don't want to intrude any longer than we have to on your family during this time, Mrs. Higgins. But I do need a better understanding of the events of last night. Please come to the station later today. Have your lawyer meet us there."

"We'll try to come by later this morning, if possible," Nikki said. "I guess we'd better prepare a bag. I'll need to call and have the lake house made ready. We'll stay there while the house is processed."

Nikki and her son went up the stairs with a police escort to pack bags. Nikki dialed her phone as she walked. "I need the lake house prepared for us as soon as possible. We will arrive this afternoon."

"Please, I don't understand. Where are my sons?" Liza asked.

"I don't know. Call us if you hear from them." Betsy said.

"Shouldn't we put a missing person report on them?" Liza asked.

"It hasn't been twenty-four hours," Betsy said. "Why don't you go to the hospital to see Addison. I'm sure we'll hear from the others soon."

"Of course," Liza said.

JOE

In the ambulance, Chef Joe sat rubbing his hands together. It was an old habit, and it hurt to do it now with his broken arm. Sweat dripped down his back. The detectives were walking toward him. He took a deep breath. *Remain calm,* he told himself.

"What happened to Coco?" Betsy asked.

"It was an accident. I swear."

"Tell me what you know."

"I made Michael a special meal at his daughter Addison's request because of his health issues. Addison takes care of her father who has medical issues. Michael got angry when I served him chicken. I made lamb for everyone else. So, he gave his plate to the dog and took Addison's meal for himself. The chicken had straw mushrooms in it. Straw mushrooms can be toxic to dogs. I loved that dog. I would never take an innocent life intentionally."

"How do we know that you didn't poison the food, trying to kill Michael? When he didn't die, maybe you went back to finish the job."

Chef Joe's eyes searched their faces. He rubbed his hands together. "I didn't poison him. Didn't he fall off the balcony? He wasn't poisoned. If he was, I didn't do it."

"We're leaving now. We need to take him to the hospital to have his arm set," the paramedic said.

"We'll be in touch in the next couple of days," Betsy said. "Don't leave town."

Joe nodded, breathed a sigh of relief. "Actually, guys," Joe said, turning to the paramedics, "I think I'll pass on the ambulance ride. I don't have health insurance."

"I would strongly advise you to come with us. Your arm needs attention. You don't want to further injure yourself. A broken bone can easily nick an artery or blood vessel, or you could cause nerve damage. The arm needs to be seen by a doctor," the paramedic said.

"I appreciate your concern, but I'm not going with you," Joe said.

"I'm going to need you to sign this refusal of care against medical advice form."

As the ambulance drove off, Joe removed from his pocket a pair of keys he'd grabbed off the entryway table and hit the unlock button. He smiled as the car lights flashed at him in response.

BETSY

As Betsy walked away from Chef Joe, a pang hit her stomach. She didn't like him leaving. Something about him gave her pause. But she had no reason to detain him. Besides, he'd be at the hospital if they needed him.

After all the suspects had left the premises, Betsy and Henry searched the entire property. The twenty-two-thousand-square-foot home would take a couple of hours to thoroughly peruse. She sighed as she followed Henry from the sitting room into the dining room. The remnants of a fire crackled away in the fireplace.

"You don't see that everyday," Betsy said.

"No, you don't" Henry agreed,

The head of an elephant mounted to a wooden backing leaned up against the side of the fireplace. Next to it on the ground was a curled up dog.

"Oh, hello little guy," Betsy said when she saw the dog. "Did you sleep here to stay warm?" She said, leaning down to pet the dog. The dog did not move. It was cold to the touch. "I think I found Coco," Betsy said, looking up at Henry.

There were deep gouges in the drywall and a dusting of the broken pieces along the mantle.

"Why it was pried off the wall?" Henry wondered.

"It seems to have been done quickly and carelessly. The Molly bolts used to secure it to the wall are still there."

Betsy looked at Henry blankly.

"They're used for hanging heavy things," Henry said.

They moved on to the next room. Henry went first, holding his gun and flashlight in case anyone awaited him there. But it was as still and quiet as the rest of the house.

"That's weird," Henry said.

"What?"

"I'm not sure what type of mushrooms these are in the trash. Joe said he used straw mushrooms, but they don't look like this. I'll have them tested." Henry put some carefully into an evidence bag.

They left the kitchen through the back door and watched Aja, the medical examiner, as she prepared to take the body away.

Betsy stood and looked at the house. The pool was surrounded on three sides by the U-shaped home. They had searched one wing of the house. Betsy walked to the end of the parallel wing of the house. French doors led inside from a covered sitting area with a stone fireplace and pizza oven. She grabbed the door handle and stopped. "Wait," she said. "There's the sheath to a knife here but no knife."

They entered a wood-paneled home office. There was a large desk in the middle with built-in bookshelves and filing cabinets on the wall behind the desk. Betsy rifled through the papers on the desk. She opened a couple of drawers.

"We'll have to have all of this examined," she said as she opened the bottom drawer of the desk. "SON OF A—!" She jumped onto the chair and slammed the drawer closed.

Rattling emanated from the drawer.

"I guess you found the occupant from the smashed terrarium over here. Sounds like it's a crotalus horridus, common name, timber rattlesnake," Henry said.

They taped the drawer shut, left a note, and called animal control.

After the office, they came to a billiard room and then a library with no clues.

"We'd better do a walk-through of the upstairs before we leave," Betsy said.

"After you," Henry said, gesturing to the staircase.

At the top of the stairs, a breezeway opened to the parlor below, connecting the two wings. A grand chandelier hung at eye level over the foyer below.

They went left first into a large game room. A huge sectional couch and video game chairs faced a large screen TV. A hammock hung from the ceiling and a basketball goal on one wall. Behind the couch, a foosball table sat next to a table covered with Legos.

Henry knelt next to the Legos. He took his iPad out and took a few photos of the table from different angles. "Have a look at this," Henry said.

There, amidst Hogwarts, the Bat Cave, a city scene with skyscrapers, and the Death Star, was a perfect replica of the Higgins estate.

"Woah, that's this house," Betsy said.

"Yes, it is. I wonder . . ." Henry trialed off as he wrote. "I'd like to have these two mini-figures dusted for fingerprints." He said, tucking them into an evidence bag. Henry plucked a mini figure that stood along the tree-lined drive with wavy brown hair, a Jurassic Park T-shirt holding a bow and arrow, and another off the lawn of the estate wearing a tuxedo with a fedora.

Down the hall, they came to a large bedroom. Trophies and ribbons for soccer, basketball, and archery sat on a hanging shelf. The archery outnumbered the others.

"This must be Kieran's room," Betsy said.

In his closet, a bow in a case with arrows sat open on the floor. The feathered end of the arrow was identical to the one that had been sticking out of Sloan.

Betsy called a uniformed officer in to gather the weapon and arrows.

After inspecting three more bedrooms and two bathrooms without finding anything, they crossed the breezeway to inspect the opposite wing of the house.

"I don't think I've ever searched a house this big," Betsy said.

"I don't think I've ever been in a house this big," Henry mused.

They passed a theater room with movie memorabilia and a popcorn machine and a yoga studio with a treadmill and Peloton.

Betsy yawned as she opened the door to the next room, a bedroom. The pink and red floral bedding was disheveled on one side. The closet was full of female clothes. The red robe that Nikki wore when she answered the door was slung onto a white tufted chair in the corner.

"This must be Nikki's room," Betsy said. Henry didn't look up from his notes but grunted slightly as an assent. "I guess they don't share a room." On the bedside table, there was a manila envelope. She put on gloves, carefully opened it, and dumped the contents onto the bed.

"I guess we've got a motive for Nikki," Betsy said, looking at the pictures of Michael kissing a voluptuous blond that was not Nikki.

The last room on the tour was the large master bedroom. The gray bedding was neatly made and had not been slept in, but Michael's shoes and coat were next to the bench by his bed. He had probably come in and started to prepare for bed. A sitting area separated the bed from the Juliet balcony that looked out over the pool. Betsy opened the door and looked down at the body of Michael as the medical examiner zipped him into a large black bag.

Betsy came back into the room and studied the sitting area.

"Something isn't right here," she said.

"What?"

"There's a couch and one gray wingback chair. There should be a second chair, right here." She stood in the spot that a chair should have been." There were small indentations in the carpet where the chair's feet should have been.

Henry nodded and wrote it down.

"Detectives," an officer called, entering the room, "we found something downstairs. Come with me."

They followed the officer down the hallway, back to the stairs, down the stairs, and down the long hallway to the office, which was situated exactly under where they had just been.

"In such a large house, I'm surprised there isn't another staircase back here. It's a long way to go," Henry said.

Inside the office, on the wall opposite from the large bookshelf, a panel of the wall was opened, revealing a hidden room. Inside, there was a wall of TV monitors. With the power out, they were all off.

"I'm calling Doug," Betsy said.

Betsy dialed Doug, the department's in-house tech wizard. He'd helped her out of more than one jam. She hated to call him so early on a Saturday.

"Hello," Doug said.

"Hey, I need your help. I've got a murder, and we found a secret surveillance room. It looks like he had the whole place rigged with cameras."

"Great. That should make it an easy one to solve."

"I hope so. One thing, they lost power here, before the murder."

"Ouch. I'll come take a look. If you're lucky, they had a backup battery in case of power outage. If not, you may only have up until the power went out or, worst case, it all deleted without a power source."

"I'll send you the address. Work your magic."

• • •

Just before nine, Betsy walked into the squad room after having a shower at home. In the conference room, Henry stared at the whiteboard, a look of intense thought on his face and a chicken biscuit in his hand. Her eyes darted to the table. Bless him.

On the table sat a large Chick-fil-A to-go coffee cup and a white bag with a chicken biscuit and a box of hash browns. She chugged the coffee, hoping it would clear the fog from her sleep-starved brain.

Henry stared at the whiteboard, on which all the names of those at the party and a list of clues or oddities from the house had been written. There had been a lot.

"There are a lot of threads to follow here, and I'm not sure yet how they fit together," Henry said.

There was a knock at the door and Doug, the tech guy, entered.

"That was fast," Betsy said. "Oh, please tell me you had some luck, Doug."

"Yes and no. We have full footage until the power goes out. But once they lost power, only the cameras that had back up batteries were able to record."

"Okay," Betsy said.

"I've got to process the footage to see what we have."

"Okay. Thanks, Doug. Maybe we'll get lucky enough to catch the murder on tape," Betsy said.

"Maybe," Henry said.

Outside the conference room, Nikki entered with Kieran and a tall gentleman in a custom suit that screamed lawyer.

"Looks like we'll get a chance to speak to the widow and son again," Betsy said.

"I'll let you know when the first video is ready to view," Doug said.

"Thanks," Betsy said as she left the room to greet Nikki and Kieran.

KIERAN

Kieran had never been in a police station. A week earlier, it would have been exciting, but now it felt like going to the principal's office. He was nauseous and guilt ridden.

"Hi, Kieran, Nikki. Thanks so much for coming in," Detective Turner said. "If you'll follow me, we just have a few more questions for you guys." Betsy led them to an interview room with a table and four chairs. Her partner Henry brought in a fifth chair.

"If we could hurry this along, we've got a long drive ahead of us," Nikki said.

"It won't take long. Where are you going again?"

"To our lake house in North Georgia."

"Okay, could you write down your contact numbers and the address? In case we need to contact you," Betsy said.

Nikki wrote it down and slid it across the table.

Kieran felt small between his strong mother on one side and the lawyer on the other. Across the table, the detectives studied him.

"When was the last time either of you saw Michael alive?"

Kieran thought back to seeing his father smoking a cigar on the covered patio. But he couldn't tell the police without explaining why he was sitting outside in the rain.

"I saw him come in after his cigar," Nikki said.

"What time was this?"

"After dinner, around eight. He goes out for a cigar every night after dinner."

"But last night, it was storming."

"We have a covered patio."

"I see."

"Kieran, who asked you to kill your father?" Henry said.

No one breathed or moved. Heat rushed to his face. *How does he know?* He hadn't told anyone, and Harris certainly wouldn't have admitted to it. He looked first at his mother and then at his lawyer.

"Don't answer that," the lawyer said. Relief washed through him. The lawyer was going to protect him.

"Excuse me!" Nikki said, standing up. "What kind of question is that? He is just a kid, and you are accusing him of murder!"

"Calm down," Betsy said.

"I am calm. Believe me, you'll know when I'm not calm."

"Where are you getting this idea from?" the lawyer asked. He gestured for Nikki to sit. She took her seat but kept her eyes on Henry.

Henry pulled his phone out and linked it to the TV screen on the wall. The shots he'd taken of the Legos in Kieran's room showed on the large screen.

"I think these Legos are a blueprint to a murder plot."

Kieran squirmed in his seat. His mother walked close to the photos. "They're just Legos," Nikki said.

"Let me explain," Henry said. "Here we have the estate, a nearly perfect model of the home. It's incredible. Did you make that?"

Kieran smiled. It had been a beast. He'd had to order tons of Lego pieces off the internet. He'd drawn out the plans. It had taken him months. "Yeah, with help."

"Who helped you?"

"Don't answer that," the lawyer said.

Henry stood up and walked over to the picture. "If you look here"—he pointed at the screen—"outside the home are two people. One is against the tree line holding a bow and arrow, wearing a Jurassic Park T-shirt. I think that one is you," Henry said.

Kieran tried to make himself smaller.

"Now, the other figure is wearing a tuxedo and a fedora, not often worn together in real life," Henry continued. "I think the figure in the tuxedo is supposed to represent your father, Michael Higgins, our murder victim. He had a fedora by the door from the office to the backyard. I think he wears the fedora when he goes outside for a cigar. I think that's when you had planned to kill him."

"Stop this!" Nikki said.

"Now, Kieran, I don't think you planned it. It looks to me like someone else planned this and explained it to you with the Legos," Henry said. "Can you tell me who?"

Kieran's eyes darted to the floor.

"The Legos paint a clear picture, Kieran," Betsy said. "Someone wanted you to shoot your dad. You were going to shoot him, only Sloan came out instead. In the dark and rain, Sloan could pass for your father, roughly the same build and height. Help me understand. Help me find the truth."

Kieran looked into the detective's eyes. He wanted to help her.

"I wasn't going to do it," Kieran said. "I had decided not to do it, but then he was hurting Yvette. Or I thought he was. He dragged her across the lawn. He aimed his gun at her and—"

"Stop talking," the lawyer interrupted.

There was silence as they all stared at each other.

"We'll come back to that," Betsy said. "Earlier, you said that Yvette and Harris had left the property together. Can you tell me what happened?"

The lawyer nodded at Kieran.

"After Yvette . . . uh . . . escaped from Sloan, she said she needed to get away. She was desperate to get somewhere."

"Where?"

"I don't know. She said it was important though. So, I went inside to get Harris, and he took her away in his plane."

"In his, uh, what?" Betsy asked.

Nikki rolled her eyes. "It's just a tiny thing. Harris bought it a couple of years ago and flew it around occasionally. It was a death trap. I never allowed him to take Kieran up."

Kieran remembered the night he'd snuck out to fly with Harris. It had been so fun. He'd never been caught, and he wasn't going to fess up now.

"What is it, exactly?" Betsy asked.

"You're the detective. I'm sure you can research it," the lawyer said. "Any other questions for my client?"

"Nikki, do you have any idea who would want to hurt your husband?"

"I don't know. But I'd put my money on that little girlfriend of Mike's. She had a shifty, untrustworthy look about her. She argued with Michael in his office. Mike may have been there too. I only heard it from upstairs in the master bedroom."

"What time was this?"

"Around eight-fifteen, maybe eight-thirty."

"But why would Yvette want to kill your husband?"

"I'm not sure. But I bet if you look into her background, you'll find something. There was something off about her."

"Anything else?" the lawyer asked.

"Nikki, do you want to talk about the photos in the envelope?"

"No," Nikki said. "I don't know where they came from."

"We're having them tested for fingerprints."

"Then you'll know more about them then I do."

"I can't imagine you were happy to see them."

"No, I wasn't. And I'm mortified that you saw them. But I didn't kill him over them."

"I'm not sure I believe you."

"What photos?" Kieran asked.

"Not important, dear. Can we go now?" Nikki said, standing.

"Yes. We'll be in touch," Betsy said.

"We're having the Legos tested for fingerprints. We'll know who asked you to kill your father," Henry said.

"A word of advice," Betsy said. "I wouldn't trust anyone who would ask you to do that."

They didn't understand. Still, it was hard to hear.

"Stop this. We're leaving." Nikki grabbed Kieran's hand and pulled him out of the office.

BETSY

Doug stood at Henry's desk when they returned from the interview.

"The first video is ready. They are linked on the cloud. You can access them there. As I process them, I'll load them. You can watch them on your tablet," Doug said.

Henry pulled out his iPad and found the video right away.

"The first one is footage of the kitchen. I've queued it up to start at seven. This one had batteries and kept recording all night," Doug said.

"Thanks, Doug."

"Sure thing. I'll get to work on the others."

Betsy sat at the long conference table.

"What, no popcorn?" Henry asked as he sat beside her.

There was no sound on the video. They saw Chef Joe standing at the island preparing food while Kieran cut vegetables. Nikki entered and spoke to Joe. Kieran left first, then Nikki.

Everything looked normal until Joe put on a pair of latex gloves.

"What is he doing?" Betsy asked.

Joe looked around himself suspiciously, walked over to a messenger bag on a chair at the kitchen table, and pulled out a Ziploc bag containing something white. He opened the bag and carefully dumped the contents out of the bag onto a clean cutting board.

"The mushrooms," Betsy said.

Chef Joe chopped them. He sautéed them in a pan and made a brown gravy, which he poured over a single chicken breast on a plate. He then threw the cutting board, knife, and sauce pan he used to prepare the mushrooms into the trash as well as the remaining mushrooms and the latex gloves, which he carefully removed.

The screen lit up. The camera wobbled.

"That was lightning," Betsy said.

"Maybe that's when the tree went down. It looked close."

Joe grabbed the plate with a kitchen towel and exited the kitchen.

Henry paused the video and moved closer to the screen. He picked up the landline and dialed.

"Hey, Aja, it's Henry. Did you get any results on the mushrooms?" Henry smiled at Betsy. "Thanks, Aja!" He hung up.

"Death caps," he said. "I thought they were. I should've trusted my gut."

"Death cap mushrooms?" Betsy asked.

"Yes. Oh, I hope we're not too late."

"Too late for what?"

"The Hunter's Hunter," Henry said as he looked at his iPad, searching for something.

"What?" Betsy said.

"The Hunter's Hunter, we've got him. I just hope we're not too late."

"Who?"

"The serial killer, the Hunter's Hunter. He's killed six people in the past few years, all over the country. He kills big game hunters, right before they go on a big hunt. He always uses death cap mushrooms."

"The stuffed elephant," Betsy said.

"Michael certainly fits the profile of his victims. That's why I asked Chef Joe about the mushrooms. But he covered himself by saying they were straw mushrooms, which would pass for death caps. I should have brought him in then and there. Look at this," Henry said, holding up his iPad. "Here is the sketch of Hunter's Hunter done by one of the other victim's family."

The picture was a dead ringer for Chef Joe. Henry read the online file accompanying the sketch out loud. "In each of the cases, he posed as a chef and worked with the family for a few months before killing." Henry put the iPad down and looked at Betsy. "By the time symptoms appear, six to twelve hours after consumption, he'd be gone. It must act faster in dogs."

"Poor Coco," Betsy said.

"Let's go get him," Henry said.

"If we're lucky, he's still at the hospital getting his arm treated."

HENRY

Henry climbed into the passenger seat of the squad car. Betsy got in and cranked the engine, pulling out into traffic.

"I'll watch the rest of the video en route and tell you what happens." He held the iPad in his lap and clicked play.

Chef Joe returned to the kitchen. He walked out the back door, closed it behind him, and returned a moment later. He banged his fist on the counter and threw a saucepan onto the stove as he prepared another lamb chop for Addison. Henry fast-forwarded as Chef Joe took the lamb chop out of the room and pushed play when he returned.

His chef coat appeared to be covered in vomit, and there were tears in his eyes. He marched out the back door.

"He's visibly upset, probably by the dog dying."

Liza entered the kitchen and began to slice the cake. She reached into her pocket and pulled out a small prescription bottle. She hastily opened it and put one and then another and finally a third pill into a slice of cake and shoved the pill bottle back into her pocket just as Kieran entered the kitchen. Liza handed Kieran two slices and sent him out with them. She carried only one piece out of the kitchen.

Henry paused the video and looked at Betsy.

"What?" she said, taking her eyes off the road for a second.

Henry shook his head.

"What?" Betsy repeated.

"We need to speak to Liza," Henry said.

"She may be at the hospital with Addison."

BETSY

The flag over the hospital popped and flapped in the wind as they walked to the entrance. Even though the storm had moved on, the wind wailed.

Betsy flashed her badge at the man sitting behind the desk. "Where can I find Joe Fulton?"

"Okay, let's see," the man said. "I'm not seeing anyone with the name Joe Fulton.

"Of course, it's probably a fake name," Henry said.

"Any broken arms this morning?" Betsy asked.

He clicked around on the computer and gave them the room number of the only broken arm they'd seen that morning. They ran to the room and burst through the door. Inside, a man in his sixties looked up at them in surprise. His arm was in a cast.

"Sorry, sir," Betsy said as she and Henry exited the room. "He never had his arm treated, at least not here."

"He probably got out of town as soon as he got away from us."

"I can't believe I let him slip through my fingers. A serial killer!" Henry banged his fist on the nearest nurses' station.

"We'll put out an APB on him. Someone will see him," Betsy said.

"I'll call it in. You need to see the clip of Liza." He pulled out the iPad and played the clip for her.

Betsy couldn't believe it. The sweet, unassuming Liza had tried to poison someone, probably Michael, but somehow ended up poisoning her own daughter. So, was it really sleeping pills like she had said or something worse? Addison's tox screen should tell them.

"I didn't think Liza had it in her," Henry said.

"Everyone has it in them," Betsy said. "Let's get Addison's room number. We need her tox screen, and if we're lucky, Liza is with her."

"We need to talk to Sloan, too, while we're here," Henry said.

"And the guy from the raid this morning."

They returned to the front desk and got the room numbers for both Addison and Sloan, who had both been admitted to rooms on the third floor. The attendant said he'd work on getting the other room number and bring it to them.

"I'm getting anxious about Cara. We've wasted too much time on this new case, and we aren't getting any closer to finding her."

"We are. Patience. These two things are all tied up together, and if we keep following the breadcrumbs, they'll lead us to Cara."

"But will it be too late?" Betsy asked rhetorically.

Betsy and Henry exited the elevator on floor three and navigated the hallways looking for the room numbers. Before they arrived, a doctor stopped them. "Are you guys here about the archery wound? Sloan Peterson?"

"Yes. Are you his doctor?"

"Yes. I am just about to check on him. He's been out of surgery for about an hour. The surgery went well. We removed the arrow. We also gave him the antivenom for the snakebite. He really had a rough night. We need to keep him overnight, but he will make a full recovery."

"I guess he's lucky the arrow didn't hit anything major," Betsy said.

"He's either the luckiest guy on the planet, or whoever shot that arrow did not want to kill him," the doctor said. Betsy looked at Henry. "His room is right here." He held the door open for them. Betsy went in first.

"Doctor," Betsy said. "You'd better check that room number again."

The doctor entered the room behind them. He looked from the empty bed to the two detectives. He checked the chart in his hand. "Nurse," he said, exiting the room. They followed him into the hallway. "I'm missing a patient. Sloan Peterson."

"Oh, he left."

"He what?"

"He left against doctor's orders. He signed the paper."

"When's the last time anyone saw him?" Henry asked.

"He left around nine a.m. Right after surgery."

SLOAN

Sloan pulled up to the loading dock of Butler's Ice Cream. He took a deep breath and put his head against the head rest. His shoulder throbbed. The snake bite had a tangy, lingering pain. He grabbed the bottle of Tylenol and shook a few out like Tic Tacs and tossed them in his mouth. *Maybe I should've stayed at the hospital long enough to get some pain killers, at least.* He looked at the neatly dressed wound. Blood was already showing through the fresh white bandage.

He saw Derrick with his stupid tiger tattoo standing on the back of the loading dock. He was holding Tara over his shoulder. She was bound, gagged, and drugged.

"I'm going to get some ice cream for the drive. Load her up for me," Sloan said.

A few minutes later, Sloan exited the store holding a waffle cone of Double Expresso Chip. He needed a boost; his body was so draggy.

"She should be asleep for the whole ride, but she is tied up just in case," Derrick answered.

"Did you hear from the boss about the change of plan?"

"Yeah. The sale moves forward this evening."

"Alright, I'm going to hit the road. I've got a long drive ahead of me."

Tiger Tattoo nodded.

Sloan got into the driver's seat and realized he couldn't hold the cone and drive with his bad arm.

"Damn," he said. He took two giant bites and threw it out the window.

BETSY

As she made her way with Henry to Addison's room, her phone rang. Betsy ducked into a small waiting room and waved Henry over. She put the phone on speaker.

"Hey, Betsy, it's Aja. We've got a match on the DNA from under Michael's fingernails. It belongs to Sloan Peterson," she said.

"Why was his DNA in the system?" Betsy asked.

"He'd been arrested for solicitation of a prostitute in 2005 but clean since then. The charges were dropped."

"Okay, thanks for the info," Betsy said. She turned to Henry. "We've got to find this guy."

"I'll call to have some officers go by Sloan's place to see if he's there," Henry said. "I'll see if we have enough to get a warrant for his home and business."

"Put an APB out on his car," Betsy said.

"On it." Henry pulled his iPad out and checked his notes. "It was the yellow Corvette, license plate, ISCREAM."

"Also, I got the fingerprints back from the Legos," Aja said. "There were only two that were identifiable. One belongs to a juvenile, no match in the system. The other belongs to Harris Higgins."

"Why was he in the system?"

"DUI, from three years ago."

"Thanks," Betsy said and clicked the phone off. "Where is Harris Higgins?"

"If he has a plane, he could be anywhere."

LIZA

To Liza, her daughter, Addison, looked small in the large hospital bed.

"Do you need more water?" she asked.

"No, Mom. I'm fine, really," Addison said.

"I can run down to the cafeteria. They have a Chick-fil-A."

"I'm fine, Mom. I wish I had a book," Addison said, flipping through the few hospital channels.

The detectives from that morning entered the hospital room.

"Good morning, detectives," Liza said. She wasn't happy to see them but smiled warmly anyway. She didn't want to talk to them but could see no way around it.

"Addison, these are the officers that helped you this morning."

"I'm Detective Turner and this is Detective Sanders. We'd like to talk to each of you separately about the events of last night."

"You mean my father's murder?"

"Addison. Don't be so blunt," Liza said.

"Yes," Henry said. "And the events leading up to it. Liza, would you step outside please?"

"Of course," Liza said, stepping into the hallway, followed by both detectives.

"You may not be aware of this, but Michael had cameras throughout his house," Betsy said.

"He had cameras? Really? That's a little unsettling," Liza said.

"Yes, it is. We've been watching them, frankly, to catch a murderer. I'd like to show you a clip," Betsy said.

Henry held up his iPad and pushed play on the video. Liza saw herself from above as she very visibly slipped something into the cake. Shame coursed through her, and her face burned. She knew it was turning the color of a tomato, betraying her.

"What did you put in the cake?" Betsy asked.

She couldn't answer that. The truth was incriminating, and she'd never been much of a liar. She opened her mouth to speak but couldn't find any words.

"I think you wanted to kill him," Henry said. "I think you wanted to kill him, but you knew he was stronger than you. So, you thought you could drug him, put him to sleep. Once he was asleep, you could sneak up to his room and what? Suffocate him with a pillow? Or stab him? Or throw him off a balcony. But there was a mix-up, wasn't there?"

Liza was stunned by the accurate analysis. This detective was good . . . too good.

"Somehow Addison got the cake," Betsy said, "and slept through the rest of the evening. Tell me. When did you realize Addison had eaten the cake you meant for Michael?"

"Maybe I should get a lawyer?"

"Why? Did you kill your ex-husband?"

"No. No. Of course not."

"So why did you try to drug him?"

It was impossible to answer that.

"I think you did it for your kids," Betsy said. "They needed him dead, but why?"

Liza's eyes narrowed. "No, they didn't. They loved their father, and none of them would be capable of anything so heinous."

"But you were, weren't you?" Betsy said.

"I don't know what you're talking about."

"Did you kill Michael?"

"No. Of course, I didn't kill him."

"Stay in town. The rest of the tapes will be ready soon. We will know who killed him."

ADDISON

Addison lay in the bed, her medical chart open in her lap. A psych eval? *They'd ordered a psych eval?* Well, that was standard practice in cases of a sleeping pill overdose, but she hadn't taken any pills. She'd told them that.

But she couldn't tell them the truth. The truth she had figured out. Her mother had drugged her. Liza must have figured out Addison's plan to kill her father. Mothers are like that. They always seem to know what their children are up to. Maybe they do have eyes in the back of their heads. Her mother wanted to protect her from herself. So, she'd slipped a sleeping pill or two into Addison's cake to keep her from doing something she would always regret—killing her father.

It was a mother's instinct. Always protecting their kids from their own worst impulses. Helping them to become the best version of themselves. Fate had rewarded her. She was free. Her father was dead but not by her hand.

The detectives entered the room, Liza behind them.

"I'll be right outside, honey. You don't have to answer anything."

"I've got it, Mom."

Liza left, and Betsy closed the door to the small hospital room.

"What can you tell us about the events of last night?"

"Dinner at my dad's, pretty standard. I fell asleep after cake, and I woke up here."

"So, nothing unusual happened before you fell asleep?"

"Well, the dog died. You should test her stomach for poison."

"Why?"

"I think the chef poisoned her. I think he meant to poison Daddy."

"Did you talk to the chef before dinner?"

"Yes."

"About what?"

"I asked him to make Daddy a special meal, lighter, lower calories."

"Why?"

"Did you know I've been working as my father's nurse for some time?"

"Yes."

"I was worried his numbers were too high. He needed to eat healthier, but he didn't want to."

"Are you aware that you had sleeping pills in your system?"

"Yes."

"How do you think they got into your system?"

"I have no idea."

"Have a look at this," Henry said. He handed her the iPad. On the screen, her mother slipped the pills in the cake.

"Can you explain that?" Betsy asked.

"No."

"I believe your mother wanted to drug your father," Henry said, "so that she could kill him while he slept deeply."

Addison laughed.

Henry continued, "We believe the cake got switched, and she drugged you by mistake. Do you know why your mother would want to kill your father?"

Still laughing, Addison waved her hand at them. "I know it's not funny. But you can't be serious? My mom is a pacifist. She's never had a fight with anyone, ever. She lives to keep the peace. No, you're looking under the wrong rock."

"When the paramedics put you in the stretcher, an empty syringe fell out of your pocket."

Stay calm. That doesn't prove anything. Wait for a question.

"Why did you have it?"

"I use syringes for his diabetes medications. I'm not sure I had it for any reason. It was just there."

"That's not normal."

"Maybe not."

"Medical school, right? So, you probably have an above average understanding of medical procedures. Did you know, for example, that if you inject someone with air, they can suffer from an air embolism and die?"

"Everybody knows that."

"I think you were planning to kill him."

They couldn't prove anything. Addison just looked at them.

"So, who do you think killed your father?"

"You're sure it was murder?"

"Yes."

"The chef tried. I guess I'd put my money on him."

There was a knock at the door, and Liza pushed it open.

"I think that's enough for now. Addison needs her rest."

"Thank you both. We'll be in touch," Betsy said.

Liza's phone rang. "Hello? . . . Harris! . . . Where are you? I've been worried sick. Are you okay? Honey, where are you? You saw it on the news? . . . I'm so sorry you had to find out that way. Okay, I'm on my way to you now."

The detective held her hand out for the phone.

"I'm with the police," Liza said. "They want to talk to you." Liza handed the phone over to the detective.

She covered the speaker and asked Liza, "Does he know his father died?"

"Yes, he's heard."

Betsy nodded. She pushed speakerphone. "Hello, Harris, this is Detective Turner. I'm looking into the events of last night. We want to hear your version. Can you meet us at the station?"

"I would," Harris said into the phone, "but it may be easier for you to come to me."

"That's fine. Where are you?"

"I'm at Piedmont Hospital."

HARRIS

Harris flipped through the channels for the hundredth time. He wanted to get up, he wanted to jump out of bed, but he was hooked up to IVs and monitors. He'd never been good at sitting still. Maybe they'd let him leave soon. They had treated him for the drugs Tiger Tattoo had injected into his neck. He felt better and was ready to get back to life. Two detectives walked into his room. He recognized them and smiled. Detective Turner checked her paperwork and stepped back into the hall, looking at the room number.

"There's some kind of mix-up here," she said. "I'm looking for Harris Higgins."

"You found him," Harris said.

"No, you're the guy who was tied to the chair in the flophouse last night. We found you. Do you remember?"

"Yes, I remember you. Although it's all a bit blurry."

"Okay, what's your name?"

"Harris Higgins."

"But—" she tried to process this information.

"Okay, Harris. I'm Detective Henry Sanders and this is Detective Betsy Turner. Can you tell us about the events of last night?"

"Happy to."

"So, you really are Harris Higgins?" Betsy asked. "Son of Michael Higgins? Who was at a dinner party for your brother's birthday last night?"

"Yup."

"What were you doing at that house last night?"

"I took Yvette there."

"Yvette? Why?"

"She asked for a ride."

"According to Kieran, you flew in a plane?"

"I have a small plane. Actually, it was Kieran's idea. He found me and told me Yvette needed a ride. He asked if I could fly her, since we couldn't go anywhere by car. It took a bit to set it up, and then we had to wait for the rain to stop. It was truly beautiful. The stars were so bright with so much of the city without power."

"So, you have no knowledge of what was happening at the flophouse?"

"Well, I know what I saw."

"What did you see?" Henry asked.

"After they tied me up, they took a bunch of girls out of there. Young, like twelve to fourteen years old. Maybe a few older. It was hard to tell because they carried them upside down over their shoulders."

"How many men were there?"

"Three."

"Could you recognize them if you saw them again."

"Yeah. One of the guys had a tiger tattoo on his face."

Henry wrote this down and then handed the iPad and stylus to Harris. "Could you draw it?"

"I'm not much of an artist, but I'll give it a try."

"Thanks."

"Do you know where they took the girls?"

"No. They just cleared out quickly and disappeared, leaving me there alone." Harris paused and looked out the window. "They took Yvette with them."

"They took Yvette?"

"Yeah, they drugged her and took her. Have you guys found her? I've been pretty worried about her, and I haven't been able to get in touch with my brother Mike either."

"Do you mind if we switch gears and talk about the dinner party last night?" Henry asked.

"That's fine."

"We know you asked Kieran to kill your father," Henry said.

Harris looked up from drawing on the iPad and studied the detectives faces. He tried not to show any emotion.

"What? No. Did Kieran tell you that?" Harris asked.

"No. He didn't have to. We have your fingerprints on the Legos."

"So, I play Legos with my little brother. There is no crime in that."

"There is when you use them to plan a murder."

"That's ridiculous."

"You must have been upset when you realized Kieran had screwed up and shot the wrong person. Then you had to finish the job yourself."

"Wait, you think I killed him?" Harris asked, laughing. "I didn't kill him. I didn't tell Kieran to kill him. I didn't even consider killing him."

"Unfortunately, I don't believe you," Henry said. "I want to know why you asked Kieran, your sweet kid brother, to murder for you? Is he more of a man than you?"

"I'd like a lawyer before you ask me any more questions." He handed the iPad back to Henry.

"Thanks," Henry said. "We'll be in touch."

"Well, it's been fun," Harris said as he picked up the TV remote and resumed flicking through the channels. He looked over at them as they left. "Try to find Yvette. She was nice, and I don't want anything to happen to her. That may not have been her real name though."

"What do you mean?"

"I'm not sure. I think she used a fake name."

"So, what was her name?" Henry asked.

"Tara, something . . . Tara Sharp."

BETSY

Betsy stared at Harris. Something had been nagging at her all day about this case, but she hadn't seen it—until now. Tara had known something, something big, and she'd blown her off.

The death of Michael Higgins was linked to the death of Jane Doe. She didn't know how, but Tara Sharp would. Tara had come in to talk to her. And now Tara was in over her head, and Betsy didn't have the information she needed to help her.

"I should have known something was going on with her," Betsy said. "She came to see us. Her hair was different. She tried to talk to me, and I didn't listen."

"So, Tara must have been convinced there was a connection between Michael and Cara. But why? We need to know what she saw that got her on the track of Michael Higgins and what she found in that house that led her to the flophouse."

She picked up her phone to dial Tara. It went straight to voicemail. She clicked it off and turned to Henry.

"They have her. They have Tara."

"Let's check her apartment," Henry said.

As they walked back to the elevator, Betsy talked through what they knew. "So, we have a girl who died of hypothermia, and we have a rich businessman who died of blunt-force trauma."

"And the rich businessman owned an ice-cream conglomerate. I imagine they use a lot of freezers," Henry said.

Betsy looked at Henry. "Freezers, of course."

Betsy's phone rang as they made their way back to the car.

"Detective Turner," she said.

"This is Sergeant Miller with the Mississippi state troopers. We've spotted the car you're looking for, a yellow Corvette, license plate ISCREAM."

SLOAN

Sloan saw the cop in the rearview mirror only a moment before he flipped his lights on. He pulled over to the shoulder and took a deep breath, trying to look calm. The last thing he needed was for this cop to look in the back or even ask for his ID.

"Good morning, officer. What seems to be the problem?" Sloan said.

"I noticed you have a brake light out."

"I do? I'll be sure to get that fixed right away."

"I should give you a ticket. But I love your ice cream so much," the officer said, stepping back to admire the ice-cream truck.

"What's your favorite flavor?"

"Rocking Chair Chip."

"I invented that flavor. It reminds me of my grandfather. We used to churn our own ice cream on the front porch at his dairy farm. Please, I don't want any special treatment. I'll take the ticket."

The officer looked down at his ticket pad and back at Sloan. "You'll get this fixed?"

"Yes, I can drop it off today after my delivery. Safety first."

"Alright. Well, I'll let you go with a warning."

"Thank you, officer." He waved to the officer, put the ice cream truck in gear, and pulled out onto the road.

JOE

Chef Joe wiped away his tears so he could see the road. He'd always known there would be unforeseeable consequences . . . but this? The death of Coco, an innocent dog. How could such a wrong come out of following the right path?

On the side of the road, a sign read Memphis, ninety-six miles. That would be a good time to make a pit stop before continuing west. He would need to ditch the car before anyone noticed it was missing.

In the rearview mirror, a police cruiser followed a few cars back. The speedometer read sixty-seven. He lowered his speed and stayed in the right lane. This car, Sloan's car, although fast, was a bit conspicuous. Within a few minutes, a second police car appeared in the rearview mirror.

"No, no," he said to himself. Sirens erupted, accompanied by flashing lights a moment later. He slammed the pedal to the floor and zipped in and out of traffic, honking his horn. What the car lacked in subtlety, it made up for now in speed and maneuverability.

He couldn't get caught, not now.

Three police cars with lights and sirens were keeping pace with him.

"Pull over," a voice boomed through a loudspeaker. He saw an exit, and, on an impulse, he pulled onto it. He floored it up the ramp and saw two police cars pull out and block the end of the exit ramp. The chaser closed in behind him. Joe was boxed in. Each of the officers sprang from their cars and aimed their guns at him as well.

"Exit the vehicle with your hands up!"

Joe did as he was instructed. He opened the door and stepped out onto the pavement with his arms up. The police ran to him and threw him against the car, pinning his arms behind him.

"Sloan Peterson, you are wanted for questioning in the murder of Michael Higgins."

"I'm not Sloan."

"What's your name?"

"Joe Fulton."

"And how did you come to be in this car?"

"I, uh, borrowed it from Sloan."

TARA

Tara awoke, shaking violently. Her first thought was that she was colder than she'd ever been in her life. She tried to open her heavy eyelids but couldn't. Her fingers were so cold. She tried to rub her hands together, but they were tied in front of her. She clenched her fists to warm them. After a few moments, she was able to gain control over her eyelids. She fluttered them open and found herself in a dimly lit room. *What kind of room is this?* The walls were metal and covered in a thin layer of frost. Round five-gallon cardboard tubs were stacked around the walls. She shook her head to clear it, trying to read the label on the nearest tub, but her vision was blurry. She was very thirsty.

She noticed a low humming sound and felt the vibration of

movement. Her head cleared slowly, and she saw the name printed on the tub closest to her: *Washington Carver Delight*. Others said *Scarlett's Red Raspberry, Muscadine Vine, Sweet Tea Chip*. She looked down at her hands and noticed a bluish tint to her skin, suddenly realizing where she was—inside an ice-cream truck. Her thoughts went to Jane Doe, who died of hypothermia, a few days ago.

They were taking her to where they took all the girls, wherever that may be. She just hoped they would arrive soon. She was so cold.

BETSY

On the way to Tara's apartment, Betsy got a call from Aja, the medical examiner. She put it on speakerphone.

"Hey, Aja, what've you got?" Betsy said.

"Two things first. There are small wood splinters in the wound on the deceased's head. Your murder weapon was made of wood. Secondly, the substance that was under Jane Doe's fingernails turned out to be ice cream. I'm still working on getting an exact flavor and brand, but it had raspberries and chocolate chips, which can't be that common."

"Raspberries and chocolate? It's gotta be Scarlett's Red Raspberry," Betsy said.

Henry looked at Betsy. "What?" he asked.

"I'm a bit of an ice-cream connoisseur. Scarlett's Red Raspberry is a flavor from Butler's."

"Yeah, I love their Honeysuckle," Aja said.

"Gotta go, thanks!" Betsy said and hung up.

The wind ripped through the common hallway of the cookie-cutter apartment building, like hundreds of others around the city. Betsy knocked on the door of the apartment that belonged to Tara Sharp.

"Tara! Hello? It's Detective Turner."

There was no answer.

"I'll try her cell again," Henry said. "Straight to voicemail."

Betsy stepped back from the door.

"Bets, we don't have a warrant. You can't just bust—"

But she wasn't listening. She stepped forward and kicked, aiming her foot for the locking mechanism. It burst open with a pop.

"We're in," Betsy said, entering the space. "Tara? Tara?" she said as she walked down the hallway. She entered a dining room that had been turned into a find-Cara headquarters. There were maps on the wall with pushpins and dates on sticky notes. There was a bulletin board with red string in a spiderweb pattern like you see in the movies. At the center of the red web was a picture of Michael Higgins.

Henry took pictures of everything with his iPad. In the middle of the room was a cluttered card table. All the papers and notebooks had been pushed to the side, and a manila envelope sat in the cleared area with *Detective Betsy Turner APD* written on it.

Betsy opened the envelope and looked inside.

Dear Betsy,

If you're reading this, then my mission to find Cara was not successful. I've included everything I've found tying Michael Higgins to the missing girls, and what I suspect is a human trafficking ring. Please keep looking for Cara. I feel like I'm so close now, and if something goes wrong, just keep up the search.

Thanks for all your help.

Tara Sharp

PS. Don't feel bad about dismissing me earlier this week. I was the girl who cried wolf.

Inside the folder was information on Butler's, how much money it made per year versus how much it spent on supplies. In Tara's handwriting was a note:

Making more than they should off the supplies they buy.

"How did she get all of this?" Betsy asked.

"She's good with computers, remember?" Henry said.

"But some of this would have been really hard to get."

Henry nodded. "Yeah, she's really good at it."

Betsy kept looking through the papers. She had a list of the trucks the company owned and the mileage they'd reported for the year. Tara had scribbled notes at the bottom.

"No way an ice-cream truck travels that distance in a year. These trucks are doing more than delivering ice cream," Henry said.

"The ice-cream trucks!" Betsy said. "It all fits! If they were using ice cream trucks to move girls, one of them could have gotten too cold."

"And gotten hypothermia," Henry said. "The ice cream under the fingernails . . . it all fits."

The detectives continued flipping through the papers. There was a list of properties owned by Butler's and Michael Higgins. The last paper was the smoking gun. It showed that a Butler's Ice Cream truck had been present for a fair, carnival, or festival in nearly 80 percent of the missing girl cases from Georgia over the past ten years.

There was a handwritten note by Tara at the bottom of the paper.

I only had time to go back ten years and in the state of Georgia. I bet the pattern continues in neighboring states, possibly further back.

Betsy sat in a plastic folding chair at the table. "She knew this, and I wouldn't listen to her."

"I didn't listen either," Henry said. "But now we know, and we need to move in the right direction."

"So, where is she now? We need to find her."

"Or—" Henry said.

"Or what?"

"Or she killed him, and she's gone into hiding," Henry said.

Betsy shook her head. "No, she wouldn't."

"She would if it meant saving Cara. It's a possibility we have to face. Plus, it might explain Mike's disappearance. If he's helping her."

Maybe Henry had a point. Maybe she'd planned to kill Michael at dinner. Maybe she'd gone to the party to kill him.

But somehow that didn't sit right with Betsy. Killing him didn't get her closer to Cara. Besides, Tara had never struck her as a murderer.

Although love had driven people to kill before.

"You don't think she could have—" Betsy started.

"I don't think Tara killed Michael," Henry said. "I mean, it's possible, but I doubt it."

"She obviously went there to get answers about Cara. What if things got out of hand and she—"

"Let's cross that bridge when and if we come to it."

Betsy's cell phone rang. She answered it on speaker.

"Detective Turner."

"This is Sergeant Miller. We apprehended the driver of the Corvette."

"Yes. Sloan Peterson."

"No, the driver is a Joe Fulton. We think he may have stolen the car."

Betsy's eyes flashed to Henry.

"We got him!" Henry said, pumping his fist.

TARA

It wasn't long before Tara felt the truck come to a stop. Her hands were bound behind her and something, probably tape, covered her mouth. They were either taking her to wherever they kept all the girls, or they were planning to kill her. If it was the latter, they'd probably taken her somewhere remote, where no one would be able to hear her scream. Maybe she could run for it. But her legs felt so heavy, almost like her eyelids.

The door opened with a blast of much welcomed heat and bright light. Her eyes squinted at the brightness.

"You got your wish. I'll take you to your sister now," a familiar voice said. She fluttered her eyes. Sloan stood in the doorway, pointing a gun. He grabbed her by the armpits and pulled her to a standing position. Tara, shaky, leaned against the stack of ice-cream tubs. Sloan pulled her toward the door. He jumped to the ground. She sat down on the edge of the truck and scooted forward to lower herself. Her shaky legs didn't catch her weight, and she fell onto gravel. Her skin tingled as the hot midday sun warmed her body. Her eyes were still adjusting to the bright day. Her muscles relaxed slowly after hours of tensing up against the cold.

"Let's go," Sloan said, pulling her to her feet again.

The sound of screaming girls forced her eyes open. She spun around for the source of the screams. Her eyes darted around, taking in her surroundings. They were standing in a gravel parking lot next to a wooden lodge, surrounded by high wooded mountains. A pine-dotted grassy lawn sloped down to a sparkling lake. Cabins lined the lake, and Tara saw a two-story dock jutting over the water. That's when she saw the screaming girls running and jumping off the high dock onto a large pillow. When one girl landed on the pillow, another girl launched off the opposite end, high into the air, before splashing down in the lake. Tara sighed and relaxed a bit.

Sloan pulled her across the parking lot and through a tall wooden sign that read, *Pleasure Island.* He marched her down the lawn toward the cabins. Wind blew her hair into her face. She tried to shake it out, her hands still bound behind her back. They walked along a mulch-covered path and around a curve in the lake. Sloan stopped in front of one of the cabins and cut off her restraints. He pulled her to the cabin and pushed the door open without knocking. Inside, two girls sat on a bottom bunk, one braiding the other's hair. A third girl sat on a top bunk, dangling her feet off. Tara studied the faces of the girls on the bottom bunk first and then the girl on the top.

"Cara!" Tara screamed, pulling herself free from Sloan and stumbling across the room. "Cara!" She looked the same, brown wavy hair, a smattering of freckles across her nose.

Cara didn't recognize Tara at first with her new blond hair. And then, all at once, she launched herself off the bed onto Tara, who fell back to the floor.

"Tara!" She screamed as they fell, tears welling up in both girls.

They held each other tightly.

"She'll bunk here with you for now. Show her around," Sloan said and left.

"Did they hurt you?" Tara asked.

"Tara? How? How did you find me?" Cara asked.

Tara pulled her sisters face back and stared into her eyes; both girls cried as they sat on the floor holding each other.

"I'm so sorry. I'm so sorry. I should've known better. It's all my fault," Cara said.

"No! It's not. Don't you dare blame yourself for the evil in others. Now, how can we get out of here?"

"Oh, no, we can't escape. It's impossible. One girl tried, and they shot her in front of all of us." Cara looked away. "I shut my eyes tight, but I still heard it."

"Oh, Cara," Tara said, pulling her tight once again.

"Did they hurt you?" Tara asked her sister.

"No, but I've been lucky."

"Tell me everything."

"Well, after they snatched me, I was terrified, obviously, but then they gave me a mentor, that's like an older girl who shows you around and helps you have fun. And then it was like summer camp. We can do whatever we want. We can swim, boat, they even take us out on a ski boat sometimes if we're good. They have a movie theater room and almost any movie you want, even R-rated ones. We all go there when it rains or sometimes at night. But we have to be in our cabins by nine. There's also a game room with video games and ping-pong. Oh, and you can eat anytime you want. There's always food. Unless you start to gain weight; then you get put on the limited meal plan and have to wear a special bracelet. It's super embarrassing. It didn't happen to me, but it happened to a few friends of mine. They were so mortified, but I told them it wasn't a big deal, and I tried not to get ice cream when they were around."

"So, no one has hurt you? Or touched you?" Tara asked.

Cara looked down at her feet. "Not me, not yet, but . . . well, I started to notice some of the girls would leave for a day or a week and come back sad, and they didn't want to do all the fun stuff anymore, and sometimes they would leave and never come back. And I started to realize that this place might be like that place in Pinocchio. Do you remember? Where they had fun but turned into donkeys, and then I wanted to go home."

"But you can't escape," one of the other girls spoke up.

"Tara, this is Nancy and Lauren. Guys, this is my sister, Tara. We all got here around the same time, along with another girl." Cara looked down again. "They killed her for trying to escape. But not in front of us."

Tara thought back to Jane, the girl who had died of hypothermia less than a week ago. If it hadn't been for her, Tara may never have made the connection between Butler's and her sister's disappearance.

"Why are you here, Tara?" Cara asked.

"To rescue you."

"But there's no way to escape. They have guards on every inch of this place and tons of cameras. I think they can even see in the bathrooms."

"Creepy much," Nancy said.

"I'm glad I got to see you again before." Cara looked down again.

"Before what?" Tara said.

"I've been sold. I met the man that bought me. He came out last weekend and took all the girls that are virgins out on the boat. I just thought he was a nice guy, but he was shopping, and he picked me. He's picking me up tonight. It's my last day here, and then I'll go live with him."

"They say he buys a new girl or two every six months, and none of them ever come back," Nancy said.

"But that could just be because they are all back with their families or—" Lauren said.

"Well, it doesn't matter. You're not going with him. We've got to find a way to escape before he comes," Tara said.

BETSY

Betsy and Henry received a standing ovation at the station. The officers raised their coffee cups in tribute and hollered, "Congratulations!"

"Pizza all around," the captain said. "You caught one of the FBI's ten most wanted!"

"Thanks, Captain," Henry said.

"We're doing a Zoom interview with Joe in Mississippi. It should be ready in a minute," the captain said.

"I can't believe we got him. We caught a serial killer," Henry said, grabbing a box of pizza off the pile.

"You're geeking out," Betsy said.

"Yeah. Because we caught a serial killer!"

Betsy sat at her desk and thought about Chef Joe. He had come across as docile, morally grounded, although obviously misaligned. You never could quite tell what was going on with people. She picked up the phone and dialed Tara's cell. Straight to voicemail. Her head swam with lack of sleep and the tangled-up case.

She placed all the papers from Tara's office onto her desk. She was going to follow the trail, hopefully catch a murderer, and find Cara and Tara Sharp.

"They're ready for us," Henry said.

Betsy gave one last look at the notes and followed Henry to the interview room.

JOE

Chef Joe was being held in Tupelo before being transferred back to Atlanta. They'd set up a Zoom call to interview him.

"Hello, Joe," Betsy said. "Why were you running?"

"Oh, I wasn't stealing Sloan's car. He said I could borrow it. You could ask him when you find him."

"I'll be sure to do that. We know your car was crashed into the tree. Is that why you borrowed his car?"

"Yes."

"Where were you going? Didn't I ask you to stay in town?"

"Yes, I was just going for a drive to clear my head."

"Why didn't you go to the hospital for your arm?"

"I don't like hospitals," Joe said.

"If I didn't know better, I'd think you were trying to run. I bet when you took Sloan's car, you didn't think we'd be looking for it. I bet you took it because it's fast and you wanted to get away from that house as fast as possible. That kind of behavior makes you look very guilty," Betsy said.

"No. It was dumb. I just wanted to clear my head."

"No, Joe," Henry said. "We found the mushrooms. It's over. We know who you are and what you've done."

"What are you talking about?" Joe said, rubbing his hands together.

"You're the Hunter's Hunter. Michael fits the victim profile. That elephant head on the wall is enough to prove that."

The world swam before Joe. He was caught. They knew it all. "I could barely walk into that room without wanting to scream at him. What kind of demented creep thinks the body parts of such a beautiful creature should be displayed? It's sickening."

"So, you admit it?"

"No. I'm just saying I didn't like his taste in decor."

"Well, we have enough to put you away for a long time. The mushrooms tie you to at least six other murders of men who hunted exotic animals."

"I didn't kill that worthless egomaniac. I'm not going to say I'm upset he's dead. His death saves the lives of unknown numbers of beautiful creatures. He deserved what he got. But like I said, I didn't kill him."

"We know you tried to kill him. We know you killed Coco," Betsy said.

He flinched and wiped away a tear.

"How does that feel? You, an animal-rights activist, and now you're the one to kill that poor sweet little dog."

His hands shook as he rubbed them together, tears flowing.

"You're as much a monster as they are," she said.

"You're wrong. That was an accident."

"But you did poison the food. The food meant for Michael."

"I want a lawyer," Joe said.

There was a knock at the door. Doug stuck his head in.

"The footage from the office is ready," he said.

"If you'll excuse us, we'll talk to you again once you're transported here," Betsy said as she and Henry left the room.

BETSY

Henry placed the warm pizza box onto the conference table, opened it, and pulled a slice from the large sausage and mushroom pie. He set his iPad up as Betsy took the seat next to him.

"Eat," Henry said.

"I can't eat. The girls are out there."

"And if you're going to find them, you'll need your strength. Now eat the pizza."

Betsy sighed and grabbed a slice. Henry pushed play on his iPad, and the screen showed the downstairs office of the Higgins estate from the corner opposite the desk. They saw a woman enter and walk around the space. When she turned toward the camera, Betsy paused it.

"That's Tara. It's really her," Betsy said.

"No doubt about it."

She pushed play.

Tara rummaged around on the desk, looked off camera, and quickly exited the space.

"Why did she leave so quickly? Rewind it," Betsy said.

They rewatched Tara, and just before she left the room, she looked out the window and then retreated.

"Something spooked her, and she left," Henry said.

They fast-forwarded until they saw the bookcase open, from the wall. Betsy looked at Henry.

"A secret passage? Did they search that this morning?"

"I doubt it," Henry said.

A shape began to emerge, and the video file ended.

"I guess that's all we've got on this one."

"It's too bad. I would've liked to see how the snake ended up in that drawer."

Fourteen minutes later, they pulled up to the Higgins estate. Henry ducked under the crime scene tape and pushed open the door. Betsy passed him and led the way to the office. The bookcase was closed. Betsy pulled on it, but it appeared to be a solid wall.

"Let's bust it down," Betsy said, looking around impatiently.

"There's got to be a way to open it. Just look around for a minute," Henry said.

Betsy started rummaging around on the shelves. She opened a humidor and found a stack of stogies. She picked up a horse head book end . . . nothing. A book lying on its side with a signed Hank Aaron baseball in a stand on top, the title on the spine read *The Secrets Within*. She opened the book and found it was hollowed out and contained a set of keys.

"Do you think these open it somehow?" Betsy said, showing the keys to Henry.

"Maybe. Look for a keyhole."

But a moment later, she heard a clink, like the releasing of a magnet, and the bookcase swung open.

"Gotcha," Henry said. He was tilting a book backward off the shelf, and the title read, *The Way Through*.

They entered through the bookcase. Inside, a spiral staircase led up, as well as down.

"I'll go down," Betsy said.

"Up it is," Henry said.

Betsy grabbed her flashlight and shone it down into the dark passage. The power had not been restored here, and it was pitch-black.

"Police," she called out as she walked down the stairs.

She heard Henry's footsteps on the metal stairs as he went up. At the bottom of the steps, a tunnel ran in one direction. She walked down until she came to a large opening in one of the walls. She shined her light inside the room, which was a wine cellar. In the middle of the room sat a wingback chair, a perfect match for the wingback chair that remained in the master bedroom. This one was covered in blood.

"Police," she said again.

She heard a muffled grunt from behind her. She pulled out her gun and returned to the tunnel. The grunt sounded again from down the hallway. There was a small door set into the wall. She pulled the handle, but it was locked.

"*Mmrrhpp.*" She heard the grunting coming from behind the door.

"HENRY!" she called out. She took the keys she'd found upstairs from her pocket and tried the first one in the door, then the second, third.

Henry arrived.

"There's someone in here," she said.

It was the fifth key that opened the door. Inside, she found a storage room with shelves of files. On the floor at the foot of one of the shelves lay a man, tied up and bound at the mouth. His eyes were wild with fear.

"I'm a police officer," Betsy said as she ripped off the tape. "What's your name?"

"Mike, Mike Higgins."

"Who did this to you?"

Mike shook his head to clear it. "I don't . . . I can't remember."

Betsy's phoned chirped with a text. It was from Doug. *The video of the master bedroom is ready on the cloud.*

TARA

It felt like a dream. Tara stared at her sister, studying every detail of her face. She made constellations out of the freckle patterns, memorizing her face. She grabbed Cara's hand and squeezed it tight as they walked across the lawn.

"You're much too happy," Cara said.

"I found you! That's all that matters."

"Yeah, but we're still trapped here." Cara led her to the dining hall that sat up the hill from the lake, overlooking the camp. They sat on the steps of the long, low building. Cara picked a stick up and began to draw in the dirt.

"Okay, so here's the lake, the border to the front of the camp. The rest of the camp is encircled by an electrical fence. There are guards all along the fence as well. They walk the fence line all night long."

"How high is the fence?" Tara asked.

"I don't know, taller than me, for sure. Maybe like ten feet."

"Okay. Does anyone guard the water?"

"Yeah, there are guards along the shore, and they have a boat that circles around the water all night."

"So, there are two options. Option one, we go for the fence. We have to tackle three things, the electric fence, the guards, and the height of the fence. We'd have to find a way to power down the fence, or the whole camp, then we'd have to figure out the guard schedule to make the climb when no one would see us. Then we'd have to climb the fence, which is not really easy with the razor wire at the top. Or we could try to dig under the fence, but that would take time. Or we try for the water."

"Either way, they'll kill us."

"We can't stay here." Tara grabbed her sister's hand and squeezed it. She looked into her young face. "A million things could go wrong, but we have to try."

Cara nodded. "But what about my friends?"

"If we can get away, we'll send the police back here to save everyone, but for now, it's got to be just us."

Tara looked out at the lake. The wind whipped her hair around. There were small whitecaps on the water.

"I've got it. I've got a plan," Tara said.

HENRY

Mike was taken to the hospital while a team had been dispatched to search the area of the secret passage. When they arrived back at the squad room, Henry followed Betsy to the conference room, pulling up the video from the cloud as they walked. The video showed the master bedroom from the corner above the door. The two wingback chairs sat in front of the fireplace, and the door to the balcony was closed. He fast-forwarded until Michael entered from the secret passage behind a large bureau to change out of his suit.

He then exited through the secret passage. Henry fast-forwarded the video until Michael returned. He sat on the bed and rubbed his temples. Sloan entered from the secret passage, but Michael did not notice him at first. He said something, and Michael flinched and turned to him. The two exchanged words. It quickly became heated. Michael's face was red as he yelled at Sloan. Sloan, on the other hand, was calm and cool. He sneered as he spoke.

"Too bad we can't hear them," Betsy said.

Michael said something to Sloan and turned his back on him dismissively. Sloan darted forward and pushed Michael hard from behind. Michael spun around to face him. Sloan's hands were on his throat in a flash. Michael's face was turning red, and then purple. He clawed at Sloan's forearms.

The screen went to black.

"What? No!" Betsy said. "Doug!"

Doug entered and saw the black screen. "I'm afraid that's all there is."

"What happened? The battery ran out?"

"Actually, the battery was still good on this one. It just cuts to black at this point. Someone didn't want us to see what happened next," Doug said.

"So, the murderer erased it?" Henry asked.

"Looks that way," Doug said.

"But if Sloan's the murderer, why would he leave the fight and erase after that?" Betsy asked.

"Maybe it was an error. Or maybe it wasn't Sloan after all," Henry said.

"But all the evidence points to him."

"We need to get a search warrant for his home and office. Let me go check on what's taking so long with those."

TARA

"I believe in our plan, but just in case something goes wrong, we need to leave evidence for the police that we were here."

The girls stood in the cabin wearing black bathing suits. Cara had shown her a drawer full of them in varying sizes.

"I'd like to cut some of our hair," Tara continued, "but I guess they didn't give you anything sharp like scissors."

"No, but they gave me a razor this morning to prepare for my new owner."

"Grab it."

Tara pulled the razor across Cara's long hair, cutting chunks out of her pretty hair. She pulled her own hair out in front of her eyes and cut a few chunks out. Tara made a small slit in a few of the mattresses, and they shoved hair into them. They put a few more on the shower drain. She tucked them into the roller shades of the windows. Tara accidentally cut her finger on the razor as she was cutting more hair. She decided to go with it and squeezed some blood onto a pillow under the case and smeared it on the floor under the bed, squeezing the small cut to force more blood out. If this room was ever processed as a crime scene, they would find their DNA. They would know that they had been here. Finally, Tara took a piece of paper off a notepad on a side table. She took a purple crayon, and she wrote the following note:

To Detective Betsy Turner:

I found Cara. She has not been hurt but someone is coming here to buy her in a few hours. We have to get her away from here. We are going to try to escape. I made a plan, and I hope it will work. Once we're safely away, I'll call you. When I was here, I saw at least one hundred girls.

If you don't hear from us, then maybe the plan wasn't as good as I think it is. Forgive me for failing.

Sincerely,

Tara Sharp

PS. Tell Mike I love him.

She shoved the letter into one of the slits in the mattress.

"Ready?" Tara asked. Cara nodded.

Tara tucked the razor with the plastic cap on into her bathing suit top. They walked toward the lake, where girls splashed and laughed as if they were at summer camp. Tara grabbed two life preservers off a rack as they walked out onto the dock. A girl jumped off a high dock onto the blob, which was what Cara had called the long vinyl pillow on the water. Tara set the life jackets down and stood on the edge of the low dock, watching for a moment before diving in.

The mountain water was cool despite the heat. Tara stayed under, letting the cool water soak deep into her bones before she bobbed back up. She swam toward a floating wooden dock where other girls lay in the sun. Tara studied the blob from a safe distance. It was anchored by four long ropes attached to a metal carabiner on the side she could see. The other side would certainly have the same, so eight ropes total.

Plus, two more ropes tied the blob to the dock. The straps were pulled taut as the wind was still blowing hard away from the camp. It wouldn't take much for it to break free. Tara swam over to the blob and slid the razor from her suit. She cut the first strap to about 50 percent, and then swam to the other straps and did the same.

Tara swam back to the dock and grabbed the two life jackets. She took them to the blob and tied them to the straps beneath the craft. They floated up toward the surface but stayed out of sight.

A loud dinner bell rang. All the girls began to exit the water. Tara and Cara swam to the far side of the blob and hid out of sight.

A guard walked over to the edge of the dock, and Tara pointed downward. They both took a breath and ducked under the blob while they saw the guard above them on the dock. He turned away from the water. Tara came up for a breath and handed one of the life jackets to Cara.

"Put this on and hold on to the blob. Do not let go. This wind is strong today."

"That's the point," Cara said.

"Yeah," Tara said, smiling. "Here goes nothing."

Tara untied the two ropes holding the blob to the dock. Then she took a breath and dove under the blob. She grabbed the first strap and cut the rest of the way through it with the razor. Then, she severed the other ties. No one seemed to be looking as the two girls relaxed against the side of the blob as it pushed them away from the nightmarish camp.

MIKE

Mike woke up in a hospital bed. His mother had brought him some food. He felt like he was just thinking about something, but he couldn't remember what.

"Mom?"

"Hey, hon, how are you feeling?"

"Weird. Was I asleep?"

"You've been in and out since I arrived about an hour ago."

"Something, there is something on my mind, I can't remember."

"It's okay. The doctor said there was some swelling on your brain. With time, you should be back to normal. They said it looks like you banged you head."

Mike ran his hand over the crown of his head and felt a bandage and a lump.

"Mom, where's Tara?"

"Who?" Liza asked.

TARA

The blob was pushed out into the wide lake and away from the tiny cove of the camp. They swam to the ladder of the first house they came to and climbed up onto the wooden surface. Cara began to cry.

"I can't believe we did it. You saved me."

"I would have saved you or died trying."

They slipped the life jackets off and left them on the dock.

They looked up at the large house built into the side of the steep hill that slid down to the water. Each level had a deck. There were lights on in the upper two levels. They took the stairs up to the back door and knocked.

"Hello, anyone home? We need help."

The door opened, and Tara was so surprised, she couldn't speak.

"Can we use your phone? We need to call the police," Cara said.

Nikki stood in the large, vaulted living room, a fire roaring in the fireplace.

"What are you doing here?" Tara asked.

"This is my house. What are you doing here?" Nikki asked. "How in the world did you get here? You know the police are looking for you? After you left last night, I found my husband dead, murdered. The police think you did it."

"Okay, we need to call them. I can straighten this all out," Tara said.

"Okay, I'll make a call," Nikki said. "There are some towels in the hall closet."

Nikki grabbed her phone off the counter, where it sat next to a small hourglass keychain.

MIKE

Mike sat up in bed abruptly.

"Mike? What's wrong?" Liza asked.

"Mom, where's my phone? I need my phone."

"We never got them back after dinner last night. They are part of the evidence now."

"Evidence?"

"I'm sorry, Mike. But your father is dead," Liza said, her voice and hands shaking.

"What?"

"He was found dead this morning," Liza said.

Mike looked down at the white cotton blanket and cried. Nothing felt real.

"I know who killed him," Mike proclaimed.

"What?" Liza said, the color draining from her face. "Who? How?"

"I need a phone, Mom, now."

She handed him the landline that sat on the table next to his bed. He dialed zero.

"Yes, I need to speak to the police in charge of the Michael Higgins investigation."

BETSY

Henry had gone over to the courthouse to talk to the district attorney about the search warrant. It would be hard to get anything going on a Saturday, but they needed to find Sloan before he escaped or went into hiding. They needed to find the girls he'd been hiding and prove that he was guilty of not only that but also the murder of Michael Higgins.

Betsy's phone rang.

"Hello," she said.

"This is Mike, Mike Higgins Jr. I know who killed my dad. I just remembered something."

"Who?"

"Nikki."

"Nikki killed Michael?"

"Yeah."

"How do you know that? Did you see her do it?"

"No. But she's the one who hurt me. She hit me over the head with a frying pan, and then she put me in the basement."

Betsy was on the road five minutes later, heading toward the address for Nikki's lake house. It said two hours, but she threw the lights on and mashed the accelerator to the floor. She picked up the phone and dialed Henry.

"Hello," Henry said.

"Listen, it wasn't Sloan, or rather it wasn't just Sloan. It's Nikki. She's the one who had access to everything Michael had. She was able to frame him from inside their marriage. She's at the lake house. I'm heading there now. Meet me there."

"You shouldn't go. Not without backup."

"I have to. I can't let them get away. Not if they have girls there. Maybe that's where they moved them."

"Maybe."

"I have to try."

"Just watch and wait. Do not go in without backup . . . Betsy?"

"Call me when you know more," Betsy said and clicked the phone off.

TARA

Michael was dead. And according to Nikki, the police would blame Tara for his death. But he was alive when she left, or at least the last time she'd seen him. Tara's mind spun. *How is this Nikki's house? So close to the camp.* The lake house must be on the property of the camp, which once again tied the Higgins family to the sex trafficking ring. But she'd believed Michael. She believed that Sloan had set him up. The Higgins' family was still benefitting greatly from the enterprise. And why just give all that money away? No. One of the Higgins was complicit in the whole ugly affair. But it wasn't Michael. It had to be Nikki.

Nikki grabbed her phone, hit a number, and put it to her ear. She smiled at the girls from the side of her face most unreassuringly.

"Missing something?" she said into the phone. "No, I'm not talking about the blob! I'm talking about the merchandise, you imbecile."

And suddenly, like a bolt of lightning, everything made sense. O'Hara wasn't Michael, and it wasn't Sloan. O'Hara was Nikki. Of course. Why hadn't she seen it before? If Butler's was named after Rhett Butler, then O'Hara was a nickname for Scarlett O'Hara. It was a woman running the show. All the numbers pointed to Michael because Nikki shared his accounts. She left his name front and center. She probably counted on him taking the fall if anything ever was discovered. And like a fool, Tara had delivered Cara right back into her arms.

Tara grabbed Cara's hand and pulled her toward the door. Nikki walked over to a credenza and pulled open a drawer. She came up holding a small pistol. "Can you both have a seat?"

Tara stopped and stared at Nikki. This wasn't how it ended. Not after she had found her sister and successfully escaped. It wouldn't end like this. She tried to think of a plan as she moved toward the couch to have a seat.

"Not on the couch. You're soaking wet. I swear, the floor is fine," she said to the girls, and then continued talking into the phone. "I've got two girls here in my living room." She sighed heavily. "Have Mr.

Green come here. Make it seem like the plan all along. I guess I'll have to kill the other one. I don't know why you didn't do that to start with. . . . No, she's too old. . . . I'll clean her up for the client." She hung up and turned to face them as they sat on the floor.

Sloan underestimated you. I told him you were a bigger threat than he thought. But isn't that a man for you, always underestimating women. Yes, I know who you are. I knew before dinner. I've had my eye on you. I tried to get you to back off with that rock through your car window. I knew no good would come out of your presence. But you presented quite the predicament. I couldn't get rid of you without drawing attention. All I had to do was hope to get through dinner without you finding anything."

Tara looked around. She had traded one hell for another.

"But then someone killed Michael. A major inconvenience to me. But at least I could blame you and hope the whole thing would go away. But you realized Michael was a patsy and had been all along. That's when you turned all your attention to Sloan, who is guilty of a lot of things. But once again, everyone always underestimates the woman. Why did you think all the paperwork pointed to Michael? All the things were in his name. He and I are legally joined, so I own what he owns.

"Is it finally starting to click? It was me all along. I traffic girls. I'm O'Hara. I made it look like my husband was guilty. No one suspects that women are capable of such greatness. I've fooled them all."

"But why?"

"I started out as one of the girls. Snatched from my village in Colombia at the age of eleven and taught how to please a man. But I worked my way up the ladder. Once I got near the top, the clients were loyal to me . . . not the pimps. I took the pimps out and ran the business as my own. My clients loved me and knew that I'd be loyal and discreet. I have a clientele that includes powerful men, very powerful men. Sloan helped me take over the operation from the idiots running it before me. He started as a client but proved himself useful. He became my second-in-command. That's when we decided to use Butler's as a front. But we needed a rich patsy, so Sloan introduced me to Michael, who had no clue what was going on. I married him, and we made him owner of it all. It was a nice, comfortable life for a while, and I even got to have a family.

"Which brings us to now. I don't want to kill you, but you'll never let Cara go without a fight."

"I'll pay you for her . . . I'll double whatever he is paying."

"You can't afford that. Besides, I never disappoint my clients. I don't want to kill you, but I've got no choice. I can't have any loose ends. I'm not going to jail. I spent too much time making sure Michael would look guilty to let you go and tell the police the truth. Sure, I'll continue to buy and sell young girls . . . and I don't feel bad about it, I don't. If they have strength, then they will overcome it and come out stronger on the other side, like I did, and if they don't, then it's no big loss. You're either a winner or a waste."

"Mom?" the voice of Kieran came from the open door that led down to the dock. "What are you doing? Is all that you said true? Mom? You don't buy and sell people? Like slaves?"

"Oh, dear, no, of course not . . . it was all just nothing."

"Who are you pointing the gun at?"

"Okay, the truth is, dear, that I didn't come to America with my family like I told you. I was kidnapped from my village when I was eleven. I haven't seen my parents, or brothers, I had two, since that day. But I have risen in power, from a victim to a conqueror, and I'm now in charge of the whole operation."

"But Dad had plenty of money. Why would you sell girls?"

"Old habits die hard. And I'm very good at it. One begins to feel useless in a big house with nothing to do."

"We have enough money. You can turn them in. You can ask for immunity. We can talk to a lawyer about it."

"It's too late for that," Nikki said.

"Who are you pointing a gun at?"

"Nobody, dear."

Tara popped her head up. "Kieran, it's me. Call the police."

"Yvette? What are you doing here? Mom? How could you?" Kieran pulled his phone out of his pocket.

"No, Kieran, no. Don't you see? I did it all for you. And look what I have created from nothing. This will all be yours. We just need to deal with them."

"You didn't create this. Dad did."

"No, honey, I did. I created this family. Don't you see? I married him to cover my tracks, and I was rewarded with you, and now he's gone, and we can live happily ever after. Don't you see? They'll tell on me. They know the truth, and if they live, I'll go to jail. Everything we have will be gone."

"Don't hurt them, Mom. Please."

"I'm sorry, Kieran, you are too young to understand, but someday you will. Give me your phone."

"No. I'm calling the police," Kieran said.

As he pulled his phone out, the doorbell rang. "They're here. Kieran, be a good boy. Take Tara up to your room. Keep her there and quiet until I finish this."

"Tara?"

"Yes, that's Yvette's real name. She is a deceitful liar. We can't trust her."

"I don't care!" Kieran screamed, still holding the phone.

"ENOUGH!" Nikki shouted. She walked over to her son and snatched the phone out of his hand. "You two need to get out of the way while Mommy conducts a little business."

She pulled the girls to their feet and marched them upstairs. "Come along, Kieran, you too." At the top of the stairs, she opened a bedroom door. "Tie her up, Kieran."

"With what?"

"A necktie from your closet. Now you guard them, honey, and we'll discuss this after. Just be a good boy for Mommy," Nikki said. "Now you come with me." She grabbed Cara's arm and left the room.

Nikki shut the door, and a lock clicked.

"Did she lock us in?" Tara asked.

"Yeah. She's done that before when she had business. I should've known it was nothing good."

"You couldn't have known. But now you do. I need your help. That was my little sister, Cara, down there. Your mom is selling her to a man who's going to hurt her. I'll never find her if she leaves with him. Please untie me so I can help her."

Kieran began untying her immediately. "I can't believe she thought I would help her. I don't want to have anything else to do with her. I lost both my parents in twenty-four hours."

"I'm so sorry, Kieran," Tara said, taking his hand and looking in his eyes.

"Follow me." He went to the window and opened it. The window opened onto a slanting roof. Tara followed him out onto the roof, two stories above the ground.

"I'm going to pretend I'm not afraid of heights," Tara said.

"It's not so bad around front," Kieran said. They walked toward the front of the house, which was built into the side of a steep hill, shortening the distance to the ground. At the front of the house, they were only about ten feet up.

They could see Sloan and a tall, dark-haired man, who must be Mr. Green, standing on the front steps. Mr. Green's hair was greased back, and he had a mole on his chin. Nikki opened the door for them.

"Welcome," she said. "Sorry for the confusion. We thought a more private setting might suit you." They stepped into the house. The door closed behind them.

Kieran turned around, grabbed the gutter, and slid his body over the edge before dropping to the ground. Tara took a breath before following. She landed with a thump in some rose bushes. The bushes cut her fingers, and she quickly wiped some of the blood along the bricks.

"What are you doing?" Kieran asked.

"Just evidence that I was here. In case—" A shiver ran down her spine.

Kieran looked at her and shook his head. "We're not going to let anything bad happen to you or your sister." He stepped toward the house and looked into the window. He signaled for her to look too. Inside, she saw the dark-haired man caress Cara's cheek as she flinched away. "We have to keep them from leaving. And we need to call the police."

"I can sneak around to the game room downstairs. There is a landline there. I'll call the police."

"What else is in the game room?"

"There's a small kitchen."

"Okay, I'm coming with you. I need something sharp, like a knife to slit the tires."

"Use this," Kieran said, tossing her his Swiss Army knife.

"Perfect. And Kieran . . . be careful."

Kieran nodded as he darted into the shadows around the side of the house. There were two cars in the driveway. Tara ran to the first car, slipped open the knife, and jabbed it into the tire. The tire was stronger than she'd expected. She had to wiggle the knife before she heard a small hiss of air escaping. She did the same with all eight tires before she went back to look in the front window to see what was happening inside.

Sloan was coming up the stairs with Kieran. "I found Kieran downstairs on the phone."

Nikki's eyes darted to Kieran. "Oh, sorry, honey. I had the landline disconnected. We just aren't here enough to justify keeping it. Please sit here while we finish up our business."

"Crap," Tara said to herself.

Inside, Mr. Green was carrying Cara. Her head was leaned against his chest, her legs dangling from his arm. A shudder rain down Tara's spine as she watched through the window. Cara's eyes were closed, her body relaxed in the monster's arms. *They must have drugged her.* He turned and carried her toward the door. Tara looked around for a place to hide. She quickly slipped away from the house and into the surrounding woods, hiding behind a large oak tree.

The front door opened. Sloan and Mr. Green, carrying Cara, exited the house, followed by Nikki.

"It should be a quick ride from here to the airport, and then you'll be on your way," Sloan said. He stopped short and his mask of calm was shattered by one of rage.

"What's this?" Mr. Green said. "All the tires are flat? Who could have done this?"

"It's nothing for you to worry about, Mr. Green. I'll have another car here in five minutes."

"This is unacceptable," Mr. Green said.

"I understand. I'm terribly sorry," Nikki said. "Let's go inside. I can fix you a drink while we wait for the car." Nikki led Mr. Green, holding Cara into the house.

Sloan grabbed his phone, made a call, and spoke into the phone. "Get a car over to Nikki's now." He took a gun from his pocket and aimed it toward the woods. The sun was beginning to set, but it was still light enough to see. Tara crouched behind the tree, holding perfectly still, barely allowing herself to breathe.

"I know you are out there. You should not have made an enemy of me. You will regret this. You won't outlive your sister after all." Sloan turned and walked inside the house.

Stalling wouldn't work forever. They were sending another car now. The police weren't even on the way. Tara had to do something drastic. She took the knife in her hands and snuck toward the house. When she entered through the open front door, Mr. Green was the closest, his back to her. Nikki and Sloan were in front of him, and Kieran, the only one facing her, stood at the other end of the room.

Tara hit Mr. Green from behind at full speed. She knocked him to the ground. Cara flew out of his arms and landed on the ground just in front of him. Tara jumped onto his back and plunged the knife between his shoulder blades, wiggling it as she'd done with the tires. He screamed out in pain.

Sloan and Nikki pulled their guns as Kieran looked on wide-eyed.

Nikki looked at the ceiling and sighed. "Kill her."

Sloan aimed the gun at Tara.

"Not in here, you imbecile. Take her outside," she said to Sloan. "I don't want to make a mess in here."

Tara crawled next to her sister. "No! I'm not going anywhere without her, you monster."

"Get her out of here," Nikki said as she turned to help the client. Nikki put her gun down on the counter as she grabbed a towel to stop the bleeding.

Tara felt her hair being ripped backward as Sloan dragged her away from Cara. She clawed at the ground before Sloan grabbed her arm and yanked her to her feet.

BETSY

Betsy pulled up to the lake house. She'd cut forty minutes off the expected arrival. But still too much time had passed. She was unaware of what she'd find inside but hoped, at least, to find the truth. Maybe she'd get a step closer to finding Cara. She hoped it wouldn't be too late. She'd seen a lot of unhappy endings in her career, and there was no guarantee this story wouldn't go that way. She walked to the front of the house and peeked inside. She saw Tara. She couldn't believe it. She heard a car pull in the driveway behind her. A man with a tiger tattoo on his face, like the one Harris had drawn, jumped out of the driver seat and aimed a rifle at her.

"Hold it right there," he said, approaching her.

"I'm a detective with the Atlanta Police," she said, holding her hands up.

"Good for you," he said. He walked over and punched her in the stomach. She crumbled forward, bending in on herself. The intensity of the unexpected blow took her breath away. He raised the butt end of the gun and slammed it into her head. She fell back onto the pavement.

KIERAN

Kieran watched as Tara stabbed that man. Blood poured from the wound and down onto the white carpet, which was drinking it up thirstily. His mom put her gun down just a foot or so away from him. He had turned on his father yesterday. Well, he thought he had when he'd shot Sloan. Now he was going to turn on his mother. He reached over, picked up the gun, and aimed it at Sloan.

"Put her down," Kieran said.

"Nikki, control your child," Sloan said, not even looking at Kieran.

"I'll shoot," Kieran said. His mother stopped what she was doing and looked at him.

"No, honey," Nikki said.

"You're going to shoot me . . . again?" Sloan said. "Your son is wearing on me."

Mr. Green turned, sighed, and said, "Enough of this." He pulled a gun from his waistband and shot it before Kieran had time to react. Pain exploded in the boy's shoulder. He dropped to his knees and cried out.

"NO!" Nikki screamed. She ran to her son, carrying the towel she'd been using on the client, and pressed it against Kieran's shoulder. "What have you done?" she screamed at the client.

"Ended this amateur hour. I'm taking my business elsewhere."

"You just shot my son! You are dead! Shoot him, Sloan!" Nikki screamed.

Sloan, pushed Tara aside and aimed his gun at the client, who aimed his gun right back at Sloan.

"Do you think you're a faster shot then me? Believe me, you're not. Nikki, the keys to the boat, and I'll be on my way," Mr. Green said.

Nikki's phone rang. She listened and hung up. "The cops are heading this way."

"Keys now," Mr. Green said.

Nikki held the keys in her hand, "Come on, Kieran, we have to go."

"I'm not going with you, Mom."

"Please, Kieran, there's no time to argue."

"I'm not going with you."

"We have to go . . . NOW!" Sloan said.

"I love you, Kieran. I'll come back for you," Nikki said, hugging him briefly and darting out the back door, heading for the boathouse. Sloan followed.

Mr. Green stumbled to his feet. He scooped up Cara to follow Nikki toward the dock. Tara sprang up and tackled him from behind. She pushed against his injury. He screamed out in pain and dropped Cara. He turned, aimed his gun at Tara, and shot her in the stomach. Tara stumbled forward and flung her body on top of Cara's. Mr. Green tried to move her, but she would not budge. Tara clung to her with every ounce of energy she had left. Kieran ran at Mr. Green, knocking the gun out of his hand. Mr. Green looked down at the girls. The blare of sirens neared.

"No one is worth this," Mr. Green said and darted to the dock, a trail of blood behind him.

Kieran knelt next to Tara. "Tell me you're wearing that bulletproof vest again." But he knew before she shook her head. He knew from all the blood that she wasn't.

HENRY

The SWAT team surrounded the property. Henry walked around the side of the house, down a steep slope, toward the back with a few other officers, and knocked. "GBI. Open up," the voice of one of the officers boomed from the front of the house.

Henry turned the corner to the back of the house and saw two men running across the lawn toward the boathouse. From this distance, he was reasonably sure one of them was Sloan; the other was unknown to him. A boat engine roared. Henry pulled his gun and ran down the lawn toward the lake.

"Freeze!" he shouted, aiming at the slower of the two suspects, the one he presumed to be Sloan Peterson. Henry got a couple of shots off as did the officers around him. The other man was just able to hop into the boat. The driver, who looked to be Nikki Higgins, sped off, leaving Sloan behind.

Sloan stopped running and put his hands up over his head. Henry put his gun away and walked over to Sloan.

"Good evening, Sloan," he said before reading him his rights and slapping handcuffs on him.

BETSY

Betsy woke up. The sky above her was dark. She looked around and hesitantly sat up. She was still at the lake house, but she'd been dragged around the side. She stood up and walked to the front door.

When Betsy entered the house, she saw Kieran first. He sat at a barstool. A paramedic was wrapping his shoulder. Blood covered his shirt. "Who shot you?" she asked.

"I don't know his name. He ran off toward the boathouse. He got her too," Kieran said, pointing down at the floor where two bodies lay in the center of the room. Paramedics were kneeling over them. Betsy walked past the paramedics and saw that the closer of the two bodies was Tara. She was covered in blood, but her eyes blinked open. She smiled at Betsy.

"I found her. Take care of her. Please. I found her."

Betsy looked at the other girl, a face she'd only known from photographs. *Cara.* She was not responsive.

"Is she okay?" she asked the paramedic.

"It seems she's been drugged. Her pulse is strong," he answered. He began to move Tara to a stretcher, but her arm held tight to Cara. "Miss, we need to take you to get help. You have to let go of her."

"What's her status?" Betsy asked.

"Critical. Gunshot wound to the abdomen. We have to get her to the hospital."

"I've got Cara," Betsy said. "Let go, Tara. You are both safe now." Tara let go, and the paramedics rolled her out the door. They loaded her into an ambulance and drove away with the siren howling and the lights flashing.

A second ambulance loaded Cara into the back. The paramedic ducked out to check on Kieran, who stood in the doorway holding his shoulder.

"Another ambulance is en route," he said.

"I'll take him. I'll follow you in the squad car," Betsy said. "Come on." She helped Kieran into the car.

She started the siren and followed the ambulance along the winding country road. She glanced in the rearview mirror and saw Kieran, tears streaming.

"You're going to be okay, Kieran," Betsy said.

"Maybe physically," he said, wiping his eyes with the back of his good arm.

CHAPTER 10

SUNDAY

SLOAN

Sloan's lawyer advised him to say nothing as the detectives came into the small interview room and sat at the interview table.

"How long have you been involved in human trafficking?" Betsy asked, looking smug.

"Don't answer that," the lawyer said.

"Okay, how about, why did you kill Michael Higgins?"

"Do you plan on telling us what proof you have of anything, or are you just going to accuse my client of every unsolved case on your docket?"

"Well, let's see, we have Sloan's DNA under the fingernails of the deceased. We also have a video of an altercation between the two of you before his death Friday night."

It was just like Michael to have video cameras hidden in his house, but the master bedroom was taking it a bit far. He wondered if Nikki knew, or if she cared. Did Michael have the entire house under surveillance? *What a complete control freak.*

Sloan thought back to the fight. Maybe he'd gone too far. His temper had gotten away from him, but he hadn't killed Michael. He had left him alive. He had left him for someone else to kill. And someone had.

"What video?" the lawyer asked.

"Michael had nearly the whole house under surveillance."

"Well, that's good news. You must have seen who killed him then."

"The last thing on the tape is you fighting with him," Betsy said.

"That's unfortunate. We fought. But when I left him, he was alive. I swear. There must be more on the tape."

"There was. Someone erased it."

"Whoever erased it must have known the footage existed. I didn't know, so I couldn't have erased it. And if I had erased it, I would have erased the fight I had with him."

"A valid point," the lawyer said. "It's obvious the killer erased the footage. The fact that they left this fight proves that Sloan isn't the murderer. The killer left it to make Sloan the fall guy."

"Let's say someone came in after you and killed Michael," Betsy said. "Who do you think that could be?"

"Any of them. They all had a motive."

"Like what?"

"Well, Tara, the fake girlfriend. She wanted Michael dead because of what he did to her sister."

"Okay, but Michael was innocent," Betsy said. "He was just a patsy for you."

"If you say so. Do you have any evidence of his innocence? Besides, she didn't know that."

"We're looking into Tara. Any other theories of the crime?"

"Let's see, the chef. He's a serial killer that targeted big game hunters."

"And how long have you known that?" Henry asked. "If you knew, you should have turned him in. Especially with him targeting your friend."

Sloan paused. "I put it together in the hospital last night."

"Nice try. We have here"—Henry dropped some papers on the table—"copies of documents found in your house in which a private investigator found the identity of the Hunter's Hunter for you. According to Nikki, it was by your recommendation that Joe was hired as the chef."

"That doesn't say much about you wanting Michael alive," Betsy said. "I think you were mad about this sale of Butler's that he had organized. When is that supposed to happen?"

"Next week."

"And now?"

"I can't possibly think about such a thing at a time like this."

"Oh, I doubt that. I think you set Michael up to be killed because that's all you could think about," Betsy said.

"If you knew Joe was a serial killer, why are you asking me questions? You should be looking for him," Sloan said.

"We already have him. We caught him heading across the country in your car."

"He stole my car?"

"He said you loaned it to him."

"That's not true! He stole it after murdering my best friend."

"Oh, Michael was your best friend now?"

"Of course, he was. That's why I couldn't have done it."

"So, Tara or Joe are your main suspects."

"They are just two possibilities. It could have been Harris or Mike. You know Michael was going to meet with his estate lawyer Monday. I know Harris was concerned that he was cutting them out of his will."

"Who told them that Michael was meeting with his estate lawyer?"

"I don't know. Word had gotten around at the office."

"Harris said that you told him. And that you told him Michael told you he was cutting them out of the will. Did you tell him that?"

"No. He must have misremembered it."

"Uh-huh."

"Anyone else you'd like to throw under the bus while you're at it?"

"Well, of course, Addison had a motive."

"She did?"

"Michael didn't tell many people, but a few days before he died, he was diagnosed with dementia. Addison didn't want to keep taking care of him, especially if he was going to lose it. She couldn't go to medical school and take care of him. She wanted her life back."

"Addison said no one knew but her and Michael."

"Well, he told me. We were close. Best friends."

"I doubt that. Michael was a very proud man. I don't think he would have told anyone." Betsy pulled some papers out of the file in front of her. "We found these documents when we searched your home." She pushed the papers in front of Sloan. "We knew something was off when we couldn't contact the doctor Michael had seen. But he wasn't a doctor at all. He was an actor. And you paid him to lie to Michael and give him a fake report. We've tracked the actor down. He's willing to testify against you in order to get immunity."

"That doesn't mean she didn't kill him. She's smart enough to make it look like an accident."

"Well, then that's proof she didn't do it. Nothing about this looks like an accident."

Betsy threw another paper in front of him. "We found these digital images on your computer." In front of him were the pictures of Michael with his lover, the ones they'd found on Nikki's bedside table.

"Now that's who I'd put my money on. She's got a temper," Sloan said.

"But you sent her the pictures. You were behind all of them, pushing them toward the murder of Michael."

"I didn't kill him!"

"You wanted him dead. You just wanted someone else to do it for you. Maybe you didn't kill him, maybe you didn't push him out the window or bash him over the head, caving in his skull, but you orchestrated his death. We're charging you with conspiracy to commit murder. We may or may not add more charges later. Is there anything else you'd like to say?"

Sloan stared at them both with a look of hatred and disgust.

"Wait," Sloan said. "I can give you O'Hara and the whole human trafficking ring with her."

"O'Hara?" Betsy asked.

"Who is that?" Henry interrupted.

"It's a code name. The girls don't know our real names."

"So, O'Hara was your second-in-command. Some poor woman you tricked into helping you run this sickening endeavor?"

"Ha. You have no clue. I'm not in charge of her. In fact, quite the opposite. I report to her," Sloan said.

"What do you mean?" Betsy said. "You're telling me that a woman is the ringleader of a sex trafficking outfit?"

"Yeah, why not?"

"A woman wouldn't buy and sell other women."

"That's not very progressive of you," Sloan said. "A woman can do anything, be it good or evil, as well as a man."

"Butler's was the front for the sex trafficking ring. So that's on you," Betsy said.

"Yes, Butler's was a front, and Michael owned fifty-one percent of the company," Sloan said.

"Yeah, but he didn't know what you were doing."

"You're right, he didn't, but do you think I'd give a controlling share to someone who had no knowledge of the truth?"

"What are you saying?"

"I wasn't in charge. I'm only a pawn in a bigger game."

"But if it wasn't you, and it wasn't Michael, who was it?"

"Come on, you're detectives. . . . Who gets the fifty-one percent now?"

"Nikki?"

"Exactly."

"Wait, so Nikki is O'Hara?"

"Bingo. She started out as one of the girls, but she turned on the pimps," Sloan explained. "I helped her. She had the clients wrapped around her finger, and they followed her to a new operation. Then, I set her up to marry my business partner. A fall guy and a cover for her."

"So why did you work for her? Why did you sell the girls?"

"It started for the money, plain and simple. My daughter was very sick. I didn't have the best healthcare as a business owner. I was paying thousands of dollars a month to keep her healthy, to keep her alive. It was unsustainable."

Betsy opened her file and checked something. "It says your daughter died over ten years ago. I'm sorry for your loss. But why did you keep at it after that? Did she have something on you?"

"Of course. She has something on everyone."

"You say she has something on everyone. Who is everyone?"

"Lawyers, judges, politicians, celebrities, lots and lots of people who won't want her to go down for this. In fact, I'd be surprised if you get close to her."

TARA

Tara's eyes opened. She took a minute to realize she was in a hospital room. Only one thought came to her. *Cara. Where's Cara? Is she safe?* The pain in her stomach reminded her she'd been shot. She called out from the bed. "Hello? Help!" She tried to stand up, but she could barely sit up in the bed.

"Tara? Are you okay?" The curtain next to her bed slid open, and she saw Cara standing there, smiling in her own hospital gown.

"You're awake!" Cara said.

"Cara!" Tara held her arms out to hug her sister. Cara flew forward and jumped into bed with her.

Pain erupted in her stomach. "Oowww!" she cried out, gasping.

"Sorry," Cara said, sliding to the side of the bed.

"It's okay. It's worth it for you." Tara wrapped her arms around her sister and kissed her on the top of the head.

"The detectives have been here asking all kinds of questions. I told them all about Pleasure Island, the house they kept us in, and all the people I came into contact with. I had used that study technique you taught me. The one where you use the first letter to make a word or phrase, like the colors in the rainbow, ROY G. BIV."

"A mnemonic device, you mean?"

"Yeah, to memorize all the girls I met. It got weird because I just had to add a word each time I met a new girl. It ended up being over fifty words long. There were many more girls than that at the camp, but I didn't meet them all. Anyway, I told the police everything, and they are going there to save my friends."

"Good job, Cara. You have been a huge help to them, I'm sure."

"Oh, also they said they need to talk to you about the murder." Cara looked round to make sure they were alone. "Did you kill someone?"

"Of course not!" Tara said.

"That's a relief. I told them that, of course, you wouldn't kill anyone. I think they believe you. Oh, yeah, and someone hired a lawyer to represent you. She came by and left her card. I'm so glad you woke up. I'm being discharged tomorrow. My foster family is here, and they are taking me home."

Tara's jaw set. "You belong with me." She hugged her sister tightly.

NANCY

Nancy sat at a long table in the dining hall of Pleasure Island, discussing the escape of Cara and her sister. It was all any of the girls talked about. Cara had told them her plan, and they had started a food fight at dinner the night before to distract the guards. By the time it was over, and they'd been punished, the blob was gone, and there was no sign of Cara or her sister. They'd done it. They'd escaped.

"Why didn't we go with them?" Lauren said.

"It probably wouldn't have worked if there had been more of us. Don't worry. Cara won't forget about us."

"But when? I don't want to stay here for another second."

Nancy looked around the dining hall. There were only two guards here. There were usually closer to eight, with more patrolling the grounds. The two guards were talking as if they knew something was up.

The sound of wailing sirens filled their ears. The guards pulled their weapons and were watching out the windows intently.

"Come out with your hands up," an amplified voice said. Nancy looked at Lauren. In fact, all the girls were looking around at each other. Lauren stood and pointed toward the back door. She silently walked over and opened it. The girls started to pour out of the doors.

"Hold it right there," one of the guards said, pointing his gun at Nancy.

"Run. He's not going to shoot us," Nancy said.

"Like hell I won't," he said, aiming his gun. Nancy raised her hands over her head and walked toward the guards.

"You only need one hostage. Go out, girls," Nancy said. The girls ran outside.

"Stop," the guard said, but none of them did. They just ran outside.

Good girls, Nancy thought.

BETSY

Betsy and Henry stood among a team of officers with guns trained on the mess hall. They'd taken the guards by surprise, one by one, as they'd come to the mess hall for lunch. Nine captured guards now sat in the back of police cruisers.

The detective saw movement around the back of the dining hall—girls pouring out the back of the building. She ran to them.

"This way!" She led them to the large vans they had waiting.

As they climbed in, Betsy asked, "How many guards are inside?"

"Two guards are in the mess hall. They kept Nancy. She volunteered herself so we could get away. Please save her. She's one of the good ones."

"I'll do everything I can. Now climb in. The officers will take you to safety."

"Thank you for coming for us," one girl said. She smiled and joined the other girls in a fifteen-passenger van that was headed to the hospital to have them all checked out.

Cara had told Betsy the names she could remember of all the girls at the camp. They had found the families of some of them, many of whom were gathered in the GBI headquarters awaiting news. Betsy had spoken with Nancy's mother that morning. She had driven all night from Florida; her husband and two sons would be flying up this afternoon. She left the moment she'd gotten the call. Betsy could relate to that. She'd do the same if she ever got that call.

As the SWAT team prepared to take the building, Betsy called out. "Wait! Let me go in. Give me a chance to get the last girl out. What she did was very brave. She saved all the other girls. Let me save her before this escalates. We both know the likelihood of getting her out alive; once you guys go in, that drops dramatically."

"Okay, but we're not playing hostage negotiations all day. I'll give you five minutes before we go in."

"Gotcha."

"I'm coming with you," Henry said.

"Thanks."

Betsy and Henry approached the door to the mess hall with their hands up. "Get back," a voice yelled from inside.

"We're coming in. We want to check on Nancy."

"Why should I let you in?"

"We need to figure out a way out of this. Right now, you don't have a lot of options."

"Only one of you, and leave your weapons."

Betsy looked at Henry and handed him her gun. She walked toward the door and pushed it open. Inside, she found two guards pacing the room, holding machine guns. Nancy was sitting at the long table calmly finishing a plate of food.

"Are you alright, Nancy?"

"Yeah."

"Okay, guys. Let's let Nancy go, and then we can make a plan."

One of the guards stood behind Nancy and held his gun to her head. "No way. She's the only bargaining chip I have."

"That's not true. I bet you know a lot about the boss here. That's who we are after. We want the big fish, not the guards."

"So, you're not arresting us?"

"Well, we'll have to work out the details, but you can still come out of this alive. Isn't that what you want?"

"This is bull," one guard said to the other. "As soon as we let her go, they'll shoot us."

"There's no reason for anyone to shoot you if you put your guns down and walk out with me."

"You'll give us immunity?"

"No. I can't promise that, but if you give me some information about the camp, the girls that came through here, and who was in charge, I promise you, we will work with you to lower your charges." The guards looked at each other. "The other option is going up against about forty police officers, including a SWAT team, that is itching to come in here and use their guns."

One guard dropped his weapon and put his hands up. He walked out through the doors toward the officers. Betsy heard a commotion as they arrested him. The remaining guard looked at Betsy. He grabbed Nancy and pulled her away from the table and out the back door.

Using Nancy as a shield, the guard stood surrounded by the SWAT team.

"HENRY!" Betsy called. Henry rushed inside and handed Betsy her weapon. He followed her as she pushed open the back doors.

"I will shoot her. Let me through," the guard said as he walked past the men with the guns aimed at him, still using Nancy as a shield. He led Nancy down the hill toward the boathouse with his back to the water. He had his arm locked around Nancy's neck; the other arm held a gun to her head. He backed almost all the way to the water, only a few feet away from the boathouse.

"He's going to get away," Betsy said.

Nancy looked at her and winked. She flashed her teeth as she bit down hard on the meaty part of the guard's arm. He immediately dropped her. She darted three quick steps away and dove into the lake.

"Drop your weapon!"

The guard aimed and fired at Betsy as he turned toward the boathouse; he shot off a couple of rounds into the water where Nancy had gone in, before ducking into the boathouse. A motor roared to life, and a speedboat flew out. The SWAT team unloaded, firing at the boat, but the driver had ducked down and out of sight. Only his hands could be seen steering the vessel. She holstered her weapon and ran over to the edge of the water to look for Nancy. She hadn't seen her come up for air. Betsy removed her holster and kicked off her shoes as she prepared to jump in. Just before she dove, she saw Nancy's head break the surface of the water by the floating dock. She climbed up on it.

"He's gone?" she asked.

"Yes."

"I'm free!" Nancy yelled. She ran to the edge of the dock and did a flip into the water.

The guard was apprehended at the other end of the lake and arrested. He was not offered a deal.

CHAPTER 11

FINALE

The GBI searched the waters of Lake Rabun for Nikki and the client who had escaped in the boat registered to Michael Higgins.

At around three in the morning, they spotted the boat anchored in a small cove surrounded by pine trees. Two search boats moved in.

"Freeze! We have you surrounded," they announced. No reply or even the slightest sound or movement came from the boat.

Guns drawn, they approached the boat. Once they got closer, one officer from each boat boarded the vessel. They found it empty save for the body of a man with a mole on his chin. He had a stab wound in his back and a gunshot in the head. He turned out to be the CEO of a Fortune 500 pharmaceutical company. His death and the things that came out about his patronage of a human trafficking operation were huge news stories for weeks.

Over the next few days, they raided the camp as well as numerous flophouses around the city. In all, more than two hundred girls were rescued, and fifty-four men arrested. They also stumbled across the meticulous records of clients who would all be tried in time, many of whom were local celebrities, politicians, and athletes. It was one of the largest human trafficking busts in history.

Nancy and the other girls who had families were reunited at the station. The girls who did not have families or were taken from other countries were placed in group homes, where they could get counseling until their families could be found or foster families could be arranged.

Nancy and many of the girls stayed friends for the rest of their lives.

The camp, Pleasure Island, was given to a charity that rehabilitates victims of human trafficking. The name was changed.

Jane Doe's identity was never confirmed. Her DNA was found inside a Butler's Ice Cream truck. The company was forced to pay for her burial. They were out of business shortly after that. No one was convicted of her murder.

Nikki had escaped. They did not find her in the days and weeks after she'd slipped through their fingers at the lake house. Of course, at the time, they hadn't known she was guilty of so much. But now they knew, and they'd found proof of each sale of each girl she had made. She'd kept meticulous records. It became clear that Nikki had been the ringleader of the entire human trafficking operation, just as Sloan had said. Millions of dollars and hundreds of girls. The general belief was that she'd killed Michael and erased the security camera tape, which would prove this. It never sat right with Betsy, who felt that Michael was covering for her so well that she didn't have much motive for wanting him dead, except, of course, for the affair. People had killed for less.

A month after the whole affair, Kieran got the following letter with no return address. The postmark was from Tampa. He turned it over to police, but no trace of Nikki was found.

My Dearest Kieran,

I'm so sorry I am not with you. I miss you every second of every day. I know I promised I'd come back for you, but it's not safe now. I will come back, and we can be together again. We can go anywhere in the world that you would like. Think about it. I have money and can make us a home anywhere you want.

In the meantime, I've found a quiet spot to wait until the time is right to get you.

I regret not taking you with me that night. I never should have left you in the lake house, but I wanted you to get the medical care you needed. I didn't have time to help you and make a fast getaway. I still think it was the best decision, but I want so badly for you to be here with me. Soon, my love. I will come and get you. Be ready to go at a moment's notice.

I love you. Don't let Michael's family turn you against me. I always did what was best for you. Always, and I always will.

Love,

Mommy

The death of Michael and the escape of Nikki had left Kieran parentless. He'd been assigned a social worker to determine what to do with him. He had enough money from the will and the estate to buy his own place, but legally, he was not old enough to live alone. The social worker planned a meeting with his siblings to see if anyone would take custody.

He loved his siblings and would have been happy to live with any one of them. But he knew he'd be a burden to them. They were too young to be tasked with parenting. He didn't want to go to a group home either, or to live with a foster family who may or may not be overly interested in his money.

In the meantime, Kieran was staying with Mike. He liked staying with him, but it was only a one-bedroom loft, so he had to sleep on the couch. He knew Mike would let him stay there permanently, and if he did, they would get a bigger place. He figured it was the best option, but he felt in the way and not really at home.

After about a month, Liza stopped by Mike's loft.

"Hey, Kieran, how are you doing?"

"Okay. I miss my mom, but I'm not sure I ever really knew her."

"You did. There's good and bad in everyone. That doesn't make the parts you knew any less true. Now you just see the bigger picture."

Kieran nodded and looked at his feet.

"Listen, Kieran, I came to ask you an important question. You can take all the time you need to answer it."

"Okay."

"I spoke with your social worker, and I'd like you to come and live with me. My house is much smaller than what you are used to, but it's too big for just me. And I miss having my kids around all the time. Plus, I've always felt a strong connection to you. Now, I know Mike, Addison, or Harris would gladly take you, and if you'd rather go with them, I understand. I just thought, with their busy lifestyle, you may do better with more of a steady, older parent type."

Kieran's eyes lit up. "Really? Yeah, I'd like that. I feel a little in the way here. Even though I love Mike. And Addison is so focused on her schoolwork now that she's free of Dad. And Harris would be a lot of fun, but I'd end up cleaning up after him."

Liza smiled. "I think you are one-hundred-percent right about that! Okay, it's settled. You can stay with me."

* * *

Joe Fulton was found guilty of six murders. He spent the rest of his life in prison, eating food that was prepared with no love or attention to detail.

Mike and Harris hired a manager to run their father's company. Mike devoted his time to creating art and getting to know Tara. He's starting to make a name for himself in the art world and has an upcoming exhibition. He plans to ask Tara to marry him.

Harris started his zip-line company that ran over the Chattahoochee River. He uses it at least a half dozen times a day.

Sloan was convicted of human trafficking. Many of the girls spoke at his sentencing. He received the maximum sentence for each case and is serving 387 years, consecutively. He now leads a gang in prison.

Addison started medical school and plans to practice psychology.

With Betsy's help, and Mike's money to hire the very best lawyer, Tara was able to get custody of Cara. She finished her computer science degree at Georgia Tech, adding a minor in social justice.

The bond between the sisters and Betsy grew stronger after the case. They all have dinner every Sunday night. Betsy always brings ice cream, but not Butler's.

Betsy found that not all people have an inner darkness. Most people, although willing to cross a line of morality, are driven by a deeper motivation of love, care, and honor. Tara had proven the great lengths one would go for love. Although, some people were still just plain old rotten. She planned to spend her time finding and capturing the rotten ones.

Betsy left the Atlanta Police Department. The case had reignited her passion for finding lost girls. She started her own private detective agency specializing in finding missing kids with the goal of finding out what happened to Hillary. When Tara finished school, Betsy hired her on as her research assistant.

CHAPTER 12

TWENTY YEARS LATER

Twenty years later, all four of the Higgins children were gathered in the small office of Liza's estate lawyer in the days after her death. After reading the will, the lawyer gave them the key to a safe deposit box. Together, they traveled across town to the bank.

Mike stuck the key into the box, opened the lid, and slid out a long metal box. Inside was a letter and a zip drive. Harris read it out loud.

Dear kids,

If you are finding this, then I have died. I'm writing this the week after the death of your father. Hopefully it's been a long time and I've had a chance to meet my grandchildren and your spouses. I could not be prouder of each of you. I hope you won't be too ashamed of me when you see this. I was going to turn myself in, but Kieran needs me. I should have destroyed it, but I wanted to hold on to it in case anyone was wrongly convicted. Please know, I would not have let anyone else go to jail in my place.

Love you,
Mom

Mike picked up the zip drive. He pulled a small gray device from his pocket, flipped it open, and placed it next to the zip drive on the table.

"I'm not sure I can get the information off this. It's so outdated." He fiddled around with it.

"You should be able to download the contents wirelessly," Addison said.

"Ahh, here we go."

A projection of Mike's home screen, with a background of three teenagers, with curly dark hair and freckles, shot onto the opposite wall. He opened an app, and they saw video footage.

"That's the master bedroom in my old house," Kieran said.

"I don't think I want to watch this," Harris said.

"We'll watch it once and then destroy it. Agreed?" Addison said.

"Agreed."

The footage rolled forward.

Michael entered his bedroom and sat on the wingback chair in the corner to take off his shoes and untie his necktie. He stopped a minute, lost in thought, before heading toward the bathroom. He turned suddenly toward the door. Sloan entered the screen. The two had a brief discussion. Suddenly, Sloan approached his partner and put his hands on Michael's neck. Michael gasped and choked, spluttering. He scratched at Sloan's face and hands. His face turned purple, and he became limp. Sloan watched him fall to the floor, and then left.

Michael lay there panting, taking deep, gasping breaths.

He looked up when the door opened, and a figure in a robe entered. The hooded figure paused, seeing Michael at the foot of the bed.

"She's surprised he's awake," said Addison. "Remember, she'd given me sleeping pills? She must have intended them for Dad. I had wondered about that."

"Why would she drug Dad?" Kieran said.

"If he had been asleep, she could have easily strangled him. She could have just put a pillow over his face. Look at her. She's reevaluating," Addison said.

"Mom? No," Mike said.

In the video, Liza turned to leave. But Michael said something to her. She turned back and began yelling at him. He was yelling back.

"Why would Mom want to kill Dad?" Harris asked.

"For us," Addison said. "She knew my life would be over if I had to keep taking care of him. I'd never have gone to med school. You were worried about the will. She must've known he was considering taking us all out of his will, or at least we thought he was. That was probably never the case."

Michael grabbed Liza and slapped her across the face. Liza slapped him back. Michael was so appalled that he threw her down on the floor. He pointed to the door. She stood, and her whole affect was changed. She was begging him.

"She's trying to talk some sense into him," Mike said. "He's not listening."

"Shocker," Harris said.

Liza picked up a small tiki statue.

"Mom still has that. She said her and Dad got it on their honeymoon," Addison said.

Liza carried the statue toward the door. Michael said something to her. He walked up behind and grabbed her. He threw her toward the bed. She struggled to break free of his grasp. She raised the tiki over her head and slammed it down into Michael's skull. Blood spurted from the wound.

Liza's hand went to her mouth. She rushed over to Michael. She grabbed a towel to stop the blood pouring from his head. He looked at her in shock as his eyes glassed over. He slumped down into the wingback chair and died.

Liza shook him, tears cascading. She looked around the room, went to the door, and locked it. Liza kept her eyes on Michael as she paced.

"She had no phone to call for help," Mike said. "She would've called for help. Right?"

"Of course," Harris said.

"I guess we'll never know," Addison said.

Liza walked out onto the balcony, put her hands on her knees, and took some deep breaths. Finally, looking up, resolved.

The tall gray wingback chair Michael had slumped into was now stained red on one side. But the chair was soaking up most of the blood. Liza tilted the chair back onto the back two legs and dragged it over to the balcony. It took her a while as Michael was nearly two hundred pounds. Once outside on the balcony, she tipped the chair forward onto the front legs, placing the top of Michael's body onto the thick cement balcony ledge. Then she swung his feet up onto the narrow cement. He was now lying across the cement railing. She took a deep breath, wiped her brow, and pushed. She flinched a second later at what must have been the sound of Michael's body hitting the ground below. She slid the chair back across the room, then left.

"Can we fast-forward?" Harris asked.

"Yeah, I think so." Mike zipped the tape forward until they saw her return. The time stamp said 10:15 p.m. Liza entered the room, took the chair, and left through the secret passage. She then looked right into the camera. The footage ended a few minutes after that.

"That must be when she stopped the footage," Addison said.

"I can't believe it," Harris said. "All this time, I thought it was Nikki."

"Yeah, me too," Mike said.

"I had suspicions," Addison said.

"What?"

"I mean, Nikki was a horrible person and did terrible things, but Daddy dying kind of brought an end to all of that. She wouldn't have wanted to shine a light on any of the business."

"So, you thought it was Mom?"

"No, I mean, I don't know. I considered the possibility. It could have been any of us, really. And now we know."

"I wish I didn't," Harris said.

"It was an accident. She did the best she could in a bad situation," Mike said. "She must have felt terrible. The weight of such a heavy secret. What a burden to have to carry the rest of her life."

"Should we tell the police?"

"No. We destroy it. There's no reason to tell the police. The case has gone cold, and Nikki disappeared decades ago. If she's still alive, she's not coming back. Sorry, Kieran."

"It's okay. She said she'd come back, and I've been dreading it all this time, but it still hurts that she never did."

"Wait! Addison, did you say you thought it could have been any of us?" Harris asked.

"Why not? Anyone is capable of unthinkable acts, given the right motivation," she said.

ACKNOWLEDGMENTS

This novel would not exist without Adam (5), who went out and bought me a laptop after the first story I scribbled down on pen and paper. He hasn't stopped supporting me since, with time and resources that could've been put to more practical uses. He encourages my whimsy, and the book is better for it.

My deepest thanks to my first readers, who read it before it had a single comma, Sally Sanders (1), Jody Thomas (1), and Jennifer Hollen (6). You helped shape the book and saved everyone lots of confusion because you added commas, like this one.

I would also like to thank my editor, Michelle Krueger (7), and my publishing coach Russell Martin.

In researching the novel, I asked several people medical, weaponry, flight, and murder related questions. I'd like to thank those that answered, Jason Hollen, Leslie Singleton (9), Adam Hallock (5), Kitty Kidd (2), and anyone else who shared their knowledge with me.

Special thanks to the writing support of Hope Callahan (7), Wayne Sanders (3), Jeannie Sanders (1), and Will Sanders (7), and the emotional support of Yi Cauble (6), Jody Thomas (1), and Jenny Hinton (6).

I would also like to thank every one of my children's teachers for giving me the peace of mind that my kids were safe, loved and learning while I invested in this project in a quiet house.

Finally, a huge thank you to the team at Koehler Books, especially John Koehler, Miranda Dillon, Joe Coccaro, and Lauren Sheldon.

Keep track of who is which number
1-9

Addison   _____

Harris   _____

Joe   _____

Kiernan   _____

Liza   _____

Mike Jr.   _____

Nikki   _____

Sloan   _____

Tara   _____

Yvette   _____

Betsy   _____

Henry   _____

Submit your answers to the form on Katehallock.com to receive the answer key and maybe even a prize if you are one of the first to get them all correct.

Type One—The Perfectionist

Motivated by the desire for perfection and order in the world and in their lives.

Type Two—The Helper

Motivated by the desire to be needed, and thus loved.

Type Three—The Achiever

Motivated by a desire to be or appear to be successful and to avoid failure.

Type Four—The Romantic

Motivated by a desire to indulge their feelings, and to be understood for their uniqueness.

Type Five—The Investigator

Motivated by a desire to attain knowledge, to save energy and resources, and to remain independent.

Type Six—The Loyalist

Motivated by the desire to feel safe and secure.

Type Seven—The Enthusiast

Motivated by a desire to have fun, experience life, and avoid pain.

Type Eight—The Challenger

Motivated by a desire to be strong and in control and to avoid feeling vulnerable.

Type Nine—The Peacemaker

Motivated by a desire for harmony in the world and in their lives and to avoid conflict.

CPSIA information can be obtained
at www.ICGtesting.com
Printed in the USA
LVHW040259010523
745709LV00021B/771